"A TRADE.... THE LIVES OF THOSE WHO LOOKED AFTER YOU FOR YOUR OWN...."

It was a pledge the human knew the Ronin assassin had already broken. He dropped to the ground and tried to think. The poison within him welled up as if fueled by fear and adrenaline, and he battled with it, panic beginning to spew up inside him, rattling at his bones and beating at his clenched teeth to be let out. He fought to breathe silently. Inside his skull, the blood pounded. He could not die here!

The human leapt to his feet. The Ronin spun about sharply, poison quills shaking.

"I have you," it said in triumph.

The human's vision went from grays and blacks to crimson. He felt white-hot. He burned so hotly he did not know how his skin could contain or withstand the heat. He could feel himself hurtling at the creature, but his feet stayed rooted to the ground.

With a shrill scream, the Ronin assassin burst into flame. The conflagration raged, lighting up the night, engulfing the creature....

PATH OF FIRE

THE PATTERNS OF CHAOS #2
CHARLES INGRID

DAW BOOKS, INC.
DONALD A. WOLLHEIM, FOUNDER
375 Hudson Street, New York, NY 10014

ELIZABETH R. WOLLHEIM
SHEILA E. GILBERT
PUBLISHERS

First Printing, December 1992

1 2 3 4 5 6 7 8 9

DAW TRADEMARK REGISTERED
U.S. PAT. OFF. AND FOREIGN COUNTRIES
—MARCA REGISTRADA
HECHO EN U.S.A.

PRINTED IN THE U.S.A.

Chapter 1

A high cold wind off the plateau region of Arizar carried with it the scent of catastrophe, of fire and ash, mixing jarringly with the freshness of pine and evergreen. A haze of smoke lay against the peaks, encroaching on the crystalline, piercing clarity of the mountains. The human named Rand watched from the observation deck of the cruiser and thought that when it snowed, which would be soon, the weather would catch the darkness and the flakes would drift down in smoky colors in mourning for the deaths they blanketed.

Choyan, humans, and Zarites alike had perished here. The window he pressed close to breathed in the chill and the odors as well as the sight. There was no glass from home that would do this. Like glass, but unlike, it was as alien as the landscape in front of him. He put a hand against it, feeling the cold. But it was the sight which iced him over with fear. He could have been here, he *should* have been here, and though he'd nearly died elsewhere, these ashes were meant to have been his grave, too.

He watched the two tall Choyan walk the perimeter of the burn scars, hunched slightly into the wind, their clothing and cloaks unfurled. He owed his life to the vigorous Choya, the leader of the small committee currently scattered across the blasted mesa examining the ruins. Yet he was linked by more than a life debt. He shared a soul with the being, a sharing he did not understand any more than he understood the manufacture of the alien glass which separated them.

He and Palaton were separate, yet one. Without being out there, he was with the Choyan. They would be talking quietly, their dual voices blending into a quartet, their double-elbowed arms pointing out and reaching to gather in evidence with a suppleness of movement he could never attain. Even sitting still, watching, Rand felt like a stick figurine lacking in richness and depth. Or a thirsty man kneeling beside a river of glass, unable to drink. *Give me whatever it is you have, share it with me, let me pilot the stars the way you do. . . .*

He blinked as the elder Choya stumbled a bit over a bomb gouged ridge in the dirt. His outer robe flapped about him, wings of a scavenger, picking out the pieces of truth fallen here and there on the burned ground. The taller, more vibrant Choya steadied him without even seeming to. Palaton, the heir to the throne of Cho, pilot of Chaos, at once alien and the very core of Rand's being. His future. His curse.

The Zarites, small, furry, supple aliens, tended to gallop after the long-legged Choyan, scattering aimlessly from time to time yet bobbing and weaving in answer to the questions being put to them, herding the Choyan without seeming to. They had met the contingent at the spaceport, bombed out though it had been, a bureaucracy ready at hand to greet the Choyan and to show them through the ruins. Like hamsters, they were, and their ears blushed and flattened, antennae to their emotions much as whiskers and tail were on a cat. They had been escorted here, via cruiser, but Palaton and Rand had both been here before—this was where their souls had fused—and they recognized the Zarites' mild deceptions even as the committee seemed to be anxiously helping and guiding them.

Rand watched as Palaton came to a stop, his bare, maned head turned into the wind as if scenting something. The thick tresses of his hair curled back from his scallop-edged horn crown. He had no ears sculpted from his fine-boned face, but he heard exceedingly well. The horn crown acted as a sounding board conductor. And there were other senses Rand guessed, as well, that he himself was lacking.

As if knowing Rand thought of him, and thinking of Rand in turn, Palaton looked back at the cruiser. His large, expressive eyes were unseeable at this distance, but Rand smiled slightly anyway. He slumped back against the window seat, wishing he were outside, treading the burned ground. He might find some sign they missed, some hope that Alexa and the others had survived, had lived to flee the raking fire and bombs which had destroyed the campus.

There had been people here, and buildings, and lovers. . . . He had not been there when the attack came. He could only imagine the screams and reaction. The buildings which had teemed with life, fellow humans hoping to be companioned to the tall Choyan who had an unknowable destiny and need for them, now crumbled into dust, founda-

tions little more than brittle lines in char and
mud. Slag pooled here and there where the metal
infrastructure had boiled away to nearly nothing.
Rand closed his eyes against the pain of his
thoughts. He had given away his life, his past, all
his heritage to come to Arizar and learn from the
Choyan, only to lose it all. The Choyan here had
been renegades and they had been struck down
by enemies from other stars. None of them had
expected this, none of them, not Bevan or Alexa. . . .

Alexa, her short curly hair bouncing about her
face, running into the night, her arms raised in
supplication to the sky. . . . Emblazoned against
his eyes even when closed, he saw her thus. Why,
he did not know, only that the vision resonated
within him, and he decided that that was what
must have happened.

She must have heard the incoming. Must have
gone to see what it was. Must have been among
the first to flashfire into ash. She had never slept
soundly or well. Private nightmares she kept shuttered within her would bring her gasping awake
during the nights he had shared with her. Had she
seen this coming? Had it perhaps saved her? If it
had, where had she gone? He could not bring himself to imagine further.

He had not been there, had been off chasing a
fugitive from the campus . . . his darker self, his
friend, his rival, Bevan . . . and they'd both nearly
perished in the attack on the main port of Arizar,
but Palaton had come to rescue Rand, had pulled
him out of the rubble, had kept the life kindled in
him.

Like mystic twins, they shared not one flesh split
asunder, but one soul, torn between them, mirror-

ing sameness and differences. . . . Rand shuddered and caught himself. He put the heel of his hand to his temple. *I am not lost. I was found.* He *found me. I am not lost!*

His body ached dully. He had a partial cast on one arm and a support which ran from his right hip to his right foot. Not a cast exactly, but as confining as one. And his fair skin was turning purple, dark green, and blue at intervals. It even hurt to breathe.

It hurt far more to remember.

He twisted his face again to the window, taking solace in watching the two Choyan stride across the damaged earth. He imagined green shoots winging upward in their footsteps.

As if he might have sensed the young man's observation of them, Rindalan paused in mid-step and put his long-fingered hand on Palaton's sleeve. His voices were reedy with age, the cords of his gaunt Choyan neck standing out as his dual voices vibrated.

"You'll send him back, of course." His robes flared about his tall, wiry frame. His large eyes glistened with the sting of the cold wind.

"I can't." Palaton halted in deference to the elder.

"What do you mean, you can't?"

Palaton turned his hand palm up and swept a gesture over the attack-scarred terrain. "He survived this. He and the other humankinds may well have been the cause of it. I don't dare send him back until we know the truth of it." He paused, waiting to see if Rindalan could pick the lies out of the meager truth in his statement.

Rindalan frowned. "You can't keep him. It would be in violation of Compact agreements. His world barely has a classification with us. No pet could be worth the risk."

"He's no pet." Palaton's lower voice took on an edge and Rindalan rocked back a bit on his heels, hearing the menace.

The High Priest of the House of Star blinked away his reaction. He hummed a bit before saying, "What, then, do you intend to do with him?"

"Bring him back to Cho with us."

"What?" The wind swirled around, snatching away the word, but Palaton heard it well enough, keenly enough, in the startlement mirrored in Rindy's eyes and the alarmed curve of his mouth.

"I can't let him go, elder." Palaton bent close, so that he could be heard well enough in the face of the approaching storm. Behind him, he could hear the Zarites scurrying about, chattering in alarm. The elements would come beating at all of them soon enough. "The Abdreliks did not attack a mere humankind colony here, nor were they attempting to decimate our furry little friends who are now so anxiously awaiting our withdrawal. Rindalan, there were Householdings here."

Rindy did not voice his surprise this time, but his brows shot up. "This is true? We had Brethren here?"

Palaton gave a nod.

"Does Panshinea know?"

"I doubt it, although he might suspect. I haven't reported it to the emperor yet."

Conflicting emotions raced across the elder's face, like clouds raced across the plateau horizon facing them. Palaton looked away for a moment, took in the leading edge of the storm, mentally calculating, like any pilot, how much time they had before it would be difficult to fly, though it wasn't his task to fly the cruiser that rested across the grounds from them. His attention came back to Rindalan.

Choyan did not colonize. It had been decided amongst them generations ago to keep their psychic powers, their *bahdur*, pure and untainted by the sort of genetic adaptation any race went through when transplanted. It made their existence more difficult, more tenuous, for they must constantly heal the damage they did to their planet, constantly balance their finite resources, constantly struggle to be as they were and as they would be.

Palaton knew a sense of relief in telling that much of the truth to Rindalan. As he viewed the carnage, his feelings had bored into him, leaving a gaping hole that nothing, for the moment, could fill. Without his *bahdur*, his genetically inherited telepathic powers, he was helpless. He could no longer master Chaos to pilot, he could not find and fulfill his own destiny—but worse, much worse—he could not save his own people and his own world from the fate which had swiped at Arizar. Those who had attacked here would attack Cho, once convinced that they had grown strong enough and the Choyan weak enough.

Palaton swore that he would somehow find the means to avenge the work done here, and the means to protect his world, and the means to restore his power so that he could fulfill his vows. Whatever it took, he would do it. By the God-in-all whom he might never be able to see again without the *bahdur* which illuminated His presence, no enemy would touch Cho without destroying Palaton first.

He fought to rein back his emotions, which Rindy would be able to read sooner or later, shocked or not. As much as he trusted the elderly prelate, Palaton knew he was alone in this. Entirely, utterly, alone. Without his *bahdur*, his own people would be as quick to bring him down as his enemies would be. He must learn to be still and silent and patient. He bent his head over the other's hand and waited for him to speak.

That there had been renegades here could have been a shock great enough to stop the old Choya's heart in his chest. It did not, though Palaton could feel a trembling in the hand resting on his sleeve.

"What Houses?"

Only three great Houses of political power and *bahdur* had survived the turbulent course of Choyan history: Star, Sky, and Earth. The Householdings of each had their own influence and agendas, and then there were those Choyan without any *bahdur* at all, or barely enough to measure, those Choyan blind to the aura of any living thing, so oblivious that they were called Godless among their own people. But which of the Houses had sent Choyan here, Palaton did not know for sure, though he suspected. He did not tell Rindy of his suspicions.

"That, I don't know. And the evidence is gone. Obliterated." Palaton turned around, drawing away from Rindy. "That boy is all I have. He might be able to tell me." He wondered that the priest could not see through him, could not see that the *bahdur* which had once blazed as brightly in him as any sun was gone, dark, blackened out . . . now housed in the boy, like a tiny flame succored against the night. All that made Palaton what he was now sheltered inside another being who no more knew what he held than a stone would. No, he could not send the boy away. Not until he could make himself whole again. But he would not confide in Rindy. The High Priest's fortune was too entangled with that of Panshinea, who had made Palaton his heir, but he knew the erratic emperor did not intend for the throne to come to him. It was only to hold the Compact at bay, until Panshinea's own power at home had been consolidated.

Rindy moved. It might have been a shrug, it might have been a jerk of protest. He said, "No good can come of this."

"I don't see as I have any choice. Do you?" Had he been empowered, he might have seen the aura brighten about the priest as Rindalan tried to *discern* the consequences of their action.

"My destiny is nearly finished, but yours lies far ahead of you ... out of my sight ... tangled by the choices you must make. This is one, Palaton. You make it too hastily."

"Haste has nothing to do with it. The boy was part of the colony here, all but bought or stolen for purposes I can only guess at. He has answers if I can find the right questions. I can't let him go. The Abdreliks are waiting for just such an opening."

Rindalan shook his head. "He will change all of us. Perhaps even the face of Cho."

"You *discern* that?"

"No." Rindy's voices quaked. "But I feel it in my aching bones, like the wind which bites at us now. You cannot do this, Palaton."

"I have no choice," he repeated.

*   *   *

Alexa moved a hand languidly through the slurry water which surrounded her. The chamber muffled all noise so that all she could hear was the water's movement, its trickle against the sides of the chamber, the dim hum of the pump and filter. A huge being slouched opposite her, submerged beneath the turgid surface, shadowing the pool. GNask had been in the mud pond first and red clay particles sloughed off him, floating to the pool's rim and then disappearing as the circulation pump sucked the water clean.

She did not have the Abdrelik's affinity for mud, though she enjoyed basking in the spa. She watched as the alien paddled onto a ledge and his head broke water. His grace underwater transformed into a massive body, poised, a hunter's, eyes always seeking for the furtive movement of prey, thick, amphibious skin with its sluglike symbiont moving across his broad cranium, his jowls drooping upon his chest, saliva-moist.

She thought, *I look at him and see myself, truer than any mirror.*

She caught GNask watching her and dropped her gaze. She was hungry. She wondered if they would share flesh together and the thought made the corners of her own mouth grow moist. *She was predator because* he *was predator and had imprinted her in his image.* The grotesque, bulky amphibian was more her father than Ambassador John Taylor Thomas, her real father, was.

But GNask was not pleased, in general, with her, with the raid on Arizar, with recent events on

Sorrow where his efforts to gain more power in the Compact had been thwarted. Her visit to his chambers might only be another debriefing and she might be sent away as she had come in, hungry, dark appetite unfulfilled.

Alexa fought to control her trembling as the warm water bathing her began to ripple away from her, concentric lines spreading. She would look like prey herself if she did not stop her tremors. She clamped her jaw tightly as GNask heaved more of his bulk out of the pond. Water streamed down his purple-green hide.

"Alexa," GNask rumbled, acknowledging her presence.

"Master."

"You have done well."

She put out an arm, slim, well-formed for a human, and let it float upon the water, hand curled in entreaty. "I failed you. I neither know what the Choyan did nor where they fled."

"Out of your failure has come a certain triumph. Arizar is cleansed of them." GNask rolled an eye at her. A tiny, pearlesque drop of saliva hung from the corner of his lip where his tusk curled it slightly open. "We take what victories we can."

The hand she held open in entreaty she pulled back into a fist. "We'd have had more if that fool Bevan hadn't bolted. I had no choice but to call you in early."

"Every victory, however slight, is a worthy one." GNask chopped his teeth together, both savoring the results of the Arizar mission and frustrated by what had not come to pass. "The cost may not be too much to bear."

"It is for me!" Alexa's voice burst from her and

then she sank back in the water, appalled by the sound of it.

GNask curled his lips back further. He looked pleased. "Ready to fight again? So soon?"

"Your enemies are my enemies."

He bobbed in the water. "Perhaps." The symbiont slurping its way across his skull put out two tiny stalk eyes, swiveled a bit, peering at her, she thought, and she shuddered at its look. Then it proceeded to feed again, vacuuming the Abdrelik's skin for fungus and microbes. "Don't be deceived," GNask said, his voice thrumming in his chest, vibrating the very water. "I like defeat no better than you do." His eyelids lowered, hooding the predator's expression. "I have, perhaps, had the wrong Choya as my target. Palaton may be even more dangerous than Panshinea."

"Palaton was at Arizar." Her voice was barely audible across the stilling pond.

"Was he?" The hooded eyelids lowered more, until they were a glaring slit. "And we missed him. How fortunate. A *tezar*'s uncanny instincts. Panshinea should have been a pilot. He would have been undefeatable if he had been. You're sure of this?"

"Is it common for a Choya to call himself by another's name?"

"Not generally, no. That's a form of deception not commonly adopted by our friends." GNask scratched a jowl thoughtfully as his eyes reopened. "And we're no closer to obtaining the mechanics of the *tezarian* drive. I close my fist," and GNask did so, holding his hand out of the pool, water streaming from between his fingers. "And the Choyan escape like this. But their choke-hold on the rest of us is not so ineffectual. They know what they condemn us to, yet they continue strangling us to death!''

Alexa flinched as the big amphibian's voice boomed. The furtive movement drew his attention instantly, rapt and keen. She held very still, fighting the instinct to vault from the pool and run. She knew his baser thoughts as if they were her own, and knew he weighed her usefulness against the delights of consuming her. She must always be certain that she was very, very useful to the Abdrelik in his presence.

GNask opened his fist and looked at his empty hand. "I want to grasp knowledge. I want the drive. The law among the stars must be the same as the law upon the earths: the strong survive. What there is for the taking, is taken. There are worlds out there, star lanes, which only the Choyan know of. They guard their secrets jealously. I will rip those secrets from them if it's the last thing I do.''

Chapter 2

Broken concrete and smoking skies. . . . Bevan woke with a start from his dreams of hurt and burning to look into a sharp muzzled face, with rounded transparent ear flaps, not unlike a rat from the streets of his youth. But this being standing over Bevan watched him with a not unkindly stare.

The Zarite reached out and put a soft-furred paw on the human's shoulder. He helped bolster him into a sitting position. The world of hurt which had enveloped Bevan in his dreams jarred him now. The alien blinked in empathy.

"Better?"

Bevan's lips ached and chapped skin sloughed from them as he pulled them apart to sculpt a word. He put a finger to them instead and the Zarite peeled his finger away gently to push a clay cup into his hand.

"Drink. You are hot."

Hot? Hot. Bevan drank, wetting his sore lips and cooling his parched throat. Not hot. Fevered. But the Zarites might not understand. He could only guess at their physiology and thought they might do the same of him. He put the mug down.

He tried speech again. "How long?" The sounds scraped along a throat clogged with smoke and soot, made raw by fever and dreams ... dreams which cloaked him even when awake. He tried to blink them away.

"Five days since we found you."

Five days since he'd left Rand to die amid the shards of the spaceport. Five days since his own clumsy effort to take flight had brought him crashing down and his rescuers had pulled him from the crushed and flaming ship. He was sore, but nothing seemed broken. He'd inhaled fumes which still made his lungs ache. Yet this he would survive, for Bevan had been a survivor for as long as he could remember, from the mean streets of Sao Paulo to the Catholic orphanage which had taken him in, to this planet and the ragged future it had offered him. This disaster, too, he would survive.

It was the thing which raged inside him that he truly feared, the thing which he could not control or comprehend.

It was this thing—fused into him by the arrogant Choyan pilot Nedar, this thing which must be Nedar's soul itself—for which Bevan had killed.

It now exacted its own toll, this soulfire which consumed him like a kind of Choyan revenge for Nedar's death. To save Alexa and himself, he had murdered and run, but there was nowhere he could hide from the burning inside. And when Rand had come after him to help, his response had been to try to destroy Rand as well. There was no help for him now. The soulfire inside him devoured all that had been human, leaving him empty and evil.

The Zarite refilled his cup. "You must stay quiet. The Choyan are here, come back to look at the burning grounds."

Bevan looked up sharply. "What? Which Choyan?"

"I do not have their names. I only know they are up on the plateau."

At the College. Or what was left of it. What did they seek there? Did they look for him, still?

"Do they know ... do you know ... who attacked?"

"Enemies." The Zarite's ears went flat, then came up again as he answered impassively. "It does not matter. When the Choyan leave, the enemies will leave."

Bevan chewed on that answer as the Zarite crept away, leaving him alone. Sunlight slanted through a patched roof, dappling him with shadow. He had thought ... feared ... that the attack had been directed at him, in anger over Nedar's death, revenge being exacted on an entire world because of something he had done. That guilt, at least, he did not have. It had not been his sin which had brought fire down upon Arizar. If not his, then whose? The Choyan were a powerful people. Only the Abdreliks and Ronins went up against them. Which of them had dared an attack?

His lips went dry again. Bevan dropped a hand down to the mug, found it filled again and waiting, and lifted it to his lips. He drank it down, thinking it a futile effort to quench the fire inside.

His eyes blinked shut for longer and longer. He began to drift. He wondered for what the Choyan searched. He fell asleep musing on broken promises.

Plummer ducked out of the broken arch doorway. A slab of concrete lay askew, hiding the building's front. It looked as demolished as any of those on the spaceport outskirts. Miffer awaited him, squatting patiently on slat-sided hindquarters.

"He sleeps again?"

"Yes. But he's very hot."

Miffer straightened, looked out over the devastated cityscape, to the far mountains. A storm front angled across that horizon. It would take a few days to reach them. They would get only a tailing of rain, not the sleet and hailstones and thunderstorms the mountains would reap. Still, the shelter they were in would be put to the test. "Keep plenty of water near him. I'll try to buy some herbs tonight." The Zarite scrubbed a hand over his pointed face. "I hope he is worth the trouble."

"The salvage crews have already paid me a consulting fee. It does us no good to scavenge if we do not know what we have."

Miffer made a scoffing noise. "What makes you think the outlander will know any more than we do?"

Plummer's voice dropped to a sharp hiss. "He's one of them. His hands have always been filled with machinery. He will know!"

"Then you do well to keep him alive . . . and awake." Miffer seemed nonplussed in the face of Plummer's frustration. "Or the consulting fees will be returned—out of your hide!"

Plummer wiped his hands down along his flanks and then on his apron. "I know," he said, a little mournfully. "I know."

A skimmer passed the next block over, its wake sending up swirls of dust and ash. The two Zarites wrinkled their faces and coughed in the disagreeable wake. Inside, the fevered human's voice rose in the murmur of nightmares struggling to be told, to be exorcised, to be understood. Neither Zarite paid any attention to the voice or the words, as if knowing they had not the capacity or the experience to understand what troubled the human.

*   *   *

In the foothills below the mountains at a second site, hail had fallen, littering the ground with white stones. Rindy looked cold as he tottered after Palaton, but he asked no quarter as they walked the foundation outlines of what had once been a prosperous Householding. Palaton stopped and the elder knew it was no mistake that the other's tall body buffered the wind and weather for him. He pulled up at Palaton's elbow.

"Nothing left."

"No." Palaton's voices were pitched low, for his hearing alone.

"The Abdreliks were thorough."

Palaton's thick mane of hair bannered in the wind. "From the preliminary scouting reports, there are no Householdings left. Rindy, the Abdreliks didn't have the time to be this thorough, not the time or the firepower. This is self-destruction."

The elder lifted his chin. He considered the implication of the *tezar's* words. "To prevent discovery?"

"Undoubtedly. And I doubt we'll find many Choyan bones within this debris. Which leads me to ask, not only where they went—but how they got there."

To cross the void, to flee this world and seek another, meant mastering FTL. It meant that the renegades had either developed pilots among themselves, or had access to pilots. That there were *tezars* who would take contracts not sanctioned by their flight schools or their emperor or even by the Compact on Sorrow, just as there had been *tezars* who had taken on the contracts of flying Abdrelik warships into Arizar, with no qualms of conscience over attacking their own.

The old Choya took a deep, shuddering breath. "I am sorry to see this," he said, and his voices trembled with emotion. "There is nothing we can do here."

"No. And the front is moving in stubbornly. You're cold, the boy is hurt . . . and there is nothing more we can find out or do here." Palaton swiveled on a bootheel. His foot ground into the mud and ashes and melting hailstones. "I think the Zarites will be relieved to see us go."

Rindy hugged his robe around his bony shoulders. "The Households here have not done well by them. I can see clear signs of genetic manipulation and repression. They're a clever people. If brethren of ours hadn't interfered here, who knows what kind of world we might tread now. Panshinea won't react well to this, Palaton."

"And you think I will?" Palaton frowned slightly, looking down at his companion.

"I know you will. I suggest," and Rindy put a knobbed finger to his lips. "Compromise."

But he signaled silence. Palaton looked away and drew in a fleeting breath of surprise. "I'll do whatever I can," he answered. He put his arm out. "It's slippery here. Let's head back to the cruiser."

Rindalan accepted the support. "It's treacherous everywhere," he remarked.

*   *   *

From space, Arizar looked unremarkable. It was a blue water world under a G5 star, eminently suitable for life in the Choyan style. Its scars were all but invisible to the naked eye and even those that showed under technological scrutiny were nothing that a year or two wouldn't heal. It had two small moons that barely qualified as satellites, but they paced one another and created sufficient screening for the starship which hid behind them. They did not screen the interstellar activity around Arizar.

One who watched his panel intently now saw the signs of a cruiser leaving the spaceport, picking up escape velocity, then leveling off as it attained deep space. He knew the ship, knew its markings, thought he knew who might be piloting it. He sucked his breath in, raggedly, as though through a grievous injury, and held it briefly, then exhaled. The exhalation made him cough and the chunky, stunned-looking Choya sitting in the pilot's seat next to the observer made a jerky movement with his arm as though startled.

The observer's attention flickered only for a second, then fixed back on the cruiser.

"Palaton," breathed the observer. Another tearing breath and exhalation. "Not yet. I don't have you yet . . . but I will. I'll have back everything you stole from me, and all you hold as well."

He grabbed at the stolid Choya. "See them, Staden? There goes the heir to the throne on Cho. I worked for it—*I* wanted it. He fought me from the very beginning . . . I should have killed him at

Blue Ridge when we were cadets, when I had a chance . . . he flew better than I, even then. Everything, better than I. I fought wars and won them, but he . . . he won causes! He could even pull victory out of defeat. What chance did I have against that?"

The quiet Choya did not answer. His flesh had paled to a grayish tone, his cheekbones had sunk into a cadaverous expression as though all his vital juices had been sucked from him.

But Nedar neither noticed nor cared. He shook the Choya, a hard jerk demanding attention. "I wept when the emperor sent for him . . . then wept again when Panshinea sent him away to protect him from the corruption of the throne and sent for me. It did not matter that I would be besmirched by the emperor's actions. No. Palaton was all. I was nothing. *He* was spoken of as the hero in exile. What was I? A *tezar*, no more and often less. He took my life from me . . . not the blade that wounded me. It is no wonder they all thought me dead and consigned me to your gentle care, to take me home for burial. I might still need you for that, Staden."

Spent, eyes burning with his intent, Nedar leaned back into the console seat, and pressed his hand over the healing wound in his flank. His voices dropped to a whisper. "They took my *bahdur* from me and left me only this, my hatred, to fire me. Will it be enough, do you think, to destroy Palaton?"

Nedar took another deep breath, harsh and grave sounding. He put his head back against the molded rest, ebony mane falling from his proud horn crown. He had seen the Abdreliks withdraw from their pounding of the planet. His canniness as a combat pilot had kept them in hiding, as it did even now. And he had seen the Choyan destroy their Householdings and flee in the wake of the strafing, flee across Chaos to the unknown, though he had had enough *bahdur* stolen from the unresponsive Choya next to him to remember the glimmer of their passage.

These things Palaton did not know. These things, and others, Nedar would find a way to work against him. For now, he needed allies. His patroness Vihtirne would strip away his pretenses all too easily. She could not be trusted until he knew his strengths. There were others he could turn to, he thought.

"Take me home, Staden. But not to rest. Not yet. Not until Palaton is destroyed." He gave in to the urge to breathe only shallowly, and to let his eyelids shutter down over his eyes, but his face did not relax, even as sleep claimed him. It remained contorted in hatred.

Chapter 3

Ambassador John Taylor Thomas strode along Compact grounds, disdaining the ground transport at hand, stretching his legs after a day in close quarters. It was a discipline of his, to walk when he could easily be carried, a discipline which kept him fit and still at the edge of his prime. A rain tinged wind pushed at his thinning hair, reminding him that not all things stayed the same, no matter how hard he worked to maintain such a situation.

Heads turned as he passed, making note of who walked and where, and that he wore a bodyshield and thus was not nearly as vulnerable as he looked. The shielding blurred the shadow which rose and fell at his footsteps. It would not hold against a full-scale attack, but for the subtlety of assassination, it might well save his life again. It had already done so once, though not recently.

Thomas threw his head back and looked at the sky, stippled with gray-white clouds, moving too fast now to scatter showers on the Compact city, and he breathed in the fresh air. Whatever Sorrow had been in its past, its makers had either been too wise to destroy their world, or they had been gone so long now that the world had righted itself. He envied them their wisdom.

His step slowed as he neared the crystallized stream which edged the compound sector he traversed. There was natural water throughout the city, brooks and ponds and lakes, and by the sheer cliffs which bordered the edge of the horizon, there would be veils of water falling from incredible heights, pounding into mountain tarns. But the crystallized streams and lakes of the city were not natural, and it was no longer water which filled them. A quartzlike material lined them, for they had been made into a tomb.

Thomas paused at the stream's edge. Most of those who lived in the Halls of Compact quickly grew used to the sight. He never had and he knew of only one or two who had ever admitted to him that they, too, had been deeply affected. One of them had been a Choyan he wished he could have trusted.

The embankment widened slightly, and under the spreading arms of a copse of gold-flecked trees, Thomas found a bench and sat. Though it had not quite been sculpted for a human body, it met his needs without too much discomfort. The overlook was intentional—here the crystal stream began to widen into the lake and bridge structure leading into the central grounds, and here the dead could be seen most distinctly.

Like a fly caught in amber resin for all eternity, the alien dead had been caught in crystal. Their faces, he thought, looked both startled and amazed. Mothers gathered young to their bodies. Young lovers embraced each other as if their youth could have staved off the impending death.

No one knew what had been wrought here—what enemy had come upon and imprisoned an entire race—or how it had been done, for the alchemy to change water into quartz was impossible, yet the evidence lay before him. What a world to lose, these people who had kept it so carefully and yet lost themselves to another enemy, unknown, unnamed.

Sorrow had been chanced upon and had been deemed an omen. *This could be your path and your death*, it seemed to say, if you do not turn your road aside. And so the quarreling aliens who found it left it inviolate and founded a treaty organization upon its lands. The bodies in quartz had been left intact, though xenobiologists and archaeologists had been probing the phenomenon for centuries without much success.

There was a movement behind John Taylor Thomas, one that he heard and felt and smelled, and he knew his appointment had arrived, but he sat very still. It never did to show fear to your enemies.

"It still gives you pause, does it, Ambassador?"

"Indeed it does, Ambassador," he replied to GNask, and then turned slightly upon the bench.

The Abdrelik had lowered himself to the foot of one of the trees. The bulk of his face wrinkled. "You may dim your bodyshield, Thomas. I think there is that which bonds us."

Cursing to himself for offending the Abdrelik, Thomas thumbed down the bodyshield to a neglible level. His time with the ambassador would be short. He decided not to fence with the alien. "Where is she?"

"Quartered. She does well, considering we plucked her out of a holocaust."

Thomas watched the piglike eyes of the other. "Injured?"

"Of course not. Your daughter is a most remarkable . . . specimen. Intelligence and common sense and the wit to know when to use either."

He felt somewhat mollified. Alexa, safe. As safe as she could be after they had imprinted her. As sane as she could be . . . after. "You have what you wanted, then."

"Not quite." GNask sucked in a prodigious amount of air. GNask was an amphibious creature and the realization of how formidable he could be underwater struck Thomas. "Our friends did not like our probing. They destroyed themselves and most of the evidence we need to make our case. However . . . I think we can cause the Choyan some trouble."

"We agreed on more than trouble. We agreed to prove a tampering charge, tampering with a Class Zed status."

GNask put the back of a beefy hand to the corner of his mouth and mopped it slightly. "We agreed that if the Choyan were tampering, they should not be allowed to get away with it. Panshinea is a brilliant being, ambassador. I'll not present a case before him without all the evidence I can get. And when I get it, you'll get your daughter back."

"A visit, then?"

Something flickered through GNask's muddy eyes. "If she wishes it," he said. He levered himself to his feet. "We'll be in contact, Thomas. And do not worry. She does well with us."

With that, the Abdrelik turned and left, hiking over the knolls and onto the grassy flat leading to outer pathways and compounds.

Thomas stood to watch him go. He closed his eyes to ease his pain. It was not as if she'd died on Arizar, though he knew the daughter he loved so much had died years and years ago when the Abdrelik had first integrated his symbiont into her body. He opened his eyes and found his hand clenched, nails biting into his palms.

GNask did not know that he had had biochemists working on finding a neural stripper to rid Alexa of that imprint should she ever be returned to him. The work was long and tedious, but the last word he had had from home had been hopeful. Very, very hopeful.

"We are not as backwater as you think," Thomas muttered. A leaf dropped from the branches overhead and struck him. He looked up, then thumbed his bodyshield back on full. He was among enemies on a planet set aside for peace. He would never forget either.

*   *   *

Rand stayed at the observation window, despite the mellow warnings on deck that it would be closed soon for shielding. His legs and hip ached a little, a tiny, fierce, burning ache that told him both that he'd been injured and that he was healing. He watched the world which had promised him everything and given him nothing grow smaller, framed by the window.

He did not hear Palaton enter but suddenly was

aware that his presence was dwarfed on deck. He turned his head and voiced his thoughts.

"There's nothing left."

"No. Very little."

The twin voices of the Choya underlined one another. He could hear strength and sorrow in both tones, the differences so subtle he wondered how he could hear it. Rand stirred, coming about. "I should have been there."

Palaton looked at him. Lines furrowed in the brow emphasized by an unruly forelock of hair and the proud, scallop-edged horn crown. "And should we have salvaged nothing from Arizar? No hope, no understanding?"

"I'm not—" Rand stopped, waved a hand as words failed him.

"No," said Palaton. "Perhaps you're not. But you *will be* and that is what counts here."

You will be. Potential. The promise unfulfilled. That was what the Choya saw in him, rescued him for. That was what the Choyan saw everywhere they looked. The potential. The realization of a tiny portion of the alien's thought process stilled Rand for a moment.

What must it feel like to look at something and see not only the accumulation of that moment, but the possibility that stretched beyond it? What if they were wrong? How could they know they must be right? They must have the confidence of the ages behind them. He pondered the feeling of certainty, what it must be like to be born with it. No wonder the Choyan headed the Compact of alien races. No wonder they were the pilots, the masters of Chaos. The only wonder in him was that Palaton had chosen to look at him and *see.*

Palaton sat in a fluid bending motion. He put out a hand and cupped Rand's shoulder, then dropped it. The gesture passed so quickly he might almost have imagined it. The Choyan were not given to casual physical closeness. Rand looked at the alien, with the sculpted bone crown that cupped and released masses of hair tumbling down the back of Palaton's large head. Had they butted heads like elk and moose in the primeval days of their race's youth? Had the crowns grown to protect the mighty brains within their skulls? And had the instinct to keep an arm's length away remained anyway? He would never know, he thought. If he did not know about himself, his own race, he could never even hope to know the alien mind.

He contradicted himself as he saw a fleeting shadow cross the other's gold-flecked eyes. Doubt and worry pooled within.

"You didn't tell Rindalan," he said, tripping a little over the elder Choya's name.

Palaton leaned back in his chair with a sigh. "No. How could I? We Choyan are all woven together, different strands of a single being, the God-in-all. He would not understand the bond between us."

Rand added softly, "He would not understand that I carry your *bahdur*."

"No." Palaton's face tensed as if he gathered himself. "No one would. I had thought perhaps Rindy might, but since I cannot know his mind . . . it's better not to risk it. Rand, this is very important. You must understand that I cannot do, will not be allowed to do, what I have to if this bond between us becomes known."

Rand lowered his head slightly. "I think I know."

"Do you?" Palaton looked away, out the observation window, where only black velvet could meet his gaze. "It is not for myself I ask. It is for Cho."

Rand did not respond for a moment, thinking of home, where one man might imagine he could make a difference, but probably could not, though, God knew, thousands had tried throughout history. But to be an emperor of a world ... his thoughts as well as his vision blurred. His eyesight, he brushed a hand across his face, knowing that temporary blindness would set in from drugs given him by the College before his flight and its destruction. The drugs had been meant to artificially bind him to a dependence on the companionship of the alien sitting next to him. It needn't have been done. Perhaps the Choyan had no real concept of friendship that they would resort to such means. He only knew that the onset of blindness was slowly creeping in, he would have to endure it, and then it would fade. He was thankful he had not received a full dosage of the drugs. His burden would be lessened.

But mental clarity was another matter. He seemed to be thinking in two minds, one of his own and the other ... he knew nothing of except that it seemed to shadow him, to contradict and baffle every word and image within his own. The voice was his and yet not his ... he exhaled deeply and it caught Palaton's attention.

"You're weary." The Choya stood. "I wouldn't do this now if I had time to do it later ... but you need to know how to protect yourself, how to shield what you carry for me." Palaton composed his face. "They'll not only destroy me, but you, if we're found out."

Rand thought dryly that he was just getting used to being a target himself, but the idea of losing Palaton jiggled an odd feeling inside of him, something akin to panic. He felt it bounce around, creating a hollowness. He didn't like it. "Tell me what to do," he said. He didn't pretend to understand why what Palaton was telling him to do would work; he listened and attempted it on his own. In the long run, it was like muffling the sound of his own heartbeat, the electric flow of his own thoughts. It was easier to do than he'd thought when Palaton had explained the method to him and when done right, offered relief. The battle of the two beings within him would at least quiet, if not fade altogether.

Rand paused. He looked up at Palaton. "Okay. When do I do this?"

"All the time," said the pilot. "Don't worry, it becomes second nature."

It would have to quickly. It tired him, and Rand sagged in spite of himself.

Palaton caught him. "You should be secured in your cabin anyway." The FTL alarm underscored his words.

"No." Rand's longing leapt into his inner voice, the voice he knew the best, the one which drove him to do what he did. "Let me see Chaos with you."

The Choya tilted his head slightly, looking down at the human. Palaton wore no facial jewelry as many Choyan did, the links in fiber-fine wiring customarily buried under the first, delicate, translucent layer of skin. His expression looked oddly naked. "No," he refused Rand.

There was no word for "please" in the Trade they spoke. The equivalent was "think again" or "reconsider" as if a bargain must be struck. The word coming to his lips angered him and Rand would not say it. This was not a deal being struck between the two of them. This was a plea. It was not right he would not be allowed to utter it. He dropped the shield he had just so painstakingly erected.

The second voice, the shadow in his mind, gave him a word. He said it and Palaton flinched as if struck. His lips parted and he paused, then his voices rumbled. "You risk your sanity. Only *tezars* can safely do what you ask of me. Reality twists. . . ."

"I know what I face. I don't want safety. I want to pilot!" Rand struggled to his feet, despite the castings and the pain that shocked through him with the effort. "I want to go where you go, to see what you've seen. I gave up my home to gain the right to do this."

A wry smile twisted Palaton's lips. "You want to see what you *think* I've seen. And no one of my people would have promised to make a pilot out of you, no matter how renegade they were. You don't have what it takes and that is not a consideration of your hopes and desires, it is a fact of your genetic makeup, something you cannot change."

"And how am I to know the experience, how are any of us to know it, if you won't give us the opportunity? No one else is allowed to do what you do."

"Because no one else can."

"The *tezarian* drive comes in a little black box. I've seen it. I see pilots carry it from ship to ship. It's a *machine*. Teach me to use it."

Palaton put a hand up to the height of his brow, where the horn crown merged, as if he might rub an ache there. He lowered his hand before finishing the gesture. "I cannot."

"I'm asking you to give me the chance to earn the right."

"It is not a right!"

His voices cut through Rand. He felt himself recoiling a little, hurt. "You're telling me that pilots are born that way. Did you know you were one before you could walk?"

Palaton's lips twisted again, slightly. "Not quite that soon, but soon. Pilots are born, not made. Like diamonds. The edges are cut, polished, surfaces faceted . . . but the gemstone begins and ends a diamond. The soulfire drive," and Palaton hesitated, then finished, "the soulfire drive can only be used by one born to be a *tezar*."

"It's not right," Rand protested. "What if one of you bleeds to be a pilot—"

"What is not possible is not possible."

"You know," and Rand fought to keep his footing, every bone in him aching, but nothing aching so much as the heart pounding in his chest. "My planet isn't considered much by Compact terms. We deserve it, I suppose, for the mess we've made. But anyone can become just about anything if he works for it. There are universes out there which . . ." Rand's voice nearly failed him, but he found it again, "are new and fresh. Which can give something back to my world, if you let them. If

we're allowed to get there. We have things of value
we can trade. *We* are of value."

"I'm sorry. I wish I could explain it more fully
to you. Piloting is just not possible to one not born
to be a *tezar*. It's nothing I have any control over.
It doesn't matter what world you come from. This
is a Choyan matter, and even within my own race,
there are many who cannot be what they wish."

Rand swallowed back a harsh response. Yet he
could not cave in, could not surrender. The desire
which had brought him across immeasurable dis-
tances would not let him deny it. Instead, he repeated that soft word of Choyan which had come
to him out of the nowhere, the shadow. "*Desanda*.
At least let me watch. For a moment. Let me see
what Chaos is like."

Briefly, Palaton shuttered his eyes. Then he put
out a steadying hand. "There is another who pilots
this ship. We shall see if Rufeen allows it. If she
does, then we'll both have a look."

Rufeen pursed thick lips in disapproval. Her
heavy Earthan body filled the cabin bulkhead. "If
any but you asked it of me, Palaton."

"Then you must respond to me as you must respond to anyone else. You're in command of this
cruiser."

Her gray eyes considered the boy leaning against
the starship corridor, just out of hearing range.
"I'm a *tezar*, as you are," she said to Palaton. "I've
seen everything. But what you ask—" she shuddered. "This is sacrilege."

"It's a request, nothing more."

"Our secrets. . . ."

"Will remain unrevealed to him," Palaton said,

and hoped he did not lie. "Do you think a Class Zed citizen can determine what the most brilliant minds among the Ronins and the Abdreliks have not for centuries?"

She blinked. "And yet," she answered, "we do not invite them into our cockpits either."

Palaton did not flinch. "He left his home," he said. "He was promised the stars by those who could not give them. He doesn't understand fully why he can never have them, why only we can master the patterns. His heart was broken by deceit, and only you and I can begin the mending by showing him what is possible and what is not, so he can gather his life and get on with it." It was more than he intended telling her, but he found a trust in the squatty Earthan standing before him, who like him had all but forsaken her House and Householding for the position of *tezar*.

Rufeen's pearl gray eyes widened a little. "Who did this to him?" she asked.

"I'm not sure yet," Palaton answered. "But they were Choyan."

Her thick lips tightened as the implication sank in. And Rufeen made a decision. "Come in," she said, giving way and raising her voices. "And secure yourselves. We're on the edge of attaining FTL now."

She did not need to tell Palaton that. He could feel it as though it carried an aura all its own. And the boy behind him, God-blind though he should be but was not because of what he sheltered inside of him, ought to be able to feel it as well. Palaton stepped through the bulkhead opening and reached back to assist Rand.

He helped Rand settle, feeling the awkwardness

of the boy in his hands, casts and all, and enfolding the webbing about him. Then he took the chair next to Rufeen. "I thank you."

She gave him a sidelong look. "You are what you are," she said flatly. "It does little good for you to ask me to disregard it." She splayed a hand over the black box instrument board, in addition to the major panel of the cruiser. "On my mark. . . . *Now*."

Rand gasped as the cruiser shuddered, piercing an invisible barrier of sorts, and before him the view went from the black velvet of normal space littered by diamond fragments of stars, to a soup of colors, stirred by an unseen hand. The skin of the cabin melted away and he found himself hanging in the weblike chair like a piece of meat about to be dropped into a stew pot. Sweat popped out on his forehead and his heart thumped in sudden panic.

The shell of the cruiser was gone. Where it went, he had no idea, but he rode through space unprotected, unsheltered. As Chaos swirled about him, he knew he would be devoured whole.

He tried to swallow. It did not help that the hands he gripped with appeared to be melting away, flesh from the bones, like wax. He looked at the back of Palaton's head and reminded himself he'd asked for this.

Palaton did not sense the boy's discomfiture. He had little opportunity to think of anyone but himself, for this was the first time in his life he had tried to confront Chaos without *bahdur*. He did not like the sensation. The turmoil, the colors muted by the absence of free-flowing light, yet created anyway, only to slowly bleed away to darkness, the wash and frenzy of a sea of havoc wrenched at him. He tried to anchor himself against the tide of confusion and panic threatening to rise.

"Tezar." Rufeen's gentle voices were laden with concern. "Is anything wrong?"

Admit to another pilot that he had lost his soul? Never. Palaton held himself still against the tide of havoc. "Nothing, Rufeen."

What could she suspect? Every *tezar* saw in his/her own way the various patterns of Chaos. Some saw a blinding confusion of pathways to take, for others there was often only one pathway with clearly delineated landmarks, or patterns, to sight. And for those unfortunate in the same manner he was now, there was only turmoil. But she could not read his soul now, she would be too entangled with guiding them safely through. As to that . . . he'd tested himself against old Rindy. Scoured of *bahdur*, he still had his inner defenses against invasion by others. A casual search would not batter those walls down. She could not press even if she wanted to.

And he would fight to the death before he would allow any further trespass.

But Earthans were the salt of Cho. It was in their genes to balance the forces they saw around them. She would not be of the House of Earth if she did not sense his tenseness and want to soothe it.

"Tezar. I know it must be difficult to let another pilot you. Would you care to take over?"

She had him caught now. He could scarcely refuse her gracious offer without revealing himself. He read her face as she looked to him briefly. No diabolical scheme narrowed her eyes, or etched her expression—yet she'd snared him as skillfully as any seductress.

Palaton opened his mouth to refuse, when Rand made a strangling noise from the security web behind them. Palaton reacted instinctively as he would for a Choyan child, leaving his chair despite the reality which melted around him as he did so. For a dizzying moment he considered an abyss under his booted feet, an abyss which fell through the depths of the universe.

Rufeen muttered to herself as she manipulated the control board. He needed no special talent to see she had become suddenly disturbed. Her movements caught his attention, distracting him from Rand.

She looked up. "The patterns are shifting."

"I would never interfere, *tezar*, I give you my word."

"*Somebody* is." Rufeen shook her head and sucked in an exasperated breath. "There it goes again. My patterns keep slipping away. I've never seen patterns like this."

"Can you bring us back in line?"

"I think so. Old Rindy must be dreaming."

Palaton started a little at her statement, but, yes, the elder prelate had more *bahdur* than almost any two Choyan put together, although he hadn't tested out to have all the talents needed to be a pilot. Could he, in a deep sleep, be reaching out to interfere? Palaton unclipped his shoulder strap. "I'll see to him."

Rufeen's chin jerked in disagreement. "I might need you here!"

"He has to be stopped." Palaton could not tell her he had no aid for her.

She bit down on her lip, then nodded. "All right. It's a short trip. I'll burn all I can."

If he could have seen it, her aura would have appeared to flare with the effort as she turned all her energy to regaining her control of Chaos. The cruiser trembled slightly and then bore to the starboard as it answered her command at the helm.

Rand answered as well, a thin wail of pain.

He caught himself as Rand thrashed in his webbing and tore lose, bolting to his feet with a cry. His turquoise eyes went wide with panic. From a pale face came an expression of such loss that Palaton's own heart quailed.

Rand put a hand out and reached for him. Their fingers touched briefly and Palaton tasted an agonizing moment of *bahdur* which was no longer his to claim ... and an alien wash of fear and abandonment.

Then the boy toppled to the deck as if dead.

Chapter 4

Palaton's heart dropped and he pitched after the boy.

Rufeen spared a glance over her shoulder. "What is it?"

Palaton had gone to one knee so quickly the joint numbed from hitting the floor as he knelt by Rand's side and put a hand out to turn the face toward him. Under the humankind's closed and pale eyelids, the eyeballs moved skittishly. His breath shallowed. Palaton found small comfort in that. "He's unconscious. It's a Chaos fugue."

"My apologies. If I could have kept the helm answering to me alone . . . will he be all right?"

"I'm not that familiar with his physiology, but I think so. He's been through too much."

Rufeen made a low sound of understanding. Palaton brought the boy up in his arms, awkward because of the healing supports. "I'll take him back."

The pilot nodded, saying only, "I have it under hand now, *tezar*. Thank you for your assistance."

Palaton accepted her gratitude mutely, intent only on taking Rand to the passenger lounge where he could make the boy comfortable. There were drugs available for the condition of acute disorientation, but he did not want to administer them until the boy was conscious. Any adverse reaction might not be apparent if Rand were already disabled.

No one occupied the lounge. Rindalan, as was his privilege, had a private cabin. Palaton wondered if the old Choya did indeed dream, perhaps of piloting, in his sleep, and if he had interfered with Rufeen. Palatan could not remember if there had been any inkling of the talent to be a *tezar* in the prelate's background. It was equally likely Rufeen fought with her own burnout of power, the dread that happened to them all, a fire that burned steadily and brightly until it began guttering and then—snuffed out, as quickly, as suddenly, as if it had never been.

He had always feared that. To reach for a light and find darkness. Now that he had darkness, it was not so terrible. The disease and neuropathy which accompanied burnout did not have a firm hold on him yet. The slow and agonizing death which the disease incurred was still decades away for him.

And if what the College Choyans had told him was true, then once his purified *bahdur* could be retrieved from Rand, he could begin again. No disease, no emptiness. His power bright and clean, like a purified torch which had once burned dark and smutty.

A miracle.

If it were true.

And if it were not, then how had they existed on Arizar, a colony of Householdings, renegades from Cho, an entire foothold of Choyan where his brethren had never been before? They had discovered the bonding between humankind and Choyan *tezars*. It was they who found that humans could be a receptacle, a filter, for *bahdur*. They thought they could offer this miracle.

And he, desperate for a future, had not refused. If he had foreseen, he would not have taken it, unlike Nedar who grasped it no matter what the catastrophe . . . even the death and destruction at Arizar, even that price he had been willing to pay. And his rival had paid the price with his own life.

Palaton would have joined him if it could have saved the others. He would not have paid that price. Even this emptiness was not worth the toll exacted on Arizar and the jeopardy placed on all Cho.

And here he was, bringing more jeopardy home to them. A charge of tampering would not be treated lightly. While he wrestled with the dissatisfaction at home, Panshinea would face the critics of the Compact.

There was a pattern in Chaos known as the Tangled Web. Most pilots saw it, though its actual placement and appearance might vary somewhat. They all avoided it like the plague. It was trouble, death, and destruction. Moameb had once told him that he had seen a Devourer in the midst of the Web, like a greedy spider, waiting to consume the unwary who got caught.

He wondered if his actions had brought them all into the course of the Tangled Web. He placed his palm gently over Rand's forehead, found it damp and cool, and removed his hand. He told himself again that he'd had no choice. That the Great Wheel turned without his help. That events on Cho unfolded without his plotting.

That assuaged only the tiniest layer of guilt.

He could always have turned his back on Panshinea. He could have accepted the beginning of his loss of *bahdur*. He could have refused to look into the eyes of a humankind and begin a bonding he had little understanding of.

But he had not.

Now he must endure whatever faced them and do what he could to right the inevitable wrongs which would befall. His mother had been an artist: a weaver, and an embroiderer. He thought of the hangings he'd seen in his youth, and of those gracing the walls of the imperial gallery in Charolon. Particularly in embroidery, the intricacy was made a stitch at a time, error as well as triumph, sometimes stippled with drops of the artist's own blood. Now, he realized the parallel of his mother's work to the fabric of one's life. Sometimes there had to be a little blood, a little struggle, for it to remain a worthwhile project.

But, as he bent over the still figure of the unconscious human, he vowed that any further blood spilled would be his own. He would not sacrifice the innocent in the tapestry of his future.

The thrum of the cruiser in its flight had nearly lulled Palaton to sleep when Rand stirred and his eyelids fluttered. The gentle awakening gave Palaton hope—those deranged by Chaos unreality often woke with twitches and convulsions as their minds fought with their bodies. He roused himself, stifling a yawn, as Rand's eyes opened. The humankind blinked rapidly several times.

Then, softly, "Palaton?"

"It is I."

Rand grabbed his arm. "I almost had it," he

said. "Almost had it ..." Weakened, his grasp loosened and the boy subsided.

"Had what?"

"I ... don't know."

"Dreams," Palaton offered. "If you have them."

Rand's eyes rolled a bit in their sockets, then the boy focused on him again. "Oh," said the boy softly. "We have them." He licked his lips. "So that's what I miss every time I take the drugs."

"That, and more. I can't expose you further."

Rand's head turned slightly to see if the observation screens were open. They were not. He shifted his weight upon the couch and let out a tiny groan. "Everything hurts."

"You hit the floor rather hard."

"Mmmm." Rand's face twisted.

"Was it worth it?" Curiosity piqued Palaton. Had Rand seen with his borrowed *bahdur*? Such a thing was unthinkable, but he had to ask.

A strange expression shuttered Rand's face. "I'm not sure ... I'll let you know," the boy said.

Unsatisfied, Palaton stood. "I'll get the meds."

"No."

Halfway across the lounge to the standard meds cabinet on the far wall, Palaton twisted in midstep. "What?"

"I'm all right now."

"You could lapse again at any moment. I cannot predict your next reaction. You could lose everything, Rand, all touch with reality and yourself. I won't allow the possibility."

The boy did not respond immediately. There was a vibration in the decking beneath Palaton's boots. Through senses other than the paranormal, he became aware that Rufeen was taking the

cruiser through a series of shifts and maneuvers.
The pilot's activities were also setting up rapid
changes in the perceptual fields of those not ma-
nipulating Chaos or those who were not capable
of it. The ripple effect would be hitting them momentarily. He did not want Rand to suffer. Palaton abruptly continued his journey, took down the
meds case, and brought it to Rand.

He forcefed the meds while the boy's attention
seemed distracted and though Rand almost
choked on one of the caplets, he swallowed quickly
and made a bitter face. It gained his attention.
"Don't take no for an answer."

"I do not," answered Palaton solemnly, "intend
to." He waited until Rand closed his eyes and
slipped into a light sleep. Then he took up a
watchful position in a nearby chair and fought the
effects of Chaos upon himself. Taking a deep
breath, he slipped into the calming meditation
he'd learned as a raw cadet at Blue Ridge, where
his true life as a Choyan and a *tezar* had begun.
His grandfather's Householding had only been a
temporary nest, a crib, a beginning. Blue Ridge
was where his heart belonged.

He leaned his neck into the molded headrest,
finding respite from the weight of his horn crown
as he did so, and let himself go. He dreamed, remembering his days on Cho as a simple pilot when
a *tezar* had garnered more cheers from the masses
than even an emperor.

Rufeen's low-pitched voices woke him. "Heir Palaton, are you available?"

There was sand in his eyes, and his throat hurt
as if he had been trying to talk in his sleep. He

sat up and keyed open the interlink between the
lounge and the com. With an eye to Rand, who
still seemed to rest quietly, he answered, "I'm
here."

"I have just requested berthing assignment. Palaton . . . there is an awkwardness. Cho will not
give us clearance to land."

Awkwardness was an understatement. "What?"

"Heir Palaton. . . ."

Heir. Not *tezar*, but heir. Panshinea's heir. The
heir to all the chaos which reigned at home in the
wake of Panshinea's brilliant but often erratic rule
and now the emperor's sudden departure to the
Halls of the Compact. Was he being refused as
Panshinea's heir? Was Cho already being torn into
pieces by factions readying to take the throne?

"Have you been given a cause?"

Rufeen sounded abject. "My apologies. I may
have precipitated this. I sent ahead for medical
facilities to be readied for the humankind. Palaton, the Congress has refused to allow an alien to
set foot on Cho."

He had hoped to bring Rand in quietly, anony-
mously, as the emperor's privilege, under his
cloak. But now Rufeen's solicitousness had tipped
his hand. Palaton took a deep breath, thinking.

Changing air pressure disturbed the lounge, as
the far bulkhead opened, and Rindy struggled in.
His robes were rumpled as if he'd not only slept,
but fought in them. His gaunt frame looked more
frail than ever as the prelate joined Palaton and
sat in the chair opposite. He asked mildly,
"Trouble?"

Before answering, Palaton put a hand out and
keyed the interlink com to privacy mute their con-

versation from Rufeen. "It appears we won't be allowed to land."

"Really?" An eyebrow arched, sending off an avalanche of wrinkles down the elder's brow. "I'd like to see how you're going to deal with this." And he folded his hands across his tiny paunch and watched Palaton with an air of dry amusement. It was the prelate's equivalent of saying "I told you so."

In this situation as well, Palaton did not intend to take no for an answer. However, he had a feeling that the berthing refusal included an armed response.

"Rufeen, have they put any teeth into their bite?"

"We'll be shot down. Shields are up everywhere. There is an offer to put a hospital barge into orbit, so the humankind can be treated. That's all the communication we've had so far."

Her response reinforced what Palaton surmised. He was not being rejected. Only the boy. He should have anticipated the response. The Choyan had never allowed mass exposure to their private lives, where their abilities might be deciphered and revealed. They had adopted an isolationist policy centuries ago . . . and they would not abandon it now for him. What few aliens had ever set foot on Cho had done so only under acute insistence from the Compact.

Rand quaked under his hand. The humankind he'd sworn to protect, even as the manling protected his power, was in jeopardy. He didn't have the time to play politics.

Rindy grew impatient. "What are you going to do?"

"Make Congress change its mind."

"And how do you propose to do that? We're talking about representatives from 483 counties, not to mention the fallow lands. Levying that kind of political weight could take months, if not years, even if Panshinea were solid in his throne."

It was a disadvantage of the Cho system of government, which was broken down into smaller, autonomous counties rather than large blocks of nations or continents. Rallying support could take a great deal of effort. Political Houses and players were deft at what they did. On the other hand, resource management was far more efficient on a smaller scale. Palaton stood up.

"Oh, I don't intend to play their game. I think I may have to appeal to a higher court."

"Higher court?" Rindy questioned. "What are you thinking of, my son?"

"Dreams."

"What?"

Palaton took the mute off the interlink line. Rufeen responded a little frostily after having been given dead air for so long. "Palaton?"

"I want you to set up a general broadcast."

"I can do that, but it won't be effective until we've decelled into space norm. And when we do that, Palaton, we'll be within range of strike missiles. They can blow us off the air, literally, if they wish."

Palaton said gently, "I'm aware of that, *tezar*." Before she could apologize yet again, he said, "Let me know when you've gained orbit and made the setup."

Rindy plucked at a thread on his hemline. "What is it you're doing?"

He considered his elder. Rindy's wide, blue-hued eyes regarded him steadily. Palaton answered, "I'm going to appeal to the masses, Prelate. To the Godless, the Houseless. I'm going to ask for a general strike, if need be, to bring us down. I intend to trade shamelessly on my reputation as a *tezar*."

"That's unheard of! Palaton, you're playing with forces you've no inkling of. Even Panshinea would never consider such a move!"

"Have I a choice?"

The elder grew quiet. He looked at the sleeping humankind's face. "Once again, I think not. But I beg you to reconsider. You will be enfranchising their voice, the voice of the masses. You will be giving them the unsaid promise that you will listen to them in the future, that you will owe them. Such promises, spoken or not, may be very difficult to keep. The God-blind do not have those rights."

"And if I tell the Congress of my intentions, will they yield to me, do you think?"

Rindalan considered the question. His thin chestnut fringe of hair lay wispily along his bold scallop-edged crown. He scratched his fingers through his hair as if stirring up concepts. Then he shook his head. "I don't think so. They're a stubborn lot."

"Then I have to go to the commons. And, having made that decision, I think perhaps it's best the Congress not know of it. Surprise will be part of the effect. Rindy, I can't not bring Rand down with me. You know that."

"I know that you seem to think that." The prelate sighed. He put his hands on his knees, bony knees which stuck up through the fabric of his overrobe. "Desperate times provoke desperate measures, it has often been said. But are you this desperate?"

"The Abdreliks and the Ronins must not get hold of either Rand or me. Only Cho can protect us."

"But can you protect yourself from Cho?" Rindy paused. "The God-blind do not have the privileges we do for the simple reason that they cannot see as we do. Our attitudes and our laws protect them and our world from their careless actions. Be sure you're not opening the door to mob rule."

"Are you accusing me of being God-blind?"

"No. Just . . . hasty." Rindy looked away a moment, as decel alarms sounded. He pressed himself back in the contour chair as though awaiting a nasty but necessary exploit. "I cannot condone this."

But he could have taken steps to stop it, and was not going to. The elder Choya closed his pale eyes against the glare of the lounge.

As the cruiser bucked into normal space, Rufeen informed him that the broadcast link had been made and waited for him. He took a moment to compose what he would say. Then he opened the comlink and began to speak.

Rindy opened his pale blue eyes and considered him as he did so. The stare was steady and quiet, the prelate's thoughts hidden away. Rand awoke to the sound of Palaton's voices and he lay quietly on the couch, listening.

Palaton finished, then closed the com link. "What's done is done," he said. "I hope it's been done well."

Rindy said ironically, "You seem to have inherited Panshinea's love for that humankind, Shakespeare, as well as his throne."

"Do you think it will work?"

"I have no doubt it will," Rindy answered him. "But I have every doubt of its wisdom."

Chapter 5

"He dares a lot."

"He dares everything," the listening Choya responded, without turning to look at the speaker, the gold in his eyes glistening with the intensity of his response.

The speaker sat with a rustle of fabric. He took off his robe of office and folded it across his lap. The room they occupied was hidden deep within the city, hidden from official eyes and official laws and even the official religion of Cho. His name was Chirek and the robe he arranged into folds would be his death sentence if he was found wearing it. The religion of the God-blind had been crushed centuries ago by a concerted effort of the Houses of Earth, Sky, and Star—one of the few things they agreed upon, Chirek thought with irony—and had retreated to a hidden, furtive profile. The request of the *tezar* they listened to might well force the Hidden Ways back into the open, and into conflict again. Yet, as a priest and a leader of the commons, Chirek could not refuse to listen. He had sworn upon taking up his duties that he would wait for that Choya who would someday come—a Being of Change—and make all ways open to the God-blind . . . restore that which had been inexplicably taken from them . . . and all would be equal upon the face of their world. He spoke softly.

"What do you think of this Choya, Malahki?"

The luminary of Danbe reluctantly turned from a broadcast he had already listened to a multitude of times that day and faced his priest. "I know him," replied Malahki. "Panshinea tried to break him over the Relocation but instead sent him into self-imposed exile. The *tezar* is honest."

"Scrupulously so?"

"Genuinely so. He does not need to take care of every word, every action, because the honesty is deeply ingrained in him. And because he doesn't take care, he stumbles. I won't pretend to you that he is not a flawed hero. And because he doesn't dissemble well, I wouldn't want to confide in him."

Danbe was now a fallow land, in a county which existed in name only on the rolls of Congress, and Malahki's position as head of that county had been reduced to nothingness, though his role among the commons remained intense and powerful. Chirek stood, and found the hidden spring on his bookcase. A tiny cabinet opened. He put away the vestiges of his religious self and shut the cabinet. "But would you trust him?"

"Yes."

"He seeks to use us."

"They all do," Malahki answered dryly. He sat back in his chair and draped a burly leg over the tabletop in front of him. "He does so without guile. And, even so, isn't this part of what we wait for? We *will* be recognized if you back us. I can bring what forces I can, but only you, Priest Chirek, can order us out in numbers."

"The Housed are not stupid. If we crowd the streets in response to Palaton's plea, we may well be exposing ourselves."

Malahki interrupted with a shrug, as if to say that Chirek told him nothing new, which the priest realized as well. He went on to say, "We can do little until the Change comes among us, giving us equality."

The Choya lifted a finger. "I cannot wait for a deliverer who may not come in my lifetime. This may be political and not religious, but who's to say we can't accomplish some of the same ends? Whether he knows it or not, Palaton has offered us power, and the means to show that we do have influence upon the Householdings. We have a *voice* upon Cho. It's time to shout with it."

Chirek stood in his library, surrounded by ancient things, maintained with a love and duty to their value, but he valued the lives of his followers no less, and so he hesitated. "There are others I need to consult with."

Malahki recognized his cue and rose from the chair. He knew that the priesthood structure within the Hidden Ways was as obscure as the religion itself, and that although he knew Chirek well, he had met few of the others in the priestly hierarchy. "We haven't much time," reminded the luminary.

"I understand," replied Chirek. "But I wished to speak with you first."

"I have the honor of knowing you respect my opinion."

"That . . . and of giving you the burden of leading our people should we decide to answer Palaton's request. You'll be exposed. I'm trusting that your reactionary background will keep the Housed from looking further and deeper and seeing us."

Malahki smiled widely. "I'm even more honored."

"Good. You'll be taking a lot of abuse if we take action."

"I wouldn't have it any other way." Malahki paused on the bottom step of the stairwell which led into this secret room. "Let me just say this: when the Being of Change comes, none of us know whether the Change will begin outside or within us. Not knowing . . . can we refuse to answer Palaton? Can we turn aside any glimmer of metamorphosis, no matter how obscure or unexpected?"

A shadow of a smile passed across Chirek's face. "You ask, already certain of what we must answer. But what you forget, Malahki, is that there are other ways for us to answer Palaton without doing exactly what he requests of us. I understand what you wish us to do. I question its wisdom, as I questioned you about Palaton's character. Try and be a little patient. I'll have an answer for you shortly, although it may not be the one you want."

Malahki crossed half the distance up the stairwell in a single bound, before looking back and saying, "Don't think me sacrilegious for saying I'll pray you side with me."

Chirek laughed. "You, praying? You've already made it clear you will act with or without me."

"Yes, but it'll be easier with you."

"Only on the surface."

The gold in Malahki's eyes gleamed. "I cannot ask for more." He disappeared through the stairwell's hidden panels and there was a sudden silence in his wake.

Chirek stood by the desk and pondered his course.

*   *   *

Vihtirne of Sky, a proud, still handsome Choya'i, was livid. She paced the marble floor of the Householding's audience room, listening to the reports of the havoc in Charolon, where commons flooded the streets. "How dare he?"

Her lieutenant sat at the wallscreen, tuning in various stations through the satellite broadcasting systems. His fingertips played over the keyboard idly, the two of them having heard most of the broadcasts earlier. He kept the sound muted. His thick ebony hair was clipped pelt short in the new style affected by the Skies, but the woman behind him still dressed in the old elegance of the naturally arrogant Householders. Her mane had been multitiered and coiffed, cascading down her ramrod stiff back, and her dress of emerald green swept the flooring as her bootheels, edged in metal, clicked impatiently.

"He has to be stopped."

Asten replied, "You forced his hand. What did you expect?"

"I?" Vihtirne paused in her pacing, turned, and raised an arched brow. Her facial jewelry, only the thinnest tracing of platinum and gold, accented the flush of her cheeks. "You value my influence with the Congress too highly. If I could stem this tide, I could take the throne."

Her lieutenant put his head back, taking his eyes off the wallscreens for the merest instant, and looked at her. She held his stare.

Then, relenting, "Perhaps you're right." She walked to Asten's side. "Still, it remains true, I can do nothing further in all of this without Nedar." Her brilliant, sapphire gaze swept over the wallscreens. "That should be Nedar's name they call. Although . . ." and her eyes narrowed. "Bringing in the Godless may seal Palaton's fate. They're uncontrollable. Palaton is a hero, but it remains to be seen whether he's a statesman of any kind. The emperor will not be pleased. Palaton may find his support eroded."

"Any statesman would pale in your shadow," Asten said. Another broadcast caught his attention and he focused the screens on it. He stopped as her hand dropped to his shoulder and gripped it with the strength of an iron claw. His lips thinned and whitened with the effort not to call out. The scene of the commons flooding the city of Charolon bled from his vision with the agony as her nails dug deep.

"Don't mock me," Vihtirne warned.

"I do not!"

"False flattery is much the same." She lifted her hand. "You are young and handsome, Asten, and I have yet to know if that is the limit to your talents. But there is no time for games. We have to find Nedar."

"He's not responded to any of the messages you had me put out. Wherever he is, he's keeping his own counsel." The lieutenant made an effort not to shrug away the pain of her touch. She had no sympathy for the weak. He had worked too hard to gain this position and her trust to lose it now. "Shall I rebroadcast?"

"Do whatever you have to to find him." Vihtirne frowned. "What's happening in Charolon?"

Asten took a cautious breath, sizing up the data coming in from the various broadcasts. "They've just given berthing permission."

"It did not take them long to capitulate, did it?" She watched the screen avidly, her lips half-parted. "After all these years, they've grown soft. I want to see what they do when I reclaim the water recycling patent." She laughed softly. "We all drink water, don't we, Asten?"

Her lieutenant did not answer. He was busy bringing up the message records to do as she had requested. But the short, fine hairs at the back of his neck rose. She laughed as she stroked the back of her hand against them.

*   *   *

A continent away, braced against the northern lands of Isaya, a Householding of Earth came to a halt, its members leaving the winter grasslands and their herding, taking conveyances and cruisers in response to a summoning. They scraped their feet free of grass and earth and dung before crossing the threshold, heads bowed, for the doors of Kilgalya were now the greatest of the doors in the House of Earth, and had been ever since the wounding of Tregarth decades ago.

If they had questions as they entered, they stilled themselves, for monitors had been set up in the great hall and they could see the streets of Charolon filling with commons in answer to a plea the communicators took delight in rebroadcasting again and again.

Old Devon stood awaiting them at the summit of the great hall. Years had bent his strong Earthan frame. His horn crown had thinned to brittleness and even curled somewhat with age. His hair shone shock-white, and his dark eyes blazed.

"This is what a House Descendant gives us to rule us." Old though he looked, Devon's voices boomed throughout the great hall and his assemblage. "They, and the Skies, choose to forget that the Wheel turns for them. We are the heirs of the Wheel. It is our House which awaits the fall of Panshinea." Devon paused then, for the swell of noise from the Choyan listening to him made speaking impossible for a moment. After the shouts died down, and the only noise in the hall was once again those muted tones from the monitors, the old Choya raised his chin, and his ebon gaze swept across the faces of his listeners. "We have our own heir, and we will not stop until he sits in place of Palaton. The *tezar* tells us that bringing a humankind here is a matter of world security. Do you accept this?"

Cries of "No!" boomed out before the question was even finished. Devon nodded in satisfaction. "If you do not, then I will not. Go to your Households. Do what is necessary to bring the Wheel into alignment. For too many centuries we who have striven for balance have been overlooked and ill-used. We will not bend our backs so that others can step up to the throne over our bodies again. There is only one restriction I put upon you: do not sully the reputation of the House's heir. Ariat must remain blameless of any action you take." The old Choya took in a great sucking breath, as though what he had said, sparing as it was, had taken all the energy out of him. He waved a hand, dismissing them. "Go and do what you have to do."

*   *   *

Beyond the obsidian gloss of the landing field, at the edge of sand and dirt, where the great domed berthing cradles lay, a tide of Choyan could be seen pushing against the invisible barrier which held them back. Palaton stood, leaving his seat on the passenger ferry, and looked over the crowd. The beat of their voices could be heard even at this distance.

Rindy arranged his robes over his knees. "I'll take the boy in with me," he offered. "You must meet the crowd you summoned."

"I have to. I'm looking at riot now. It would take very little to loose them—" Palaton sat down. He felt stunned. He had done nothing to earn such devotion, such a following, and he felt helpless in its grip. Though he had hoped for a massive strike, he did not know his words would fill the streets of the capital with commons from all over the world.

The Prelate looked at him. "You knew and yet you didn't know."

"I don't think anyone could know about something like this." Palaton twisted his neck slightly to watch the horizon as the hover ferry droned its way across the field.

"This is not a criticism of you, my son, and yet you should hear it: Panshinea would have known. Vihtirne and many others would have. Perhaps they could not have commanded it, but they would have known, would have expected this."

Palaton came around until he could meet Rindy's stare. "Is this for me . . . or for the *tezar* who may well be Panshinea's permanent heir?"

"Does it matter?"

"Yes."

"Then you must find the answer out yourself, because I can't tell you that." Rindalan nodded. "Only they have that answer." He paused as the humankind groaned and began to move on his litter. "It's best you don't expose him to this. If he's seen as your weakness. . . ."

"Thank you, Rindy." Palaton leaned forward, elbows on his folded legs as the boy awoke and looked around, a bit bewildered.

"We're dirtside," he said.

Rand croaked a sound, then swallowed and began again, "Already?"

Rindy chuckled. "You slept a good bit of the trip," he said.

The boy's face twisted. "I feel like I slept inside a chalk quarry." He sat up and swung his feet over the side of the litter. The ferry shuddered under his movement. Those quick, turquoise eyes turned to the windows and took in the sight.

It was a hot summer's day outside Charolon. The bright cerulean sky held not a wisp of cloud to mar it and the towers of the city speared the horizon beyond the spaceport berthing cradles. The green of the early spring still covered the greenbelts which crossed the city's girth, though the air was hot and dry. Birds arrowed across the outbuildings, their shadows dappling the ground below like dots of much needed rain.

Rindy took a deep breath as if feeling the boy's awe at what he saw made Rindy himself experience it anew. The boy broadcast, not with power, but with the expression on his unetched face and in his luminous eyes. Only humankind had eyes like the Choyan. Perhaps this explained some of Palaton's natural empathy toward the humankind. The priest reached forward and patted the boy's knee. "You'll be with me," he said. "Palaton has supporters to greet."

Rand looked at him quickly. The wide, guileless eyes sized him up before Rand turned back to the window, saying flatly, "All right."

Rindy said ruefully, "I'm glad to have won your approval."

Palaton looked to them both, and stayed silent.

Just inside the security outbuilding that shut the commons away from their arrival, he could see the contingent of palace security waiting to meet them. A Choya'i stood to the fore, tall, her bronzed hair clipped back from her horn crown, her stature formidable, her uniform severe, and, like a brilliant gem in a simple setting, her beauty shone through. Jorana, come to see him home. Palaton wondered if he dared assume anything else about her presence.

As the hover ferry settled onto its pad, its hum fading, the gullwing side doors opened. Jorana stood in their frame and he could see her gray-blue eyes, always more gray than blue, widen a bit.

She beckoned attendants forward, the cabinet badge on her right shoulder winking with the movement. The Choyan who snapped to her soundless order did so with pale faces, for how often was it that a cabinet member came personally to direct security forces?

They wheeled out a chair for Rand, who collapsed into it a bit more quickly than he had expected. Rindy, in his stately, aged way of moving, emerged after the humankind and Palaton followed. He ducked under the archway of the hover's door frame and then straightened to find Jorana looking at him.

"It is good to see you, *tezar*, after thinking you lost." Her voices were deceptively formal, their tone an invisible barrier as effective as the sonic one which guarded these buildings.

"And good to see you, too." He did not bother to hide his own emotion at their reunion. The look of wonder which lit her face for a brief second was his reward.

Jorana dropped a shoulder and turned about to look down on the humankind. Her face ran through a gamut of expressions, from distaste to curiosity. "And this," she remarked, "is our problem?"

"None other."

"He doesn't look so worrisome to me. They looked smaller on the broadcasts from Sorrow." She leaned slightly away from the litter, body language at odds with the casual tone of her voices. "I will be curious to know why you've brought him and just why he is so valuable to our world security."

Rand's gaze flickered up at the Choya'i.

She examined him so intently, and without speech, that he reached into himself and shielded himself as Palaton had taught him, fearing that those cold gray-blue eyes must surely be spearing right through the truth of him. "I'm sorry."

"Really?" she said finally, her Trade accented with irony. "Then perhaps we should have left you to the Abdreliks and the Ronins."

"I'm not that sorry," Rand muttered. "Just for the trouble I've caused."

The corner of Jorana's mouth twitched. "If not you, then someone would have. We Choyan do not lead calm lives." Her gray-blue eyes lifted up, took Palaton's measure. "Though perhaps some of us are more prone to trouble than others. What more have you planned?"

Rindalan offered. "I'm taking the humankind with me. Palaton will stay behind to greet his supporters. May I suggest, O learned one, that you leave the bulk of the guard with him?"

Jorana gave the Prelate a long stare from under her eyelashes as if deciphering the other's motives. Then she nodded briskly. "That would seem to be best. They're all yours, Palaton."

"And their mood?"

"Who can say of the God-blind?" But a darkness passed through her eyes, and she did not elaborate. "As for the Housed . . . you've made enemies you cannot afford to have." Jorana touched his forearm, briefly. "It's not too late to turn the tide. Go back. Take your charge to a Compact base. Return to a position of neutrality."

Palaton shook his head once. "What's done is done."

"Do you think so?" Jorana looked him over. Her gaze lingered, more intimate than her touch on his arm. "I would persuade you differently."

"I don't want persuasion. I need support."

"Then I'm here also," she answered. She cleared her throat and added briskly, "The communicators are broadcasting from the general lobby. Once outside, my forces will be needed to move you bodily to the conveyance. Don't let the press rattle you . . . keep moving past them to the conveyance. Then let the commons parade you to the capitol building. They've gone hungry a long, long time . . . it will take a while for them to feed on this."

And she would know well, this remarkable Choya'i who herself had just come out of the God-blind, the Houseless, the commons. He nodded. "All right. I'll meet you later." He touched Rand on the shoulder. "You'll be fine."

The boy's head jerked in answer to his own. Palaton left them, guards bracing him, and made his way to the general lobby, where he could see the communicators and imagemen waiting for him. There was a swell of sound as physical as any tide rushing to meet him as he stepped through. For a moment, he gloried in it.

Rand could see little of the city through the phalanx that remained between him and the shielded windows of the conveyance. What he did see surprised him. Charolon looked old, a fortress city, surrounded by high-rises and courtyard buildings, not unlike major cities on Earth. The technology he had expected, if it was there, stayed hidden. He leaned back with a sigh.

The elder Choya's gaze settled on him. "What is it?"

"Nothing. Just that I—well, I expected something different. Something more."

"More?"

"You're so much older. . . ."

Understanding dawned across Rindalan's face. "Ah. You expected floating towers, slide walks . . . miracles of technology?"

"Yes."

The Choya folded his hands across one knee. "The simpler way is better. Less pollution. We build with wood and stone, for example, because wood is a renewable resource, and stone can be reshaped many times. The buildings here," and he unwove a hand and beckoned, "are made of vegetable fiber, then reinforced. They will break down after five decades or so, and then be replaced."

"Vegetable fiber?"

"Genetically enhanced and ribbed. Giant gourds, if you will, cut to size and glued into place."

"You grow your buildings?"

"Put that way, I suppose I would have to say yes."

Rand craned his neck to look again. "And who lives there?"

"This section of Charolon is inhabited mainly by the masses whom Palaton called upon to strike." Rindy moved uncomfortably as the conveyance swayed over an awkward bit of road. "More correctly termed, the God-blind."

"Because they can't sense God."

The Prelate dropped his chin affirmatively. "Succinctly put, yes. All those of us who are Housed can see the God-in-all. But there is a lesser strain of Choyan who cannot. Of necessity, they remain lesser. Their blindness can, and has in the past, caused our world great difficulty." Rindy gave him a piercing look. "Just as you've done to your world."

Rand pondered what Palaton had already told him, coupling it with what Rindy said now. How would his world be, indeed, if those who had been so unheeding could have seen the presence of God in everything they'd fouled? He looked at the tenements they passed. "Do you let them live among you, anyway?"

"Homes are not Houses," the Choya answered, and the emphasis put out by his dual voices left the distinct impression on Rand that Houses were lineages, like royalty.

"What if you're born into a House, and you can't see, or you lose the seeing. Are you driven out?" Behind his question lurked the worry of how much he would have to protect Palaton.

"No. Sometimes it skips a generation. And among the Godless, there are also born those who can see the God-in-all. We have testing every few years to determine the ability. But there are enormous power struggles on Cho among the Householdings. No one is driven out intentionally, but quite a few fall from power."

Rand looked at him speculatively. "Can you see God in me?"

"Most assuredly. All living things, or things once alive, hold the God-in-all. Some more vibrantly than others. I would hardly be a priest if I could not see God."

Rand put out his hand and stared at it. Rindy laughed and the boy flushed, then put his hand back down at his side.

"Is it daunting?"

Rand chewed a bit on his lower lip before answering. "I'm not sure," he said slowly. "I wondered if you could also see . . . evil."

"The anti-God Ummmm. Evil is easier to detect by action than by sight. But then, evil has always been more difficult to deal with than good."

"A universal truth." Rand put his head back on the conformed seat. The headrest intended for Choyan heads and necks stretched above him.

"One of many that binds us together. The Compact is composed of more similarities than differences."

Rand's gaze flickered back to him. "I think," he said, "that you would like to think so." He lapsed into silence and Rindy would have liked to let him keep it, for the manling looked weary, but he could not.

"We separated you and Palaton," he said, "out of necessity. He would never allow what we must insist on next."

Turquoise eyes watched him. Rindy patted his robe over his knees, arranging the fabric as he arranged his words. "Cho does not accept alien visitors lightly. We have had fewer than a handful over the last several centuries."

A squat black building rose on the horizon. A barrier along its perimeters gave it grounds undisturbed by the commons who had been rampant along the streets. Its ebony windows reflected back the Choyan sky. Rand saw it framing Rindy's head, intense and disquieting. He realized they were heading toward it.

"I had no choice about being here," Rand said. He felt his voice thin with apprehension. He tried to still the tide rising in his chest.

"And, unfortunately, the heir gave us no choice about accepting you. But that does not mean that we cannot take precautions."

Gates opened with a deathly quiet. The conveyance passed within. Guards who had been pacing the vehicle now spread out and took up stances within the barrier, as though bracing it. As they drew close to the building, Rand could see Choyan issuing from a side door, and they wore protective clothing similar to deep space suits, or like the garb firemen wore when facing environmental disasters. Rindy leaned from his seat.

"I will stay with you," the Prelate said.

As a friend? Or as someone who had decided to learn all that could be wrung from him? Rand swallowed questions that he knew would get no answers and concentrated on the shielding Palaton had taught him. He had no doubt he would need it desperately.

Chapter 6

Hat turned away from the wallscreen, snapping off the communicators' comments with a great deal of satisfaction as the room went both dark and silent at the same time. Like kites, he thought, they would circle above Palaton until nothing was left but bones. Or about Charolon until nothing was left of it but black powdered stones. They were gossip mongers, little better.

And what more was he than a nursemaid, the Earthan added, as he heaved to his feet. This wing of Blue Ridge was empty, quiet and anticipatory. It had been scrubbed within a layer of its original tiling by the cadets who'd abandoned it half a year ago, in waiting for the next class. They would be here as soon as Palaton, as Emperor's Heir, passed on the results of the various Choosings from around their world. In all the time Hat had been at Blue Ridge, first as a cadet, then as a *tezar*, and now as master, no one but Panshinea had ever judged the results of the Choosings. He wondered if there would be a discernible difference this time. How odd that a classmate would be judging them.

Not that he had ever been a *tezar* the equal of Palaton or Nedar. No. Modesty was not a part of

Hat's makeup. He was practical, solidly rooted like the earth and stone of his House. Having left that Householding for Blue Ridge, he had never looked back. He doubted that he even heard from his family for anything less than a major death. He'd given them all up for the life of a *tezar*, and then when he'd been asked to give that up for the cadets, he'd been happy to do so. He was happier here as a master and teacher and, yes, nursemaid, than he'd ever been as a *tezar*, a conqueror of Chaos. Moameb, the old master, had read him well and when asked to take over the elderly Choya's position, leaving space had not been a sacrifice for him.

And so it made it ironic that he, who had never particularly cherished his *bahdur* and all its uses in defining Chaos and piloting FTL drive, he would never lose his *bahdur* as a *tezar* would, burning it out, suffering the atrophy and death of the nerve pathways that conducted those psychic powers until there was no power and there was only aching, agonizing illness and death awaiting. The fate of a *tezar* would never be his, as it had been thought to have been Palaton's.

He had never thought Palaton gone, lost in *bahdur* burnout, though his disappearance had never ceased to be grist for the mill of the communicators. In truth, the weeks and turnings of Palaton's travail had passed to Hathord like all time passed, measured by the growth of the classes of cadets at Blue Ridge. If he had worried about Palaton, perhaps he might have joined in the speculation, but he had not. No Choya or Choya'i he had ever known had burned as brightly as Palaton. Therefore, it was impossible for him to imagine the void without him. Palaton would not simply flicker out. He would smolder for decades before his brilliance was lost. Hat just knew it would be that way.

As for Nedar, the war pilot would undoubtedly go down in flames as well, but in action, not in solitude waiting for inevitable disease and death. Hat just knew that would be the way as well.

Although he had not heard from Palaton in years, Nedar came back to Blue Ridge from time to time. He had, like Palaton, rooms in the graduate quarters. His quarters were kept locked and unoccupied until the arrogant Choya returned to throw them open. When he possessed the rooms (Nedar never occupied a space, he *possessed* the place with all the vibrancy that was possible), the cadets would come to see him, a Choya of incomparable ability, a legend in his own time as Palaton had also become. To Hat's pleasure and surprise, his old classmate welcomed the cadets. He regaled them with tales of Chaos and listened patiently to their questions.

The only thing he would not discuss with them was *bahdur*. It was considered a breach of etiquette anyway and few ever tried, though it was always on their minds, like sex. How did it feel when it burned bright and how did it feel when one began to lose it, to grasp for it, to have it fail you. . . . How does it feel?

Those questions Nedar would brush aside with a steely, dark glance and simply leave hanging in the air. Usually the cadet who asked would fall prey to embarrassment and leave, not to return that evening or perhaps during the entire term of

Nedar's stay. Even the brash knew when they had overstepped Nedar's bounds.

That look of rancor had never been turned toward Hat nor did he ever fear that it would. He and Nedar were friends, though how such a thing had been fated, he could never be sure. He had come to Blue Ridge only because he had the talent to do so and because the resulting contracts would be invaluable to his family. Nedar had come because the Salt Towers refused him and, despite his arrogance, he had an inborn need to pilot that was as necessary to him as breathing. Hat had seen that in him right away.

He'd also been friends with Palaton, but Palaton had many acquaintances. He was not given to the dark moods which singled Nedar out, but he felt those of the other Choya keenly.

As Hat rambled through the empty corridors, he thought of those early days before the friendship had begun. The fear of flying clenched a bit in his stomach. He could fly, but he did not want to. No. Nursing the cadets here, sharing in their joy and fears, that made him much happier. Flying used to tear the very insides from him and he could tell no one of it.

Then that dark day when one of the cadets had died early, far earlier in training than any cadet had ever died at Blue Ridge, brought his fears colliding with the future. It had been a horrible, horrible accident. Death was always waiting in the shadows at any of the pilot schools—they eventually flew blind, relying on nothing more than the wings of their thrust glider and their *bahdur*, the beginning of the final tests for those who would become *tezars*. Months of mathematics and phys-

ics would follow once wings had been won to
make a pilot of universes, but here at Blue Ridge,
one first had to learn to fly the uncertain winds of
Cho. When the sensory deprivation began, there
was always a death or two. That had been
expected.

This had not. And in a way Hat had never
learned, Nedar had somehow been a part of it. No
one knew of it but Hat and Moameb, the elder
tezar who then ran Blue Ridge with the aid of his
staff. Hat had been sent as a runner to fetch Nedar
to tell him that he had been found faultless. No
one else would ever know Nedar had even been
under a cloud of suspicion.

So Hat had come upon Nedar in his rooms, silent, brooding, drinking, and the stink of fear
shrouded him. He sat in his swivel study chair,
his booted feet propped up, a glass in his hand.
That a Choya such as Nedar could be afraid had
struck Hat speechless and he'd just stood on the
threshold of the other's rooms.

Nedar had eventually looked at him. "What
have you come to tell me?" he'd demanded.

But in his voices, Hat heard that which could
be pitied. Nedar *feared*.

"If I fail here," Hat said, "I can never go home.
I fear that every day."

Nedar dropped his feet to the floor. He let a
pause hang in the air before answering, "What has
that to do with me?"

And then Hat had given him the news that the
investigation had been concluded and he had been
found blameless.

From that day forward, something else, unspo-
ken, had passed between them. It remained to this

day and so, when a voice, low and guttural, issued out of the shadows, Hat turned to it unafraid. He had been more than half-expecting it.

"Nedar! You've come home."

Hat banked the fire in his study. He watched the flames' reflection upon the etched planes in his friend's face. Nedar had always been handsome. Now his face was sharp-edged, almost painful to look at, his eyes smoldering and sunken within it. The *tezar* nursed the drink in his hand, barely sipping at the amber liquid now and then as if only to moisten his voices.

The tale he'd been told astounded him: renegades, a hidden colony, the luring of *tezars* to their Householdings in order to maintain a legacy of starflight. Destruction and torture . . . Hat sat back in wonder.

"No one has said anything of this," he voiced. "We had never heard of Arizar before the Abdreliks accused us before the Compact. And there has never been any mention of colonization."

"And there won't be, publicly. They were scoured from Arizar, Hat, burned to ashes too difficult to sift. There was no evidence left for the Compact. I wish I could say I was sorry, but the renegades were merciless in their own purposes. They intended me to die," finished Nedar. "My body was given over to be disposed of. But I was not dead! My *bahdur* stayed kindled within me, an ember that I drew on, until I gained enough strength to fight back and free myself."

The gauntness, the hunger in the eyes, now Hat understood them. "Nedar, I—"

"No. Listen to me. If I stay, I'll bring that danger to you. Palaton has returned as well . . . and I don't yet know if he is an enemy or if they used him as badly as they used me. But I do know this—" And Nedar's intensity burned him more hotly than the hearthfire they sat near. "He was there. He was alive when I was taken for dead. I cannot trust him until I know the truth."

"Nor I," blurted Hat without thinking. He bit his lip as silence followed. "How did you land? We were shielded against—" he stopped. Against Palaton.

Nedar smiled. The warmth did not reach his eyes. "I came down in his wake as soon as the ports opened. Not far from here, actually. I knew I wanted to come home to Blue Ridge. You know it's the only true home I have."

"And you may stay as long as you wish. You know that, Brethren."

"As long as it doesn't threaten you or the cadets. But no one, Hat, can know I'm here. Not even my House or Householding. I will not unwittingly bring danger on any of you."

Hat had been on the edge of his chair. He sat back a little now. "You can't think that Palaton was part of it."

"I don't know what I think of our friend." Nedar took a shallow drink. "A hero can be duped as easily as a fool, if he's blind enough. Panshinea has strings on him, or thinks he does, if our emperor has made him heir. We both know our emperor has no intention of relinquishing the throne as long as he's alive. But if I know Palaton, he thinks he can break those strings, or at least resist the dance when the emperor begins to tug on them. Who knows what lured him to Arizar."

"I understand."

"Do you?" Nedar murmured. "This will be difficult for you, Hat, if my enemies come tracing me."

"Blue Ridge takes care of its *tezars*. To protect and serve, even our own. It's about time." Hat stood. "You can stay here until after hours. I'll have dinner sent in."

Nedar saluted him with his nearly full glass. "Thank you." He leaned back in his chair and half-closed his eyes, watching the fire.

Hat shut the door gently so as not to disturb him.

*   *   *

They did not want to touch him. He saw that in their faces, even through the protective face masks, as they reached for him and took him away from Rindy. Rand let out a word of protest, but the elder Choya looked sternly at him as if to say that he carried the honor of humankind and Palaton with him, and Rand bit his lip as he read the other's expression. Within the black box, he was led to a gridded room. They stripped him, even of the braces and bandages, laid him down on a grille and, after examining his eyes, gave him a pair of ocher-colored lenses to wear. Then they passed him through a series of light waves, standing behind a barrier as though he might carry the deadliest of plagues.

Rand lay on the grille and tried to think of other things. Despite the light which battered him and hurt his eyes even through the protective glasses, the room was chill and he shivered as he suffered the sterilizing. They spoke about him as if he couldn't be listening, but they spoke Trade instead of Choyan and he could not help but hear.

"What do we have on these things?"

"There's a lot from the Quinonans' data base. They did a fair amount of field lab work before they were stopped by the Compact for tampering. Want me to bring it up?"

"Do that. Let me take a look at him."

There was a pause, during which the female technician, at least he thought it was a female, he couldn't tell behind the suits, snickered, saying, "Well, we know he's mammalian and has external sexual genitalia—which, I would say, is fairly cold sensitive."

He felt his body heat with a flush that must run from head to toe. There were a few more scraps of sentences as they worked on their data base information. He overheard, "He can't be too contaminated. This is Bay station bandaging. They would have done some decon work."

"Save that. Get it over to sterilization and we'll rewrap when we're done. No sense in wasting new material on him."

No, there was no sense wasting anything on him at all. Rand turned his head as a light bar passed over him, blasting him with its brilliance. He narrowed his eyes to a slit. He was being watched from behind a barrier.

They saw him move.

"Lie still!" Aside, "We'll have to run that scan again. I want him strapped down if necessary."

Rand licked lips gone suddenly dry. He forced himself to stay in his current position, even though the leg they had unbraced ached horribly and he could feel a twitch in his thigh muscle.

It must have shown on the scan, for one of the Choyan asked sharply, "What's that?"

"Muscle spasm, in all probability. Yes. That's one of the limbs we took braces from."

"Note that, for rehabilitation. It doesn't seem to cause him much pain."

Rand thought of asking the Choya if he wished to trade places. The light bar basted him again and he managed to stay still as it passed. There was a long moment and then the head technician said, "That's done. We'll need a physical exam. Any volunteers?"

The female spoke with a shudder in her voices. "Not me."

The second tech said, "Cavity searches, orifice registration, the full works?"

"We need it on record."

A sigh. Then, "I might as well as long as I'm suited up."

Rand watched uncertainly as one of the tall, suited figures separated itself from the other two behind the barrier and strode toward him. The Choya pulled a recessed drawer from under the gridded table and Rand heard a rattle of instruments.

He bolted upright. Pain lightninged up his leg and into his hip and he spasmed in agony. The Choya's gloved hand shot out and pinned him in place. "If you insist on partaking of our hospitality," the masked face told him, eyes hard as gems, "you will have to suffer some of the disadvantages as well. We won't have plague or pestilence brought in, deliberately or accidentally."

Rand gasped as he fought to bring both his pain

and fear under control. "Just what ... do you think I am?"

"As to that, I'm not sure. I'll have a better idea when I've read the Quinonans' field report. You're a Class Zed. That's borderline enough for me." The suited Choya laid him back down and leaned over. "It's pleasanter if you relax."

They were no gentler with him when the sterilized bandages and braces were brought back in. The Choya who'd been working on him stepped back with a grimace that could be easily read behind the faceplate. "I've done enough dirty duty. Trista, you get in here and rebandage him."

Rand lay sore and bruised, draped weakly across the gridded table. The Choya had treated him no better than a piece of meat. The bandaging was a relief only in that the operation seemed to be a preliminary to letting him dress and get out of there.

The female technician worked brutally efficiently on him, retractioning leg, arm, and shoulder and wrapping him as quickly as she could. The first had returned to the work desk behind the barrier. Her supervisor called to her, "Hair, skin, and urine samples. All other bodily fluids."

Trista made a noise between her teeth. Rand lifted his head. She clubbed it back down with the palm of her gloved hand to his forehead. "Stay down," she ordered briskly.

He felt the scrape of a scalpel across his inner thigh, bringing the skin up raw and tender. "I can give you," he began, but the Choya'i interrupted briskly, "I'll take what I need," and she proceeded to do so with a catheter.

He gritted his teeth on both the anger and the hurt rising in him. When she'd finished, she leaned over. Her eyes were a strange yellow. "I'll have your clothes brought in."

"How about a little vivisection?" he spat out.

Her eyes shadowed darker. "Don't worry. We'd do it if it was called for. I haven't taken an alien apart and put it back together in a long time." Her head snapped out of his line of vision as she stepped back. "Wait here."

Rand hadn't the ability to leave, much as he wished to. He lay still, listening to the other techs argue about the reliability of Quinonan reports.

"This can't be right."

"What can't?"

"Even taking that he's got single pan brain capacity, look at this."

There was a Choyan laugh, dry and short. "According to this info, Kirlon stonework has more esper readings than humankind. I can't believe it."

"Nothing more sophisticated than occasional resonance sensitivity? Are you sure?"

"This is Compact data, confirming the Quinonans'."

"No wonder the Abdreliks are drooling. These guys fail in the Compact and GNask is looking at a big stew pot for dinner."

Rand's stomach clenched. They thought of him as no more intelligent than fodder. What use did Palaton have for him, then? What did the *tezar* see in him that these other Choyan did not? And where was Rindy in all of this?

After long moments, the female tech entered the room, his clothing draped over a metal extension.

She dropped his clothes on the end of the exam table, saying, "Dress yourself."

She did not ask if he needed help, nor did he ask for any. He had to lean upon the table heavily to stay upright, but he finished the task he began.

Rindy appeared beside the barrier. "Doctors, are you quite finished?"

The tallest of the suited technicians turned to the Prelate. "I'd like to run some general IQ tests and a few esper exams."

Rindy looked at him consideringly. Then he shook his head. "We have full Compact data available on that score. It would be useless and time-consuming. I think I must insist you remand him back into my custody if you're quite finished with the decon sweep."

The tall Choya with the gem-hard eyes said dryly, "If we'd been any more thorough, he'd be dead," and turned away.

Rand did not doubt him. He sagged onto the arm Rindy held out for him. The elder Choya looked down at him. "There are some trials in life," Rindalan stated, "which are unavoidable."

Rand could not answer him. He concentrated only on putting one foot in front of the other. From behind his shielded *bahdur*, he could feel them as they watched him leave. Hatred and contempt. He wondered what humankind had done to earn it, or if the Choyan thought of all aliens in the same light.

Chapter 7

"Who on the Blasted Plains authorized him to be treated like that?"

Palaton's angered tones brought Rand's sagging eyes open wide for a moment as a pair of imperial guards lowered him to the couch of the quarters selected for him. Rindy had already bowed a Choyan courtesy and left them in the corridor. Only Jorana stood to take the brunt of Palaton's outrage.

She stood with purpose, gray-blue eyes watching as the guards saluted her and left. As they passed beyond her range of vision, she turned smartly to Palaton and said calmly, "I did."

"You did? *You did!* And what did you succeed in proving? This is my ward. I gave my word to protect him—"

"From your own people, as well?" interrupted Jorana mildly. She pushed a clump of bronze hair from her brow which had escaped from its hair clip.

Palaton's ire transmuted into a few Choyan phrases which Rand had never heard, did not understand, and had no doubt it would be useful to know someday. The Choya'i's face pinked under the onslaught, but she did not step back. She waited until Palaton finished, then said, "I could get no one to guard him willingly elsewise. You bring him out of Chaos into turmoil—would you have him be a target and unprotected simply because our guards are xenophobic and I could not control or convince them otherwise? This way, at least, I have a number of Choyan I can count on."

Palaton took a deep breath. "*I* will guard him."

Jorana looked from Palaton to Rand, who lay awkwardly where he'd been placed, his braced leg sticking out in front of him, his arm and shoulder almost at right angles to his rib cage. "And you've done an admirable job of it, so far."

His jawline worked as though he chewed on words but could not quite spit them out. Jorana waited with a half-smile curving her lips, then stepped back as though she deemed the duel finished. "We have business to discuss, heir to the throne."

Palaton crossed the room and arranged Rand more comfortably, then drew a light quilt over him. "Will you be all right?"

Rand nodded wearily. He murmured, "They hate me."

"No. They fear you."

"And there's a difference, isn't there?"

"Among civilized people, yes." Palaton adjusted a pillow under his head. "Or so we hope."

"I'm not going anywhere," the boy said. "For a while." Rand put his head back on the crown-rest pillow and closed his eyes.

Palaton took the signal to leave and joined Jorana. Without a word, she led him from the palace wing and back downstairs.

Palaton followed silently to the room he'd come

to know as Panshinea's library, with the hidden entrance from the outside atrium, and a fireplace that usually blazed brightly in the emperor's presence, rain or shine, but now was empty. Jorana's emotion filled the room instead. He did not have to have his *bahdur* to feel it himself.

"You shouldn't have brought him here," Jorana said, and her voices vibrated on both the levels of anger and concern. "Nor called on factions you can neither control nor predict the actions of. Do you have any idea what you've done?"

"I couldn't not have brought him here," replied Palaton evenly, though he did not look at her when he said it. "He's a pawn, without the defenses to protect himself. He has answers to questions we have yet to ask and because he holds those answers, he is a danger both to himself and to us."

"To *you*," Jorana corrected.

His eyes came up then, to her face, and he saw the storm cloud of emotions running across it. He did not have to empathize to be rocked by the force of her expression. "To Cho," he repeated firmly.

She took a step closer. "You jeopardize all we've worked for. I kept you alive for this."

"To be Panshinea's puppet?"

"No! To be his *heir*. And you are. It was his vanity to think he had all the time in the world to consolidate his throne and his line . . . a vanity that exemplifies why the House of Star suffers."

Palaton blinked. He said blandly, "Even for you, you speak frankly here. I would not put it past Panshinea to have his own palace thoroughly recorded."

Jorana half-spun away from him. "I know where I trespass—unlike you."

Indeed, she knew exactly what she did within the palace grounds. If she felt free to talk within this room, then so could he. There was meager solace to be found in this conversation. "So you think I trespass?"

"You presume."

"Jorana, I didn't have any choice."

"And what," she leveled at him, "will you do with him?"

"Keep him safe. Hope he's happy. Give him the future that was stripped away from him."

"There is no future here for him. Consider what you've done, Palaton, very carefully. We are still at a stage where it can be undone."

He did not answer her charge or take the hope she offered him.

"Make no mistake about what Panshinea has offered you . . . he's not going to give you the throne. You're his heir only so long as he needs you. But he does need you."

Palaton watched her. He answered, "And make no mistake about why I presented myself as his heir . . . Cho needed the stability. I'm not opportunist. I think you know that of me."

"I know that you're a *tezar* first and a politician last. Calling on the God-blind. . . . For all his faults, our emperor is a brilliant politician. He juggles as well as anyone I know. Even he wouldn't have dared as much. Malahki has taken up residency on the steps of Charolon to await audience." Jorana sucked in her breath. "Panshinea won't leave you even the crumbs of yourself."

And what would she think of him if she knew

he did not even have the *bahdur* to defend himself? He wondered how she could look at him now and not see the weakness of his aura. Did she see only what she expected to see? He wanted to tell her what had happened to him on Arizar, how he'd been offered hope and help, and now was stripped of his very essence, of all that made him a Choya and a *tezar* and held only a thin thread that he might reclaim it. Would she then accept the boy and help him? Softly, he asked, "And what would you leave of me?"

"It's not what I would leave of you . . . it's all that I would give you. I may be newly risen, I may be out of the ranks of the Godless, but my *bahdur* shines as brightly as any of the Housed. We could build what Panshinea cannot."

He felt her embarrassment and shame, begging for a liaison he had already refused her years ago. He ached to tell her of his emptiness, to see if she could fill him, and knew he didn't have the right. He shook his head. "I'm in no position to offer anyone a future. The resolution of the humankind's future and Cho's trust are my priorities now. Are you willing to wait, knowing that even then I may not offer you what you wish? I can't ask you to tangle your fortunes with mine."

As gentle as it was, it was still a refusal. Jorana sat then, a movement that translated as near collapse. "Rindy came back with you. Did he approve?"

"No. He put one of his tablets under his tongue and gave me a sour look while I tried to explain it to him."

She put her chin up. "You speak with humor, but you can't mean it."

He spread his hands. "I won't change my mind. I *can't* change my mind. If there is humor, it's that of acceptance. The boy is from a Class Zed planet. To let him go now, with the little he knows and understands, will bring a tampering charge against Cho. Not against me. Against *Cho*. There are those in the Compact who would love to prove such a case."

"We're strong enough to do without the Compact."

She left him speechless for a second as his own jaw dropped. Jorana did not blink as they stared at one another. Then Palaton caught himself. "Perhaps," he agreed. "But I don't think the Compact is strong enough to do without us."

"And must we Choyan carry the burden of the ills of all races?"

"If necessary." He spread his hands flat upon the empty desktop between them. "The people sealed within Sorrow faced an enemy we know nothing about—and who may return. As good as we are at making war among ourselves, there are none of us who could manage such a death for an entire race of people. Would you have any of us, Ronins, Abdreliks, Ivrians, Gormans, any of the others, face that enemy alone?"

The defiance bled from Jorana's finely planed face, dissolving into sadness. "You're noble."

"No. I just recognize the burden inherent."

"I disagree with you." Jorana thrust herself out of the chair, standing over him once more. "We've been staring into the frozen waters of Sorrow for generations. Most of us don't even see the faces staring back. But you do. No matter what I say, you'll do what you think you have to do, even if it destroys you."

"I'd like to think it won't go that far. But, yes. I'll do what I have to do."

"It's too bad Panshinea doesn't have this room recorded." Her glance flitted around the study. She strode to the exit. "He could learn from you."

"Jorana."

She paused at the doorway. "What?"

"Do I have your support in this?"

She shook her head, mane cascading to her shoulders. "No. Not for the boy. But I'll do whatever I can for you. You're my burden, I guess."

She left quickly, the door shutting soundly at her heels. Palaton waited a long moment, then realized he had been holding his breath, and let it go.

He sat down at Panshinea's desk. It had been cleaned of any of the emperor's business, and a fine layer of dust overlaid it. He whisked the dust away with the side of his hand as if he could dismiss his own fears that quickly.

Everything that Jorana had said had merit. He could deny none of it. He wondered what she might have said had she known the entire truth. How much of her foresight stemmed from power, and how much from shrewdness? It scarcely mattered if it helped him navigate the chaos of Panshinea's reign. He sat poised on the brink of calling her back and confessing. There was something inside of him that would not let him do it.

The door opened hesitantly. Gathon, the only Sky to hold power under Panshinea, looked in.

"Ah," he said, "here you are, Palaton. My greetings are tardy."

Gathon was of that breed of Choya who aged well. He held enough flesh to keep his facial features from growing gaunt, but he did not grow huge the way an Earthan might. Yellow-white streaked his Sky black hair, more white than Palaton remembered, but after all, they had not seen one another in years upon years. The dark, pebble brown eyes still watched with a penetrating gaze, and the minister held himself well. He did not yet feel the weight of his horn crown upon a feeble neck. Weight he might feel from his many responsibilities as Minister of Resource, but he looked as if he had held up well. He put a hand up as if to ward off some of Palaton's examination. "We need to talk, if you're not too tired from the journey."

Palaton shoved his chair back a little from the desk. "All right."

Gathon came in and sat down opposite him. He folded his hands in his lap, at ease, almost with the serenity of a Prelate. Perhaps he had found a measure of religious peace in dealing with the land's well-being, Palaton thought. "What can I do for you?"

Palaton tilted his head. "Serve me as well as you've served Cho and Panshinea."

The minister smiled tightly. Like Palaton, he did not wear facial jewelry under the translucent panes of his facial skin. Age etched his expression sharply for a fleeting moment.

"I do not necessarily serve both Cho and Panshinea in the same breath," Gathon said. "Or in the same task. Much as you serve as a *tezar* and as you may serve as an heir. I am not for you, Palaton, but neither am I against you. I will help inasmuch as I can. That having been said, I would like to give you my first recommendation."

Palaton held his tongue. Gathon waited a polite interval before continuing, "It's in both our best interests to get Malahki out of Charolon."

Palaton remembered only too well the luminary of Danbe and the incident which had forced Panshinea to drive Palaton away from Cho for so many years. He was somewhat surprised that the God-blind reactionary was still alive. This could be a difficult consequence of his actions. The revolt and Relocation of Danbe had been a bloody one. Malahki would not be an easy Choya to dismiss. "And do you think Malahki will listen to me?"

"You summoned him. I expect you will have some influence on whether he returns to his county or stays and goes underground yet again."

Palaton took a deep breath. It was time to pay the price of his support. "Done. First thing tomorrow morning. Soon enough?"

Gathon looked at him from deep, dark pools of brown. "It shall have to be."

"Anything else?"

The Minister of Resource looked at his folded hands. "What of the humankind?"

"What of him?"

"Does he have . . . full run of the palace?"

"He's not an animal, Gathon."

The Choya looked up. "Of course not. But neither is an alien a usual guest within these or any walls on Cho. What can I expect?"

"Expect nothing. He's here under my protection for a short time."

"Tampering charges from the Compact cannot be taken lightly."

"One guest does not constitute tampering with an entire people!"

Gathon stood up slowly, gathering himself. "I would hope not. He'll need protection. I'll arrange it with Jorana's staff." He paused. "You are not needed here, Palaton. Your emperor left a well-oiled machinery of rule in place."

"I gathered that. I don't seek to unsurp that rule."

"Then, knowing that, and knowing that you are not asking what Cho can do for you, you might ask yourself what you intend to do for Cho."

"What can I do?" Palaton spread his hands.

"Panshinea chose to stay on Sorrow. He chose to leave you behind, here. What are you that he is not? You are that rare Choya who has been able to step beyond the Houses and the God-blind. You are a *tezar*. We have not had a *tezar* as an heir in several centuries. Know yourself, and perhaps you will understand the needs of Cho as well." He bowed and left, back ramrod stiff as he strode through the doorway of his emperor's library.

Palaton watched him go. It was no accident Gathon had accosted him in the only sanctuary in the palace where Panshinea had no "ears."

Unsettled, he sat very still for a few moments, his head bowed in deep thought. He had to believe, he told himself, that it was also no accident he had been made heir to the throne of Cho. Whether by Panshinea's design, or his own, or by the God-in-all, he was meant to be where he was now. He *had* to believe that. And, believing, he must then explore the future of his involvement. Palaton clenched a fist. Did Gathon challenge him—or did Gathon sentence him to no future at all?

Chapter 8

Bevan struggled to open his eyes. It would do little good to use them, he knew. The drugs that the College had given him to prepare him for becoming a Brethren lay over his sight like a dark storm cloud. The cloud he had become used to, steeled himself for it—it was the unexpected rainbows which accompanied it which he could not bear to see.

He passed his hand over them. Lying on his back, there was little to see beyond the ceiling of the hut the Zarites called home. But he could hear the whispering voices of his hosts, moving about him in shadows, living as quietly and surreptitiously as they could with a stranger in their midst. He lifted his head and the prism dance of colors began. Every organic object in the room haloed with an aura of light. He squinted his eyes against the brightness. The Zarites paraded before him in a profusion of auras. Bevan closed one eye to dim his vision. Nothing could he see clearly or sharply . . . but everything pulsated with color.

He tried concentrating on the nearest blob of serene blue. From out of its haze and vague outline, the Zarite Thena, who'd been nursing him, emerged. She leaned over him and helped him sit upright.

In her soft drawl of Trade, she asked, "How are you feeling?"

"Better." He gulped down a wave of disorientation as her face dissolved into brilliant dots of color and then coalesced into facial features again. He blinked and for the barest whisper of time, he saw normalcy about him. Then the storm clouds boiled up again, and the balls of prism color began to bounce about again. He felt Thena push a clay mug into his hand. He knew thirst and drank greedily whatever drink it was she gave him. He would kill for *bren*, he thought, or coffee. Yes, coffee like that which could be bought from the street vendors and corner cafés of Sao Paulo, once his home, coffee rich and dark and steaming. . . .

The residue of liquid in the mug began to spit and boil and hissed into steam. He dropped the mug with a shout as it grew red hot in his hand and then exploded into shards.

Thena immediately grabbed up his hand and wrapped it with a cooling cloth. She made a tsking sound through her rodentlike teeth.

"What happened?"

His Zarite nurse lapsed into crooning sounds as she soothed the compress about his hand. He looked to the dirt flooring and saw the clay shards around his feet. Color oozed from them as if it were blood, crimson, alive, ebbing life.

"I did that."

"I think so, yes," Thena said. "Even in your sleep, things . . . shatter. Break. Catch fire."

"It's bleeding. . . ."

The Zarite's translucent round ears pricked forward in puzzlement. "It was just a mug. How could it bleed?"

"Can't you see it?"

Thena said patiently, "See what?" She patted his hand.

How could she not see it? Bevan blinked away watering tears and stared at the broken object. The red haze oozed away, soaking into the dirt floor, as Thena grabbed a whisk and dustpan and efficiently cleaned up the remains. He put his free hand back to the nestlike bed to steady himself.

His uniform from the College hung upon his body. He'd always been slender, now it seemed to him he must be nothing more than skin and bones. He could hear his breath rattle through his lungs, his blood *swishing* its ways through the canals of his body, the beat and tempo of his heart, and even the air drumming upon his ears. It was as if life had suddenly become too much to bear, too loud, too harsh, too strident in its demands upon him.

He narrowed his eyes to focus on Thena, trying to drive away the aura obscuring her Zarite features as she came back to him. He saw the worry, a cloud of its own, pressed upon her expression.

"You are sick," the nursemaid said, "with a poison we cannot drive out of you."

The poison of Nedar's soul or whatever the Choya had driven into him was what rattled through him. He doubted if the Zarites had a cure for that. "I'm getting better," Bevan told her and heard his deep and raspy voice as if it belonged to a stranger.

She shook her head. "The disturbances are getting worse. And ... there are strangers come to Arizar, searching."

"For me?" All thought him dead. Even Rand, in all probability.

"For whatever they can find. The Choyan came, and left, after looking at the ashes of their Brethren. They tell us nothing. . . . They are masters. They owe us nothing. They came and lived among us and we used them as much as they used us. Now . . ." her glance slid away, then came back to meet his. "Some of us are glad they are gone and some of us are afraid. Will we remember wisely what they have taught us? We don't know. But we do not want them back!" She led him to the table and chair. A Zarite kit scooted from under the table in an explosion of peach and white fur and cloth. A door banged in its wake as Thena sat him down.

"What about the others? What others? Spaceships, probes . . . ?"

Her ears moved. "Danger, I'm told. Much danger comes with the others."

He could see her fear billowing in the aura about her as well as hear it in her voice. He did not doubt it for a second, though his ability to see it surprised him. "What are you going to do?"

"We're not sure. We may have to move you again."

This was the third Zarite household he'd been in. The first he scarcely remembered. The second was little more than a blur.

"Tell me about the others." Concentrating on Thena seemed to help clear the cobwebs. It would be important to know who was coming after him.

Her lips flattened about her teeth. "They come

in darkness. The ships are brought down on the outlying lands. And they kill those whom they question."

No probes or drones, then. Someone was using FTL to access the planet. *Tezars* on contract were forced to remain neutral over their objectives, until the contracts had expired or were breached. The others could be Abdreliks. Or maybe Ronin. Without the Choyan here to protect the Zarites, they would become fair prey. Or ... perhaps it was his presence which drew the seekers. Perhaps if he went off-world ... the Compact would sooner or later step in, as well. Arizar might become like Earth, classified Zed, on probation, worthy of joining the Compact of those who flew the stars.

Except these worthy people did not fly the stars. The technology they had, they had cunningly stolen and adapted from those Choyan who'd mastered the planet. Difficult, if not impossible, to tell how they ranked in developmental technology. The Compact might adopt a neutral stance, not protective and refusing interference. Who, then, would protect them?

"I can't stay here."

"You're not a master. Where would you go?"

"Where I came from." Bevan stared at a bowl of food as Thena pushed it in front of him, followed by a new mug of cooling drink. The Zarite *tsked* at him again. He began to eat mechanically, the taste of the food overwhelmed by the sea of colors it swam in, some of them downright unappetizing looking. After as many bites as he could stomach, he said, "When do you want to move me?"

"Tonight. Soon it will be dark."

He nodded. Thena hesitated, then put a hand gently on his head. It felt like a benediction. "I will miss you," she said. "You were as helpless as one of my kits when they brought you. I think you will conquer this poison."

He wished he had the confidence she exuded. She stood over him until he cleaned the bowl. Light had gone from bright to waning before he stood and she helped him to the outside latrines. Once outside, the sharp outline of mountains to the east of the small village of Zarites cut off the setting sun abruptly, and darkness fell like a scythe across the area.

As he fumbled to zip zippers and buckle buckles, Thena made a hissing sound through tight lips. Her back to him out of his sense of modesty, she was looking away, through the gray and black shadows of outlying huts.

He sensed the tension in the sound. "What is it?"

"I . . . do not know." Zarites were not nocturnal, but her night sight had to be better than his, which was as haunted as his day sight.

He left the latrines and joined her. He could sense not only her worry, but a sharp inquisitiveness coming their way, a curiosity clawed and dangerous, crawling steadily after him. He felt the search prickle his skin.

"Get inside with the kits," he said.

Thena hesitated. "And you—"

"It may be the others come to move me. Don't worry."

Another sharp intake of breath. Then his nurse-maid made up her mind and left him, to protect her own.

Bevan stood alone. He did not believe it was a Zarite searching for him through the early night. He remained motionless for another moment and felt the menace waft over him and slide away uncertainly, then touch him fleetingly again. He lifted his empty hands and looked at them in the dimness, deciding what he could do when the enemy came to meet him. How could he protect himself when it was all he could do to stand? All he could reliably do would be to keep moving and provide less of a target. He had to lead the hunter away from those who had helped him. He lurched away from Thena's hut.

He heard a Zarite shout and then a squeal. Red flares burst skyward from the far side of the huts. Bevan stumbled and went to one knee in the damp grass. His breath came short and quick. Winded, so soon. Only a few steps and he was done for. Where and how had he hoped to run?

Something passed him in the night, a shrub away. Leaves whispered sibilantly against its going. He smelled a musky scent, not unpleasant, but ... strange. The difference tingled through him, pinging off alarms in every sense he had of danger. Then, nothing. The hunter had passed him by.

And then the sound stopped. Whatever it was now stood beyond him, but not so far away that a good lunge would miss him. Bevan fought to catch his breath. His panting must be heard ... surely. The drumming of his heart. The telltale growl of his stomach as it digested food it had not wanted in the first place.

As he crouched, waiting, still and quiet, his sight adjusted until the twilight was only a gray mass and he could see almost as well as in the daylight, though the insistent colors had gone. And if he could see. . . .

Bevan moved imperceptibly in the gloom. His ankle protested the change of weight as he moved from one crouch to another. Grass dampened the cloth covering his knee. He looked up and saw in silhouette the creature stalking him.

Slender and willowy, with a mane of sharp, quill-like objects draped about its neck and shoulders.

Ronin, he thought. It could be none other. The Ronins carried a deadly poison in their quills. It was against Compact law for a Ronin to go off-planet without being de-quilled or at least de-toxined.

Bevan stretched his lips in a humorless smile. Why was he positive that a single touch of one of those quills would be fatal? Why not? What use to send a Ronin after him without all the weapons available at its disposal. Laws that could be made could be broken. The creature moved like an assassin, coming after its target through darkness and deception. Its intentions had to be equally as deadly.

A click of teeth. The Ronin moved as if alerted by his very thoughts. The face in profile disappeared as it turned to seek him out. The quilled headdress rose in readiness.

"Come out," it said, in heavily accented Trade.

Oh, no. No, he wouldn't do that. Bevan stayed quiet and watched the creature pivot about, searching. It sensed him, but it did not know exactly where he was. Could it be that Bevan's night sight was better than the Ronin's? He might yet have some advantage.

Bevan went to his stomach and crawled a length away. The Ronin swung about, still looking in the wrong direction.

"A trade," it said. "The lives of those who looked after you for that of your own."

A pledge already broken before given, from what Thena had told Bevan. He dropped his face to the dewing grass and tried to think. The poison within him welled up as if fueled by fear and adrenaline and he battled with it, panic beginning to spew up inside, rattling at his bones and beating at his clenched teeth to be let out. He fought to breathe silently. Inside his skull, the blood pounded crimson. He could not die here!

Bevan leapt to his feet. The Ronin spun about sharply, quills shaking.

"I have you," it said in triumph.

Bevan's world burst loose. His vision went from grays and blacks to crimson. He went white-hot. He burned so hotly he did not know how his skin could contain or withstand the heat. He could feel himself hurtling at the creature, but his feet stayed rooted to the ground.

With a shrill scream, the Ronin assassin burst into flame. The conflagration raged, lighting up the night, engulfing the creature. It had no chance to run or drop . . . nothing. One split second and it was a raging torch.

The stench of burned flesh and plastics filled the air. Bevan toppled to his side at its scent and coughed, as smoke billowed up and around. The Ronin stayed upright, fated to burn like a candle.

The pyrotechnics brought the Zarites creeping out of their huts. Thena pillowed Bevan's head in her aproned lap as their voices shrilled through the air, counting their own dead.

The Ronin had been busy. Five had been struck throughout the village. Four were dead outright, one, lying in drool and foam, arched in convulsions, as it died a slower death, quill poisoned.

Thena smoothed his hair away from his forehead. Light flickered over them from the blaze of the enemy who burned like torch. "You cannot stay with us," she said. "We must find a way to get off off-planet."

Bevan hardly heard her. He watched the creature burn. He had done that. He knew it. But how?

Chapter 9

Morning came hot and clear over Charolon. Palaton rose with the sun, probing his memories, his mind seeking for that which he could no longer intuit. He settled for a steaming hot cup of *bren*, eggs, and fried bread, a pilot's breakfast. Gathon had left a stack of messages for him, out of courtesy. As Palaton looked through them, he saw they'd all been handled even before he arose.

The only matter which had not been handled was that of the God-blind, huddled by the thousands upon the streets and steps leading to the palace. Huddled and waiting for him to meet with Malahki, their chosen delegate.

With his throat still warm from the *bren*, Palaton went out the front door of the palace and descended the half-dozen steps which separated the emperor's domain from the former luminary of Danbe. Malahki had been sitting. Roused from a game of triblow by the jostling and sudden attention of the press communicators, he looked up and then got to his feet.

Palaton remembered a fiery orator from a God-blind river valley community who had stubbornly refused to relocate his people despite the recommendation of the Resource Board and the direct command of his emperor. The massive Choya who faced him now had changed little. The lustrous ebony mane had not grayed, though perhaps it had thinned. The elaborate horn crown, as forceful as Rindalan's, had still not been shaved to the more delicate form currently in fashion, and the brown eyes heavily flecked with gold still bored into him, seeking and lively.

They grasped hands. Calluses from the frequent playing of a hand *lindar* rubbed Palaton's fingers. He smiled at the memory of drinking dandelion colored wine with Malahki and listening to the luminary strum and pluck a lifetime of music from the *lindar*.

So long ago and yet like yesterday. He thanked the God-in-all for saving Malahki's life in what had become the bloodiest forcible Relocation in recent Choyan history. Letting Malahki's spark go out would have been a criminal shame.

A shadow flickered behind Malahki's intent stare as he dropped the handshake. "Do you remember," he said, "the throngs of children who came out to greet you when you brought the emperor to Danbe?"

Palaton nodded. "I could not forget."

Malahki turned and waved a hand over the crowds behind them and across the square and beyond view. "They are here again today," he stated simply and dropped his hand.

A roar from the commons. It shook and echoed among the pillars of the massive stairs leading to where they stood. The recording gear of the communicators immediately swung into position to catch the noise. Palaton found himself startled as well as moved. He could not say anything until the roar died down for, even as close as they stood, Malahki would not have heard it.

While they waited for silence, Palaton thought of Rindalan's and Jorana's warnings. He looked over the crowds. Thousands filled every standing space he could see. He feared for their safety and wondered at the devotion they held for Malahki, for it was obvious he had brought them here.

When the noise abated, he said to the Choya, "Will they let us speak, do you think?"

"We have been waiting for this opportunity." The gold in Malahki's eyes sparked a little.

"Then come with me. I know a garden behind these walls where we can sit and talk." He held a palace pass in his hand. Its buttons gave a warding against the various sonic barriers that fenced and secured the palace from intruders. He waited until Malahki took the pass and fastened it to the front of his light summer jacket, then Palaton turned and felt Malahki following.

The roar of the crowd and the shouts of the nearby communicators crashed like waves upon the shore as he had guards secure the front doors behind them. Inside the muted walls of the palace, ancient fortress that it was, little could be heard but a faint baffling. Malahki stood stiffly until Palaton dismissed the guards and said, "This way."

The intricacies of the imperial palace had been designed to be mazelike, but Palaton knew the garden well. He did not take Malahki there through the library where he had talked with Jorana and Gathon the day before, but through the farthest wing of the palace and then through a garden gate. There, the morning was still shadowed, dew lay heavily on the grass, and the beau-

tiful eyes of sunrise were just opening their
rainbow colors to the first rays dipping over the
rooftop.

They sat on stone benches which had been used
so often through the centuries that they had been
grooved by the sitters. The benches faced opposite
one another, close enough for quiet, intimate
speech.

"You must send them home," Palaton said.
"Charolon can't take care of them on the streets."

Malahki's mouth twisted. "She could, but she
won't. We are the commons, the God-blind, the
Godless. We had no voice, but you gave us one.
For that, Palaton, we would all stay here and die
of neglect."

Palaton shook his head. "I haven't given you
anything. You took it by sheer numbers, made
them pay heed by the very force of you. But if you
stay, if the Congress begins to fear that force, there
will be more blood in the streets than was shed
beside the River Danbe. You know that, Malahki.
You knew that when you answered my plea."

"We won't leave."

"You have to. I have no power. I am nothing
more than a pawn to take up a place in Panshinea's absence."

Malahki sat back on the stone bench. He threw
his arms up on the carved back. He dwarfed it
with his bulk and his energy. "I wondered if you
knew what you were doing when you asked for
our help."

Palaton answered wryly, "I'll admit that I did
not anticipate the response."

"Your honesty is refreshing." Malahki's eyes
narrowed. "But that won't keep me from taking

advantage of you. We're here. Acknowledge us, acknowledge our voice, or we will never leave, even if all that is left is our blood staining the gray rock of Charolon."

"You wouldn't do that."

"I wouldn't have to. The city guard would do it for me. What do I care if I die martyred if it makes you Housed, you high and mighty, *look* at us once in a while."

Palaton knew a moment of despair. Malahki did not care for his own life, he could see that written in the Choyan frame dominating the bench opposite him. The other had an agenda and Palaton realized he could not turn him aside.

"Delay," he said, "in whatever it is you plan to do. You must."

"I think we've been put off long enough. We've waited centuries upon centuries. We are more than slaves, yet less than you. How can you preach patience?"

"Because I haven't any choice! All of us are on the brink of change which could well be catastrophic. I'm here to try to stem the tide but a moment . . . just long enough for us to be prepared, to survive what is coming."

Malahki hesitated. Uncertainty dimmed the brightness of his eyes. "Disaster will make Brethren of us all."

"A disaster like that would leave us open to all the sharks of the Compact. You know that, you have to know it."

"I know that we brought home a *tezar* the Congress wanted to keep in exile, despite the appointment of the emperor. We did that . . . and it won't take them long to realize that as well. And if we can do that, we can help to put our next emperor on the throne."

His threat hung in the air between them. Palaton said, "I cannot hear treason like that."

"Hear, no. Feel . . . possibly. It's been a long time since a *tezar* was made emperor."

Palaton looked away. "Malahki, don't sign your death warrant with me as your witness. I won't take any responsibility for this."

"But you must! You're the one who awakened us to the possibilities. God knows, I've tried . . . but it was your plea which caught their conscience, which motivated them to do what they could, however small it seemed at the time. I have told them it takes many grains of sand to form a beach—but it was you who gathered them here. Why let them go? Why let them fall from your grasp?"

"Because I will not take up that responsibility! Malahki—" and Palaton got to his feet, unable to contain himself. "I *cannot*."

"A Housed Choya with a conscience." Malahki's stare raked him over. "I never thought to see it. I will preach patience. I will ask them to leave. But I will not force them, not will I give them empty promises. *That* will be your responsibility. Fulfill them or fail them, Palaton. You're on your own." He lumbered to his feet as well. He gave a crooked smile. "I'll follow the garden wall out."

He had to duck his head to pass below the arch. Sunlight flooded the garden abruptly after him, as though he, like the high walls of the palace, had been blocking it from entering.

Palaton stood frozen, trying to contain the emotions which had risen in him. What would he do if the God-blind did not disperse? How could he bear the brunt of another bloody massacre, an event which Malahki seemed to relish, if only for the martyrdom?

There was only one other to whom he could appeal . . . one who held sway over both those who could see God and those who could not though the church's position had always been to stay neutral. But Rindy would listen to him, that he knew. Palaton found himself standing with clenched hands. He forced them open at his sides, and looked about the garden. The eyes of sunrise, in all their myriad colors, looked back at him. For a moment, he wondered what Choyan hand had first planted the flowers, in what long ago century. That brief thought gave him comfort. They had survived. One only needed garden walls thick enough.

Beyond the gate, the white and gray stone of the ancient fortress looked like chalk cliffs in an old and forgotten canyon, hemming him in as he traversed it. Silent, too, was this portion of the palace, far from the intrigue and hubbub of the front steps. Malahki sensed the movement in the shadow on the far side of the wall before he saw it in the corner of his eye. Nonetheless, he came to a halt, weight balanced, ready for a fight if need be. He calmed at the sight of the graceful Jorana moving into full view.

"I wondered," said the luminary of Danbe, "if I would see you here."

"I did not dare disappoint you," answered Jorana. She held her chin high, defiantly, and her full bronze hair was severely cuffed back from her face. She wore her uniform and cabinet badge and there was wariness in her voices as well as her eyes. "What do you want from me?"

"I," said Malahki teasingly. "I dare command a Housed and a cabinet member?"

She whirled on her heel to leave. He put a hand out. "Wait, Choya'i! Temper, temper."

Jorana's mouth tightened before she relaxed it to say, "I have duties."

"Yes. Yes, you do." Malahki's voices throbbed with double meaning. "Have you forgotten your roots so soon? Was it really so long ago that you were one of the commons, hoping to pass your test and become Housed?"

"Not long enough." Jorana stayed, tense, her body poised for flight like that of a bird balancing on a wiry branch.

"I would expect not. I have not come to criticize your progress, Jori, only to remind you that you have not long to attain your goals. Palaton's bloodlines are an excellent cross for you—and, more than ever, he can use the political strength your position can give him. You will suit him well. Have you tried to convince him of that?"

"He's been in exile."

The corner of Malahki's mouth twitched. "That," he answered, "I know."

Jorana's chin dropped a little. "He sees me. He knows I am here."

"There is no better time than now ... Palaton is getting a baptism of fire while Panshinea stays out of range. You can help him consolidate his position. And you can console him through his difficulties as well." Malahki's voices dropped slightly. "I wish I had such consolations offered to me."

She trembled. Her eyes flashed as she looked up. "I did not crawl out of the commons so you could pimp for me!"

"And I have never suggested such a thing. Cho is faltering. She needs the powerful leadership of a Choya and a Choya'i. I would like to see that Choya'i be you." Malahki's gold-flecked eyes grew stern. "Your care was in my hands. I raised you well. Talent or not, you would still be one of us had I not done what I did for you."

Jorana said numbly, "I haven't forgotten. You took an orphan from the river and gave me life. You sent me to Niniot to be educated. You made sure I was sponsored for the Choosing. Don't you ever suggest to me that I've forgotten." Her eyes grew suddenly moist. "Oh, God, Malahki—I love him. If he asked me to die for him, I would."

"Ask him to give you a future."

Jorana looked away. She brushed a tear from her face. "I asked him once, a long time ago. He refused me. I cannot ask him again, not yet."

"Then, if he won't give you a future, you must take it from him. Take a child from him and leave. We'll shelter you. You have every potential. You might bear the child we're seeking, the Bringer of Change."

"No." She shook her head. "No, don't ask me to do that."

Malahki put out his hand and caught her wrist. His grip imprisoned her as she rocked back on her heels and pulled to break away. "There are drugs. . . ."

"No. I won't do that to him."

"Send word to me, and I'll have them smuggled to you."

"No!" Her eyes brimmed and tears dropped from them like a summer shower. She went limp in Malahki's grasp.

"Send to me when you're ready," the luminary repeated. "We'll be waiting." He let go of her abruptly and left, moving into the garden passage, his dark mane of hair the only streak of shadow in the lightening garden.

Jorana put her hand to her lips and tried to stop them from quaking. "God," she said under her wavery breath. "If only the river had taken me."

Chapter 10

rrRusk stood impatiently, waiting for GNask and his human shadow to appear in the audience room. The ambassador had acquiesced to speak with him, but the fleet commander knew that forcing the issue with his superior would cause him many difficulties later. GNask had ambitions and if rrRusk could plan his strategies correctly, he would ride the tail of that comet. He had no more ambition than that. Let GNask bear the brunt of government. Abdreliks preyed on each other as well as on lesser kinds of life. rrRusk knew well the tendencies of his own people. He found pride in it. They were all fit. They did not mate for sentimental reasons. They had few weaknesses.

What they did not have to continue conquering worlds was the *tezarian* drive, that black box of wonder devised by the Choyan. A simple feat of engineering and navigation kept the Abdreliks from their desire, and all the decades of trying to decipher the drive and its workings had failed. The box was simple enough. It augmented standard instrumentation panels whenever used. It was how the Choyan used it, rrRusk had become convinced, that made the difference.

He stomped a heavy foot in impatience. His skin

itched. He'd given up his symbiont to go into space and the various antifungal creams were never as efficient at purging his skin as the constantly feeding symbiont had been. His flesh crawled now in this artificial atmosphere and chafed under the tight spots in his uniform, at the neck, armpits, waist, and knees. He fought the impulse to scratch maddeningly.

The far door opened and GNask's impressive yet graceful bulk entered. rrRusk came to immediate attention. The ambassador had not given up his *tursh*. His symbiont rode the side of GNask's fleshy neck, at rest, its small stalklike eyes tucked in. The *tursh* was as much an antenna to GNask's emotions as the ambassador's booming voice.

rrRusk relaxed just a fraction. He caught sight of the humankind wandering behind GNask, small, fragile, a delicate morsel, and felt his jowls begin to grow moist at the thought. She gave him a look as she put her chin up, her dark curls bouncing away from her pale face, and in that look was a kind of amusement. Did she sense his hunger? And if she did, why did that amuse instead of frighten her? Disconcerted, rrRusk almost did not catch the ambassador's first words.

". . . commendations on the job done at Arizar."

"I accept your remarks on behalf of my fleet," rrRusk got out. He paused. "My pilots refused to do more than they had contracted for. They agreed to disrupt an unauthorized colony. They balked at capture."

GNask showed his primary tusks. "That explains the small failure of your expedition. Can it be, do you think, worked out?"

"Perhaps. There was much anger among the pilots. Choyan do not condone colonization, particularly of their own. The *tezars* keep to themselves, but I sensed their rage." rrRusk watched the girl dart from one side to the other side behind GNask. She captured his eye quickly, with her preylike actions, and he had to force his attention back to his superior.

GNask noted his distraction. He turned his massive head and barked a single word at the girl. With a laugh, she drifted to a stop at his heel. The ambassador turned back to rrRusk.

"Convince your pilots that it is not only in our interests, but in their best interests, to continue to track down these renegades. Their actions have cast aspersions on the actions of all Choyan. If the Compact were to set forth tampering charges, it would weigh heavily on them. Those who still refuse to honor their general pilot contract can be switched to other needs. But there will be those, rrRusk, that you and I can sway. There are Households on Cho in financial disarray. *Tezars* are becoming rare in many families. They need money. I can meet those needs, once you ferret them out."

"Loyalty has its price."

GNask looked him full in the eyes. "Always," he said solemnly. "And its rewards." The humankind behind him peered out again, coal dark eyes smoldering in her pale face. But there was nothing furtive in her movements this time. The eyes were hard, assessing rrRusk until he felt a momentary discomfort. The emotion provoked a strange reaction within him, he who had rarely backed down in his own water. He changed his estimation of the small being. What a huntress this one must be among her own kind! He almost did not hear GNask's next words.

The ambassador stated, "Until tampering charges are proved or disproved against the Choyan, Panshinea has given up his position on the security council. That means, rrRusk, that you and I will have opportunities that we have never before been afforded."

rrRusk made a tiny move, signifying his pleasure at being held in the other's confidence. "It would be well to take advantage."

"We will." GNask's heavy brow furrowed deeper. "It would be a shame, would it not, if Cho's own internal situation disintegrated to the point where Compact security forces had to intervene?"

rrRusk again felt surprise. "I will be ready," he pledged, "to move once you feel such a situation has arisen."

"I thought you might. Choose your *tezars* accordingly. There will be no second chances." GNask turned his back to the commander and rrRusk knew he had been dismissed.

He left, with the feeling of the humankind's dark eyes boring into him, taking an alien measure he could not understand, and it bothered him. He was not used to meeting his match among inferior races. She had done nothing overtly to challenge him and yet . . . his opinion of her had been inexplicably changed, remolded.

He wondered if GNask knew what he had in the humankind, if she'd ever turned the full brunt of her eyes upon the Abdrelik who thought he had mastered her. He noted his thoughts for future advantage.

*   *   *

Rindalan wearily finished translating the code of the transmission from Sorrow. Panshinea's fury burned its way through every word, and the Prelate sat back, every knob in his spine aching with fatigue. The chair's headrest helped bear the weight of his horn crown. He thought again of having it shaved down—God-in-all knew it was the style these days—but he'd been born with its munificent burden and he was loath to change now, even though he felt too fragile and brittle to bear its full weight.

Shaving his crown down would not lessen the burdens Cho and Panshinea had placed upon him, and that, Rindy thought with a sigh, was his real problem. He rubbed his eyes. Coupled with the emperor's rage at Palaton's actions among the Godless was a buried appeal to come back to Sorrow, to aid Panshinea in his effort to consolidate the Choyan hold upon the Compact.

"Those days are nearly done," Rindy murmured to himself. "Pan, old friend, you will have to admit it soon. The *tezars* will have to share their ways. We need new blood. We are thinning, dying out, and there are no Choyan coming forth to replace us. Well . . . perhaps to replace you. Yes. There seems to be no shortage of potential emperors."

Rindy reached out and took hold of his mug of *bren*. It had cooled considerably while he had decoded his message. The elder sighed again. He detested cold *bren*, yet he was loath to get up from his chair to find the warming plate and reheat it.

"Cold comfort, then," Rindalan said and saluted

the message board in front of him. His stylus rolled off the keypad on the arm of the chair and came to a crooked stop on the side table. The elder considered the stylus before returning to his mug. He would have to summon Qativar in the morning. He could trust no other to aid Palaton in his place. As much as he disliked travel, he would answer Panshinea's plea and go to him.

Rindy thought of the days when he had ministered to flocks of Choyan, young and old, and those memories were fond ones. Now he had but one or two in his ministry . . . but those, he told himself, affected the welfare and future of all. Was he or was he not derelict in his duties?

He was old. Shortly God-in-all would judge him for his decisions. That time would come soon enough.

In the meanwhile, he could only follow the course he'd set for himself.

Rindy put his empty mug down, and his eyes closed in sleep before his fingers uncurled from the cup.

*   *   *

Bevan dreamed of Sao Paulo, but he woke to the fresh, clean, and bitter cold air of Arizar, blinking in confusion at the difference between his dreams and waking reality. Sao Paulo, warm, humid, teeming with the smells of the poor who overwhelmed its streets. Arizar, almost virgin, cast in winter coldness, air not yet fouled by hundreds of millions burning fuel to cook, to produce technology, to incinerate garbage.

He blinked again, and the confusion of time and

place left him. Gooseflesh rippled his café au lait arms. The blue sleeves of the College uniform had torn away, exposing him to the frigid air. Around him, he could hear the chatter of the Zarites, punctuated by soft squeaks and coos. They carried him litter-bound and he bounced from time to time as they skirted rocky terrain. He sat up carefully and peered over the litter's edge.

"I can walk," he announced in Trade.

The Zarites looked up at him, the bearers showing their teeth in their effort to keep the litter steady. Bevan felt like some potentate being born through the streets of Baghdad.

The Zarite who seemed to be in charge of his procession, a soot-colored male with pale yellow eyes, looked at him from his position to the fore. He wielded a walking stick with great effectiveness, but now the instrument paused in midair, as if in thought itself.

Then the male shook his head. "No," he said flatly. The walking stick descended and the brisk pace continued.

"Well, then, how about breakfast? The sun's up and we've been at this since mid-evening."

The walking stick hung in air again. It came down with a thump. "All right," said the Zarite. "Food and water."

Bevan held on as the litter descended to the ground and he could clamber out. Pouches and bundles were opened up and passed around by the time he could join the circle of nine who escorted him.

Thena's cooking was abundant and good. Though his companions mostly spoke Trade to accommodate him, he had gathered enough Zaritian to understand some of the side comments made. He garnered the impression that food was his bearers' wages and they thought themselves well paid by his nursemaid's efforts.

Bevan curled his legs under him and appreciated the flakey-crusted vegetable casserole himself, cold though it was. As tiny chips of crust cascaded upon his lap, he brushed them off reluctantly, tempted to wet a fingertip and capture every morsel. The Zarite sitting next to him pushed a second hunk of casserole into his hands, as if sensing his appetite.

Bevan half-finished it before he spoke. "What's the plan for when we reach the port?"

The head male glanced his way, pale eyes steady. "What kind of plan should we need?" he asked, nibbling at a crisp green fruit to punctuate his response.

"As bombed out and damaged as the port is, they're not going to let us take a ship." Bevan spoke slowly, so his meaning could not be mistaken.

"All things among us are one," the male said enigmatically. "There will be no difficulty. The only difficulty lies within yourself."

Bevan had been raised within the solid walls of the Catholic church. This sort of reform Zen type of philosophy did not leave him with a comfortable feeling. "Look, we're talking a cruiser, a pilot, and fuel."

The male peeled back his lips, showing his rodent incisors. "The ship will be available. Fuel is sufficient. I am told the underground tanks suffered no damage. As for pilot . . . that is your concern."

"Where am I going to find a Choya with the *tezarian* drive?"

The circle of Zarites stared at him as if he had announced himself to be God and spoken in tongues. The leader shuttered his eyes a moment, hiding his thoughts away, then looked back at Bevan.

"You must pilot. There is no need for other."

Bevan sputtered. Fine flakes of crust swirled out like a snow cloud. "Maybe you don't have a need for a driver, but I like to get where I'm going."

The Zarite tossed the core of his eaten fruit away, stood, and dusted his hands. "Then that is your concern," he said. He retrieved his walking stick. Breakfast appeared to be over.

Bevan sat there frozen by amazement, not sure he liked the division of chores. Sure, getting a cruiser seemed like the harder part, but finding a pilot rated a close second. A paw tugged on his elbow, and he got to his feet reluctantly.

Double vision set in abruptly, prisms flashing across the faces of the Zarites around him. Bevan swayed in sudden disorientation. They pushed him over the rim of the litter and into its bed. With a bark from the leader, the bearers hefted their burden and set off at a jog.

Bevan clung to consciousness. One thing at a time, he told himself. Something would work out. Perhaps he should adopt the Zarite philosophy which appeared to be that all things were available to those patient enough to wait for them.

But his Catholic orphanage background had ground another belief into him, that of trial and retribution, of sin and redemption, guilt and confession, a great wheel of action and consequences.

Whatever happened to him now was redemption for the heinous sin he had committed. He knew that. The hell he had earned he now carried with him.

Chapter 11

"Congress has requested your presence after today's session."

"Me?" Palaton asked, and one of his eyebrows climbed slightly.

"You and the humankind," Jorana answered.

"Ah. They want a look at him." Palaton pushed aside his readouts of the *tezar* contracts, initiations, and fatalities over the last decade. This conversation sounded as though it might take most of his attention. He leaned back in Panshinea's chair. This, more than the fragrant carved wood chair in the palace throne room, was the center of Cho's rule, he realized as he did so.

The monitor framed Jorana's visage. The image was one of the few vanities he'd ever seen about her, and he wondered why she would tune the monitor's framing in that way. But she was Choya'i, and their ways were sometimes even more baffling than those of the aliens he'd met in his career. "Gathon suggests that they wish a formal presentation of you as heir."

Palaton could feel a sudden frown. "That is an imperial ceremony, not a Congressional introduction. Impossible to do without Panshinea and probably illegal, as well."

Jorana pouted her lips ever so briefly. "Argue the subject with Gathon, then. I'm only the messenger. By the way, I've been able to find a round-the-clock guard for Rand, someone who will stay with him dawn to dusk and be on call after that."

"Who?"

"His name is Traskar. He's a former *tezar*. He's not normally on duty here in Charolon, he's agreed to come in from Niniot."

That the Choya had been a pilot meant that he would be free of the xenophobia Palaton feared. But he disliked having a Choya around who'd been burned out, and was perhaps ill or unstable. He had no recollection of the name. "Where's he from and why is he grounded?"

Jorana grinned at Palaton's question. "He schooled at Salt Towers. He lost both arms and a leg in a bombing raid about forty years ago."

"I see." Prosthetic replacement was fairly sophisticated among the Choyan, but Traskar's wounds had been so extensive that he would have been hampered and retirement would have been recommended. Flight training at Salt Towers meant that, at one time, Traskar had been among the aristocracy of his House. His own loyalty to Blue Ridge chafed a bit at that, but if Jorana recommended him, she must have reasons. Palaton knew he should trust Jorana's judgment and that his questions reflected that he did not. "He sounds like a good prospect," he said.

"I thought so."

Palaton had had no time for Rand other than to check on him briefly in the morning, and the manling had not been awake then. "Will you brief

Rand on the appointment? I haven't had time to check on him."

Jorana nodded. "He's doing fine. It's difficult to watch him. He's so awkward. The splints don't help, of course, but he's so spindly and all at angles."

"They're not a graceful race. It's all in the eyes," returned Palaton.

"Not only the eyes, but the hands have been busy. So far he's discovered the passive heating and cooling system, the recessed wall lighting, the entertainment console, the automatic *bren* brewer, and the all-hours Congressional broadcast. Not to mention the bath masseuse. He's as curious as a *chiarat*," the Choya'i commented. "And I did not know humankind had a hankering for *bren*."

"This one does. You'll let him know when to be ready?"

"I will." Jorana ended her call and the monitor's soft edges lingered after her image faded to dark slowly.

Palaton found himself staring at the darkened surface, considering what the Congress really wanted of him. They would want a look at Rand, perhaps, to see a humankind in person. The various delegates would be no more sophisticated than the counties they represented. Palaton hesitated to expose Rand to scrutiny, but he knew that to refuse Congress at this juncture would be even more unwise. He had defied them enough, now it was time to ease into the position Panshinea had occupied.

The emperor of Cho was not only a leader, he was a judge. He would settle disputes which could not be settled by other means and he would judge those settlements which had been made to discern the fairness. He was the final appeal on all decisions and sentences, and he was the final recourse on policy concerning the natural resources of the planet they all worked so hard to maintain. They did a balancing act and although colonization might relieve some of that necessity, the adaptation effect on genetic selection had always posed new problems, and Cho had decided long ago not to colonize.

For all matters which would pass before him, he was nothing if Cho could not trust him. And it would not trust him if he was revealed. How could he think to stand before the five hundred plus members of Congress and pass their examination? No matter how well he dissembled, there would be someone who would know he was an empty shell. He had to have Rand at his side. But he did not know if it would be enough. Palaton bowed his head in deeper thought.

Rand looked in amazement at the vest Jorana held up for him. "What is that? It looks like an armored jacket."

"It's your batteries." The Choya'i helped him shrug into it and pulled it into alignment so she could fasten it. The buttons appeared to be magnetic. The seam closed without warning and with very little notice of where the opening lay. Rand patted it. The garment was heavy enough, but flexible.

He had been waiting all day for something to happen, anxiety gnawing inside him, looking for Palaton or Rindy for company, left to himself and to the wonders of the apartment which faded quickly after initial inspection. Water here was not more unlimited than it had been at home and the energy systems were remarkably similar, yet the Choyans had thousands of years of technological civilization beyond Earth's meager time line. Where were the real wonders? Now that Jorana and Palaton were here, they had precious little time to answer questions as they prepared him to appear before Congress.

Palaton eyed the vest. "It fits well enough."

"What does it run?"

"Bodyshield." Jorana's voices were muffled as she stepped behind him and tugged and pulled. Then a shimmery effect enveloped him. "I had this cut down from a child's suit ... if I can just get it to fit ... there! It's up."

Rand looked at the two of them through it. "What can it stop?"

"Most lightweight projectiles, bodily assault, light and sonic waves. It won't stop the projectiles, but it'll disperse most of the energy and keep the damage to a minimum."

The shimmer disappeared. Rand slapped a hand on his flank. "I think this thing can do the job without the shield."

Palaton laughed. Jorana looked at him. "You're wearing one, too," she said.

"It'll ruin the lines of my uniform!" Palaton stood resplendent in the colors of Blue Ridge, his chest lined with chevrons and badges of service.

"Think what an enforcer could do to those lines," she retorted, holding out a Choya-sized vest.

Palaton looked wryly at Rand and then, with a

shrug, stepped to her and shed his summer jacket. "At least let me wear it underneath."

"That will buffer the activation." Warning underscored her tone.

"I'll take that chance," Palaton answered dryly. "I'm willing to risk that any Congressman can shoot that well."

The Choya'i looked up as her fingers briskly strapped the vest into place. She tugged and pulled strongly enough so Palaton gasped in spite of himself and she made a face at Rand behind Palaton's shoulder as if she had done it on purpose.

Rand watched the two of them, sensing a bonding that neither wished to acknowledge, yet that existed between them as concretely as a chain. A tang of homesickness went through him as he remembered the way his own parents had reacted to each other with almost the same familiarity.

"What's the matter," Jorana asked. "Got pilot's ribs?"

Palaton looked at Rand. He said, with a great deal of dignity, "Pilot's ribs are an affliction reserved for those who crash-land. My craft usually comes down intact."

"Providing, of course, you ever get it off the ground." Jorana slapped the vest into position, was rewarded by an "oof" from Palaton, and stepped back. "Put your jacket on and see if you can trigger the shield quickly enough."

Palaton shrugged into his jacket and the shimmer appeared almost immediately. To the look of faint surprise on Jorana's face, he responded smugly, "Pilot's reactions."

She conceded with a shrug of eyebrows. She checked her chronographer. "It's time."

"What about Rindy?"

"He's waiting for a transmission from Panshinea and, I suspect, he's more tired than he's willing to admit. He said facing Congress was a bit more than he could handle right now," answered Jorana.

Palaton ran his palm over the last seam on his uniform. "I know how he feels." He looked at Rand who answered with a salute.

"What's that?"

Rand explained it. "Ah," said Palaton. "Quaint gesture. I suggest you keep it to yourself. It's not far from a street slang which commons use and it is not considered flattering."

Rand felt himself blush as Jorana laughed behind him, and pushed him toward the door.

The retired *tezar* guard came to his heels alertly. Traskar was tall, though not next to Palaton, who was the tallest Choya Rand had yet seen. The older pilot's face had been lined by sun, the filaments of his facial jewelry in onyx and gold disappearing into heavy wrinkles. Rand could not tell where Choya left off and artificial limb began, but there was a stiffness to his movement that most Choya did not have, except for aged Rindalan. His gray-streaked brown hair was plaited back into a thick and lustrous ponytail. He wore the imperial colors of red and crimson, but his chest was devoid of service badges, except for an insignia which he had proudly told Rand delineated the Salt Towers flight school.

"Conveyance?" asked Traskar in crisp accents.

"No," Jorana told him. "They're to take the Emperor's Walk. They're less expected that way."

The guard checked his timepiece. "In that case, we had better hurry. We have somewhat limited mobility." And the wrinkles deepened on his face as if it hurt him to admit a loss of agility.

Rand had only met with Traskar briefly, for the guard stayed outside the quarters, but he felt as if he should not let the other suffer. Traskar was one of the few Choya he'd met who would look him in the eye. "I'm sorry," he apologized, taking the blame, "but with these splints I can only move so fast."

The Choya stared down. He had green eyes with a multitude of brown flecks in them, as if nature could not decide whether to gift him with one color or the other. "We will slow for you," the guard said solemnly. He held the door open to let them pass.

It was an underground slidewalk. The summer heat had settled within the passageway and though jets of air attempted to cool them in spits and spurts, Rand felt his forehead dampen as they gained the entranceway. Jorana had left and it was just the three of them.

Traskar suggested, "Bodyshields."

Palaton scratched his chin thoughtfully. "It'll be hotter."

"But safer," the guard returned. He had the holster open on a hand weapon the Choya called an enforcer, and Rand thought privately that it looked like it could do a great deal of damage, shield or no. *"Tezar,"* the guard continued, "you are also the heir now."

Palaton sighed as if disliking to be reminded, and a shimmer surrounded him. Rand found the button Jorana had guided his fingers to before and activated his own. What breeze there had been instantly ceased.

Palaton ducked his head under the lip of the tunnel entrance and Rand saw, with surprise, that he'd had to do so. Traskar also bent his head somewhat as he escorted Rand inward.

The walk was not functioning. Palaton approached a panel inset in the wall. Trade as well as what Rand presumed to be Choyan was inscribed on the instruments. The automatic mode seemed to be malfunctioning, for the panel had gone to manual. Palaton manipulated the panel, but the walkway stayed within its roadway, still and motionless.

Palaton's lips pursed for a moment, then he looked at Traskar. "The solars are down. There's a power drain."

"Fans against the summer heat," the other responded.

"No doubt. We shall have to walk it, indeed."

"Ambush?" suggested Rand.

The two Choyan looked at him. Sorrow rather than wariness rode their expressions, but Palaton smoothed his face out quickly. "No," the pilot said. "Other problems. There are always power outages at midsummer."

"Can't you bring it back to automatic?" Rand asked.

"No," Palaton said shortly. "That's not possible anymore." Palaton led the way down, leaving Rand to wonder if solar energy were the backup manual power source, what could possibly have been the automatic power origin.

The walkway tunnel blossomed into a tremendous underground mall, which was silent and empty. There were no shops here, but the entire palace could have been swallowed up easily. He saw stations for water and latrines and wondered if this had been intended, at one time, to be an evacuation shelter of some kind, perhaps for imperial staff from one end and Congressional staff from the other. It had been light outside, and within, small globes lit as they approached and faded to a minimum of illumination as they passed. A bronze railing loomed in the foreground. Rand slowed as he saw that it fenced an immense series of craters.

He paused at the nearest rail. "My God," he said, leaning over and looking. A star cruiser could have been berthed in the crater. "What happened?"

"This," Traskar explained, "is a war memorial."

Rand whistled softly. "Who won?"

"We did," Palaton answered dryly. "Else we'd be up to our asses in Abdreliks by now."

"The Droolers did this?" The craters must be pre-Compact history then. Centuries old.

Traskar agreed. "Aye, and more." The guard slapped a wide palmed hand down on the railing next to Rand. "Took out the Congressional halls that time. Never again."

"Or so we hope." Palaton stepped away from the railing and strode on again. He paused to adjust his step to Rand's shorter and hindered stride.

Beyond the craters, as globes came to life, Rand could see the infrastructure of an incredible building . . . towers and spiraling walks in midair, hall-ways and courtyards, machines which lay sparkling and half-destroyed in the golden gloom. Overhead trams hung from arches which spanned the building. He spotted what he thought were robotics in disarray, technology he had not seen on Cho in any form.

All of it lay beyond the railing, consigned as a memorial, dusted by the ages even sheltered here, underground.

It took them a great deal of walking to pass the wreckage. Rand watched it. He wondered how the Abdreliks could have attacked with a Choyan pilot guiding them.

He must have voiced his wonderment aloud, for Palaton answered. "They didn't. We all had FTL navigation then. We spanned our own heavens, each of us, without knowing there were other races who could do the same. The Abdreliks had poor success with their navigators. The Ivrians range closest to us in reliability, but only on short FTL runs, bordering on known space. Our first contacts were brief, abrupt, and hostile. The Ab-dreliks, particularly, are . . . were . . . an avaricious race. They took a great deal of discouragement and might never have come to terms if it had not been for the discovery of Sorrow."

Traskar said, with a growl in his lower tone, "That war gave us the mastery, though."

Palaton looked back over his shoulder. "That it did," he said slowly. "We were forced to the limit and discovered just what we could do with Chaos. After that, after the Compact was settled, the oth-ers saw how easily we could travel vast FTL dis-tances without navigational worry and began to contract for us to pilot them as well. The Ivrians continue to work on their drives, but ours is unquestionably superior because of its accuracy." He looked over Rand at Traskar, as if willing the guard to say something else, but the guard grew silent.

The walkway began to slope upward. Rand felt it in his knees, particularly the one forced to remain straight by the splinting, and in his lungs. Palaton and Traskar adjusted their speed for him once again. He grew heated inside the bodyshielding. His shirt would be soaked with sweat by the time they reached their destination.

An intricate piece of sculpture edged the slidewalk. Rand paused both to look at it and catch his breath. "What is it?"

Palaton eyed it. "A light fountain."

The wiry tracings remained dark, however, despite their approach. Rand put a hand out and touched it. It was almost ethereal in its beauty and he wondered what it must look like dancing with light, even to his dimmed vision. "It's incredible."

"One of five throughout Charolon," the pilot said. "Sculpted by Cleota the Fair. No one can bring them to light any more."

"They're broken."

"No," Palaton answered slowly. "We seem to lack the ability to activate them."

Rand looked at him quickly. "I don't understand."

A darkness flickered through the other's eyes. "Neither do we. Come on. The Congressional session will be ending soon. We don't want to keep them waiting."

The guard drew Rand away to follow in Palaton's footsteps. Rand turned back once, to look at the faint, gleaming outline of the war memorial as the vast shadows in the underground cavern threatened to swallow it forever. Whoever had built that building, the walkway, the fountain . . . was something more than the Choyan who lived here now. Was this why the Choyan rarely allowed visitors dirtside? Was theirs a civilization faltering and growing dim itself? Did they secret themselves away to hide behind a reputation built centuries ago which they could no longer uphold?

Palaton looked back and their gazes caught. The Choya's fair face darkened with a humanlike flush as if he had, for the briefest moment, an inkling of what Rand thought. Then he blinked, breaking the contact, and turned away, to lead Rand out of the passageway and into the still light summer's eve.

Chapter 12

As they moved through lengthening shadows, it became perceptibly cooler inside the shielding. Rand wiped his brow on his sleeve, hoping new sweat would not immediately drench him. The streets were nearly empty. Conveyances sat idling, resting on the pillows of air on which they rode, floating eerily above the street lanes. He eyed the nearest one. Technology humans did not quite have yet for long-term, maintenance-free operation, but it was not so far from their reach. Another generation and they would have it, efficient and well-tooled.

Questions had him grinding his teeth with the effort to keep silent, but he did not let them go. He instinctively felt Palaton would not answer, even if he could. The Choyan quickened their pace and he stumbled after, bones aching and muscles trembling. He determined to keep up, caught himself, and fell into step. As they did not wish to reveal their weaknesses, neither did he.

The winged building which replaced the wreckage he had passed underground had neither the beauty nor the size of the first. There were no soaring walkways for interconnection, no trams balanced upon gossamer cables, no windows facing in impossible directions. He did not know how old it was because it had the outer appearance of age, but he knew that part of that had to be facade. Stone and marble and tile gleamed dully as the sun, still hot, sank lower on the horizon.

He saw figures separate themselves from the shadowy columns and approach cautiously.

"Broadcasters," said Palaton, and there was a sneer in his voices.

Traskar stepped ahead of Rand. "They won't come much closer," he said.

Rand looked for the camera gear. There appeared to be none. "How do they—" and his question cut off. He saw now what appeared, like a third eye, in the center of their broad brows. If it was a camera, it was so thin and flat it could be worn like a headdress. They wore vests like the ones which powered his bodyshield and he wondered if they powered the broadcast signals. Would they be relayed to a nearby station, amplified and then rebroadcast or taped? Or had they the ability to broadcast directly to any receiver tuned to them?

They did not draw close, but Rand felt their camera eyes upon him acutely as the three of them passed and began climbing the shallow steps to the front of the Congressional hall. He had his *bahdur* cloaked, yet it fed him the emotions of distrust and fear and resentment coming from the watchers.

Palaton paused till Rand drew even with him. Casually, yet protectively, he let an arm drop over Rand's shoulders, and the bodyshields merged into one large shimmer. "Steady," he murmured.

Rand nodded.

They passed under a flying arch and over a threshold which, momentarily, canceled out their bodyshields. A mechanical Choyan voice intoned, "Expected and admitted."

He had felt nothing and looked about for the sensors. Nothing met his inspection. Traskar had fallen in behind them and his heels struck the marble flooring with a military staccato. Their bodyshields had resumed the moment they crossed into the lobby. Palaton said softly, "Take your shield off. Jorana may be right concerning security, but this is diplomacy."

Rand did as bid. In the bright light of the lobby, his vision grew less accurate, and the shimmering protection had worsened it. He did not miss the shield as it evaporated. Palaton dropped his arm from his shoulder and took his shield down as well. "If you have to bring it up," he warned, "split seconds count."

"If I have to bring it up," Rand answered, "I'll be diving for the floor first."

Palaton didn't respond, but Traskar let out a gravelly laugh.

He could feel their eyes upon him, these representatives of the Choyan counties. His stomach knotted and his pulse quickened. Now that he looked upon them, the Housed elite of Cho, he could see the difference between these Choyan and those who had thronged the streets on the broadcasts he'd watched in the solitude of his room. The horn crowns were defined and elegant, not coarse and brutish. The clothes were cut in styles he did not know, except that the fabrics were rich and lustrous in colors he could not name, which blended into one another and then raced away like droplets of water along a waxed surface, separating again. He realized that these were among the aristocracy, even among their own, and their gazes were sharp and considering of him as he passed.

These were those chosen to know what was best for the planet and its people because they had the inner sight, and the ambition, and the destiny.

And, from the emotions filtering through to him, the conceit, the greed, and the shrewdness. Rand blinked as he fought to contain the power Palaton had given him. He resisted the impulse to shield himself again. It would not work against these probing thoughts.

Palaton slapped a palm against a richly burled door. It opened to him, and its twin by its side, revealing a vast gallery. At its center clustered podiums. The aisles were wide enough to drive a car down. The ceiling domed far overhead, and he could see the tracing of the setting sun through it.

Traskar said, "I'll be on standby here, sir."

Palaton nodded, a bit absently, Rand thought. He touched Rand's shoulder again. There was a definite warmth as they connected and Rand knew a panicky moment when it seemed as if all that filled him went flooding to his shoulder, to drain into that touch, to abandon him, to flee. He felt as though he were dying, and his knees began to buckle.

Palaton's power, seeking return. He had fought it instinctively, but now he wondered if he might have been able to let it go, to pierce that curtain which separated them. Too late, for the tide surging in him returned to normal, and the moment passed. Rand looked up. Had Palaton felt it?

The Choya did not look at him, but kept his attention on the audience which was rising to their feet as they entered the aisle leading to the center podiums. Rand felt the intensity of his purpose.

Though not all seats were filled with Choyan, they weren't necessarily empty. Here and there thin, transparent screens stood in place. Rand's head turned as he went by.

Palaton slowed. "Broadcast screens," he said. "For those who wish a proxy presence. The screens are not necessary to transmit an image, but are a courtesy for those of us on the floor. Sometimes it's difficult telling the transmitted images from real presences."

One screen activated as they drew even with it, and Rand found himself looking into a three-dimensional projection of an older Choya'i, her silvery hair combed back from a brow so delicately adorned with crown that it was almost nonexistent. Real or projection, her eyes drilled into him, and he felt the force of her will all the way through him. Yet, through her seemingly solid body, the screen could be faintly seen.

There was a momentary gap, as she received the transmission that he returned her look. The Choya'i nodded almost imperceptibly. Rand felt Palaton's hand on his splint, drawing him onward.

"Don't take time to make either friends or enemies," Palaton said under his breath.

A rising tide of noise followed them, gaining strength as they came to the podiums in the center of the hall. The floors were sloped downward, so that they stood in an amphitheater, which offered an equally good view from everywhere, except perhaps where they stood, a position where someone was always at their backs. He could feel sudden, steely tension in Palaton's lean body as they reached their objective.

The empty seats filled. The inactive screens came alive. Only in a few, rare spots, could Rand see true emptiness. When the hall filled, the voices stilled. A massive Choya stood, his shock of white hair in such disarray that it was nearly impossible to tell if he were horned or not.

"Welcome to the heir," he said. His voices boomed, bass drums in double, and Rand winced slightly at the sound.

"Welcome to the heir," the audience rejoined. Palaton bowed slightly.

"Thank you for bringing me home," he answered, as if there had never been any trouble at all coming back, as if this multitude of five hundred or so had been responsible for working a miracle.

Palaton never raised his voices, but Rand could hear the faint echo as they were broadcast to the far edges of the hall. He felt awe and quenched it by thinking, *Hold on. The Greeks knew how to do this.*

As if by recalling this, his mind descended into a maelstrom of questions. Who had been their Egyptians, their Greeks? Who had birthed their civilization? What secrets had they left behind them, besides light fountains, which these modern-day descendants no longer knew?

Palaton reached out and touched Rand again, catching up his free wrist. "May I present to you, noble assemblage, the humankind I have taken under my protection. He is known to me as Rand."

Rand felt a heat inside him, as though every pore had been invaded, and the concentration went to the core of him and burned there, telling him of the penetrations. The *bahdur* inside him coiled as though it might strike, and he worked on the control Palaton had taught him.

Palaton looked on him mildly, and there was pride in that look, Rand recognized with surprise. He swallowed back the turmoil inside of him.

The white-haired Choya sat abruptly. "Him I do not choose to greet."

Palaton's fingers tightened about Rand's arm. Rand knew that dizzying, sinking feeling of *bahdur* about to abandon him again, and realized that some of it must indeed be escaping to Palaton— he felt it, too, and that was why the pilot kept taking hold of him, as though he could sip bits of it back, like taking drafts of a steaming cup of *bren*. With the realization, he felt some of Palaton's shock as well as his tension.

"I apologize to the Congress," Palaton said, straightening, but not loosing Rand. "I cannot tell you of the particulars of the guardianship, only that this manling is under my protection, and that his safety is vital also to the safety of Cho. Compact or not, we have enemies we have held at bay for centuries, and we have done so because we are both smart and prudent."

The majority of those within the hall had seated themselves. A wiry old Choya'i, with a permanently humped shoulder remained on her feet long enough to shout, "I am not one to accuse a *tezar* of hastiness, but the decision you made alone was one for all of us to consider."

As she sat down, Rand saw a projection screen

at her back, and realized she was not what she seemed, though it made her objection no less vehement or immediate. Cries of agreement followed her presentation.

Palaton did not wait for the cries to cease before he bellowed, "There are times in a crisis when there is no place for democracy. This was such a time."

The shock-haired Choya snorted loud enough to be heard at the podiums. "Prove it," he said.

Palaton bored a look at him. "I am a *tezar*," he threw back, "and not accustomed to having my judgment questioned."

"You are the heir, and you had damned well better get used to it," called back another Choya, one of flaming red hair, and bold, twisted horn. He wore black and silver and had not, Rand remembered, gotten to his feet at all when they entered.

Palaton turned slightly toward him to retort, "I am the heir, not by reason of birth, but because I am a *tezar*, and I saw a duty, and I fulfilled it."

"Then I might have been heir as well," responded the redhead.

"So you might," said Palaton, "if you had had the courage to do it, and Panshinea had accepted you."

Color to match his mane rose in the other's face, but his lips clamped shut and he did not answer again. A murmur had arisen at Palaton's words, and then died out again.

"I took the Emperor's Walk today," said Palaton into the quiet. "I saw dust and disarray. I wondered how long it had been since most of you had seen the ruins and remembered what it means to us."

The old Choya'i said, "Don't chastise us, Palaton. We also serve who stay here and sift laws through our hands and weigh the meager resources of a dwindling planet. You travel the stars. We traverse the narrow roads of possibilities dictated by what is left of Cho." She rubbed her humped shoulder as if it pained her. Her image wavered a bit as though her movement disrupted the broadcast.

"Our people," responded Palaton, "are still our greatest resource, and I suggest to you that a goodly portion of them are overlooked by you."

His words dropped like a bomb and Choyan exploded to their feet. In spite of himself, Rand took a step backward as voices rose in volume. He saw Traskar straighten and come down the aisle a step or two as if anticipating trouble.

The shouts drowned out one another until they died down again, and Rand was left with only a partial coherent sentence, ". . . they cannot know what is good for them . . ." before all had grown still again.

Palaton said, "I have not done for them what you will not."

There was a grumble of mollification, as though the Congress had been somewhat appeased, though not entirely convinced.

"Send them home," came a call from behind them. Palaton swung about to place it.

"I have asked," he returned. "I will ask again."

The shock-haired Choya stood. "We have voted, Palaton," and his words fell like chimed notes in the silence. "For censureship. You have been asked here today to receive this verdict. Your acceptance as heir remains unverified until such time as we can come to agreement. I will add, for my own sake, and the sake of my Householding and county, that it is hoped you will be candid with us as soon as it is possible as to the purpose of your guardianship. We are Choyan. But even though we are who we are, it is not necessary that we carry the burdens of a thousand thousand worlds who do not choose to rise above themselves."

Palaton dropped Rand's wrist. It had gone numb and prickly at the same time. Rand felt a shock as though he'd been slapped.

"What does he mean," he whispered to the pilot.

"He means," answered Palaton grimly, "we're on our own."

Chapter 13

Rand dreamed of a love spooned close to his body, curled about him, caressing him and whispering in his ear. The night kept his eyes closed, he could not see who welcomed his body with such passion and intimacy, but he knew the touch. Alexa, who'd been lost on Arizar, the first and only lover of his memory.

He dreamed he opened his eyes and saw her looking at him, her pale face, framed by short, curly dark hair which gleamed blue-black in the darkness. He said, "Why are you here?" because toward the end of their days at the College, she'd turned from him to Bevan and the two of them had locked him out of their intimacies and he had never understood why.

"Because," whispered his dream Alexa, "you're alive and Bevan is not."

His voice stuck in his throat. Her lips moved over the curve of his neck and the words tumbled out, following her, "But you're dead, too."

"No," Alexa told him. "No more than you. I'm alone. You're alone." And she moved her hand about him, stroking him lightly.

Even in his sleep he began to rouse and his senses blurred dream with reality. The black, white, and gray of night became shot through with a golden fire. The haze swirled around him, curtaining him away from her eyes, settling about him like a shroud, separating the two of them from their lovemaking.

"No!" he protested, trying to shrug off the curtain blanketing him. Alexa withdrew further until she stood by the side of the bed, her slender form pale in the shadows.

"Find me," she whispered. "Please."

"Alexa!"

"Where?"

"Look for me." She held out a hand in entreaty, childlike, despite the lushness of her womanly form. "Please."

He tried to call out again, but his voice strangled in his throat. Her form shimmered and disappeared in a golden torch which dwindled even as it burned.

Rand bolted up in the Choyan bed, breathing hard, his voice stuck in his paralyzed throat, his effort to call out harsh in his own ears. He blinked several times. His body had responded to the memory of the lovemaking. Rigid and aching, he swung his feet over the side of the bed, unable to return to resting.

As he swallowed down his emotions, his eyes adjusted to the room, but the golden fire he'd seen seemed shot through everything, a pixie dust coating which lingered everywhere he looked. The blindness creeping in on him made it difficult to distinguish light from dark, but now, if he concentrated, the golden fire settled on the outlines of the furniture and various objects in the room, delineating them. He could see, yet could not.

His arm and leg itched abominably. They had ridden a conveyance back from the Congressional Halls, but he'd gone to bed aching and sore. Now the braces irritated him to the point where he felt he could no longer stand their constraints. He shrugged off the arm brace tentatively, flexing his limb. The soreness had all but abated. He worked his wrist and his fingers gingerly.

He bent down and unfastened the leg brace, fumbling for the straps and catches with only his fairy dust vision to aid him. His leg held him as he stood, wavering, then more solid upon his feet. His bones told him they would ache when it grew cold and damp, ache like an old man's rheumatism, but now they were healing, young and green, and he felt as though he had been freed.

Alexa had not been here. His mind knew it even if his body did not, and his body's enthusiasm gradually waned as he made his way about the Choyan quarters. But how real the dream had been. His throat caught at the sensations still draining from him, the pain of losing her yet again.

Had he thought of her because he was alone, abandoned to Palaton's guardianship by a planet which did not care for either him or his people's struggle?

He found a chair and sat in it abruptly, his legs buckling from under him, not from lack of strength but from the shock of everything. Alexa had fed emotionally from both himself and Bevan, but in the end she had abandoned him, too. He had never understood her explanation. "You're not dark enough," she'd said and left him. And, although he was fair while Bevan had had a South

American's skin, he knew she hadn't been talking about color.

She had often dreamed violently, startling awake in the night, with a half-scream or a smothered snarl, tangled in the bedsheets as though she had wrestled to gain consciousness. Their love-making had always been best when she'd come to his dorm room, shared his bed, cuddled with him until drowsiness threatened to claim them both, and then left, for there would be no rest if they slept together.

Going to Bevan had not changed that in Alexa. Bevan had told him. What demons did she fight in her sleep, what demons had she hoped to meet in Bevan's own darkness to match her own, and why had he, Rand, not been good enough to help her? Why would she call for him now . . . and did he hear her spirit, her memory, or had she somehow survived the holocaust on Arizar?

Rand sat, trembling as the summer night grew cold and damp with morning fog, and wondered. When the sky outside his window began to lighten, he felt a need not to be alone, got up and dressed, and trespassed the rooms which had been given to him for other boundaries.

Palaton heard the whisper of a trespass at his doorway. He turned his head, saw the figure which had broached the security system, and smiled despite his first worry. "You've had a long day," he said, "if you're just heading to bed."

"And you," answered Jorana. She stripped off her coat of office and the belt of arms she wore. The enforcer made a dull thud as it hit the floor where she dropped it. She came to his side, leaning upon him, her scent dusky. "Should I leave?"

"No. I don't think so." He pushed himself back in his chair, and reached for her, drawing her into his lap. "I thought you were angry with me."

"Always," she answered. She stroked a forelock of his hair back from his brow. The caress of her fingers tangling in his hair sent a pleasant wave through him. "You're a *tezar*, and I know that, I know you'll always be leaving me. But that doesn't keep me from worrying when you'll be back."

He listened to the slow beat of her heart for a moment before answering. "Before we start this again," he said, "let's talk about expectations."

"I have none."

He tilted his head back, eyeing her. "None?"

She traced the quizzical expression on his face lightly. "No. I can't ask that of you, can I, as long as you're entangled with Panshinea? And if I did, your answer would not do justice to either of us. You're not free."

"And you? Are you free?"

Her frown passed quickly, marring the smoothness of her forehead for only a second, yet he saw the tracings of deeper lines there, of the subtle aging of a Choya'i. "I know myself," she said, ducking over him and kissing him at the base of his crown. "There's freedom in that."

He could not answer that, for the echoes of her accusation went far deeper than she knew. What would she say to his bastard birth, forbidden by the Housed, his ignorance of his father and the genetic capabilities passed down to him? What would any Housed Choya say? For that, and the *bahdur* stripped away from him, made him less than the commons who ranged the streets of Charolon. He would be as nothing in her eyes. Would she still love him then?

He closed his eyes and let the touch of her hands take away the fear which had begun to pulse like blood through his body.

Rand came to a halt in the vast maze of hallways. He knew which way he wished to go, which direction it was that pulled at him, but the strangeness of the night and the corridor stopped him. He put his hands to his eyes. A wave of need threatened to overwhelm him, then it receded and left him staggered, his back to the wall, his skin awash with the tingle of the emotion as it ebbed away.

His heart pounded for a beat or two, then steadied. It was as though he had two bodies, two hearts, two skins—and nothing separated them. Then he would be torn apart, but even before that, he could barely stand it, because that which was himself and that which was the other was alien and yet not. It was as though what he was becoming could not live within his human skin.

Rand put his chin upon his chest and concentrated. It had to live there. It was his trust. He'd promised to keep it until there could be found a way of returning it and if it changed him somehow, then that was the price to be paid. He waited, withdrawn, until the emotion bled away entirely and he knew he could continue. The emptiness which drew him remained, and he knew only that he had to answer it, though he had no hope of filling it.

He took a step out from the wall into the corridor and came to a halt, throwing his head back, stopping in fear, for a Choya stood there, had been standing there, for how long?

He did not see the Choya well, his sight dimmed and startlement muting the fairy dust illumination. He swallowed hard, for it appeared a weapon filled the left hand of the Choya.

But the lines of the being relaxed somewhat, in shadow silhouette. "The humankind, I trust?"

"Yes."

"You should not wander. Jorana's troops are nothing if not effective. Imperial protection may be the only safety for you . . . but even they will shoot in the dark."

"I didn't mean. . . ."

The Choya cut him off, disinterested in hearing excuses. He leaned forward slightly and Rand was struck by a pair of pale blue eyes, intense, driving all notion of his face from his mind. "Do you know where you are?"

"No. But I know where I'm going."

The pale blue eyes receded into shadow again. "Commendable for any intelligent being. Then I shall not bar your way."

Rand thought to stride on, but a hard hand gripped his shoulder. "You are a stranger in Charolon. Don't walk in the night any longer than you have to. There are those of us who do not welcome strangers, and those of us who would find you easy prey."

A cold bolt followed the words, a bolt stabbing through Rand with the intensity of an attack and he stifled a gasp of alarm and tried to center himself. This was like the scrutiny he'd faced before hundreds that last evening and yet different. Ruthless. It did not care about what damage lay in its wake, or if it was perceived as intense or a casual brush. Rand licked his lips and concentrated on repelling it, sending it aside gently. A thought flashed across Rand's mind, a thought with a voice so unlike any he had ever felt before that he knew instinctively it was not his, had not come from within, but perhaps from this towering Choya. *He has a mind of stone,* and the thought had a kind of cold satisfaction.

And the attack ended as abruptly as it had begun.

Rand swallowed and said only, "Thank you for the advice."

The hand loosed him and let him go on his way. He fought the impulse to turn back and see if he was followed, by glance or otherwise, but Rand couldn't find the courage to do so. There was a weakness in his newly healed limbs and he had to find Palaton or collapse in the hallway.

Palaton woke, his bed still a nest of linen that smelled sweetly of Jorana. They had made, but not consummated, their lovemaking, and he woke with an ache and hunger for her sharpened by her visitation. As his eyes cleared, he saw the awkwardly planed figure standing silently across the room in a corner, watching him.

Palaton thrust himself out from the covers. He cursed first in Choyan, then found Trade coming to him. "How did you get in here?"

"Does it matter?" Rand asked softly.

"Of course it matters." With dignity, Palaton gathered a sheet about his waist. "There's enough security on these quarters to kill a battalion of assassins."

"I simply walked through."

"Walked through?" Palaton's gaze narrowed. "And where are your splints?"

"They bothered me. I took them off." Rand's voice sounded thin, tired, and troubled. "And, yes, I just walked through."

Palaton approached the doorway to his apartment quarters. The alarm system indicator showed it to be fully armed. He hesitated to tempt the system, the sonics barrier was set for severe incapacitation. He would not want to be caught in the barrier himself. He looked back toward Rand who had pulled up a large upholstered chair beside the fireplace and sat down.

"Did you feel anything?"

"My ears buzzed a little."

"That was all?" Palaton's voices rose a little, incredulously.

The young man shrugged, a movement that would have been elegant in a Choya but looked disjointed in a humankind.

"Remind me to make a note that humankind hearing systems are not as . . . vulnerable . . . as our to certain sonic ranges."

Rand's face twisted. "I'm not sure that would have helped."

Palaton paused, halfway across the room, his mind on business, but a note in the other's tone catching his attention. He crossed the room and took the chair opposite Rand. "Why are you here?"

"I needed to not be alone. And . . . I sensed you, also, not wanting to be left alone."

"And so you found me. How?"

That shrug again, so awkward that it made Palaton's skin crawl to see it. "I just did."

The wings and hallways of the palace were immense and intricate, though Rand had been placed not too far from the apartments given to the heir. Palaton shook his head. He groped for a rational explanation. "Between us, there is power. You know that."

"I followed it, then." Rand looked toward the large, curtained windows, where sheer panels let a translucent dawning through. "Maybe that's how I got through the security system."

Using his *bahdur*? Palaton did not like the thought. He chose his next words carefully. "Did you draw on me?"

"No, I . . . I just answered a call. I knew I had to be here. I knew that I, or you, couldn't be alone."

Palaton sat silent for a moment. "But how did you know that?"

"I don't know." Rand's turquoise gaze considered him. "I don't know where I end and you begin. I don't know if I'm me or you. I had this dream, you see, from my own memories and it was abruptly jolted away, and I was bothered by it. So I sat up in my room for half the night and then I knew that what I dreamed was from myself, but it was also from you." He paused, and looked toward the bedding. "Did you have a companion who left too early?"

"And if I did," Palaton said wryly, "I would hardly make it known."

"I'm not asking if you failed. I just want to know if . . . I don't know." Rand buried his face in his hands and his next words came out muffled. "I don't know if I'm me or if I'm you."

There was no precedent to know what *bahdur* did when infused into another, particularly an alien another. The thought that Rand might be using, squandering, his reserve of *bahdur* haunted Palaton, but he did not want Rand panicking. He had felt the flow between them on that Congressional podium, the gifting of his power, a spark, even if only for a moment. Palaton felt for the first time in days that there was hope of becoming whole again. "There is nothing to separate you from yourself," he said. "You carry my essence, like a flame carries heat, but unlike a flame or that heat, it won't consume you."

Rand's face lifted. His expression hardened. "Think not? Do you know what I dreamed yesterday?"

"No," Palaton answered quietly.

"I dreamed of flying. Not in a starliner. I dreamed that I was set off from the mountaintops, thrust leaping into the air, in something like, oh, a glider, and I rode the winds. There was golden fire under the wings and rippling over the landscape, and I could read the thermals from the shape of the sparks, how they flowed. I stayed aloft forever. I never wanted to land. But that wasn't me flying, that had to have been you. Even my dreams aren't my own ..." he paused. Rand raised a hand to his face. "I'm nearly blind today. The neural blockers have set in. I don't know how long it will last. But ... I'm not blind. Everywhere I look, fire outlines it. I can see because you burn, you all burn, everything in this room burns, and because it does, I can see it."

Palaton held his breath a moment. The boy saw through *bahdur*. He was no longer a passive receptacle. But how could Rand, be using it? Compact data scored humankind extremely low on all esper testing, despite their personal mythology. Did his *bahdur*, cleansed by Rand, burn so brightly it now spilled out? And if so, how could he hide what was occurring from his peers? He faced an alien who had been God-blind and now was not. But what should he tell him? What could he tell him? He did not see with human eyes. He did not know what Rand saw. "Perhaps it's a side effect. You may not be able to rely on it."

"There's nothing here I can rely on except you and maybe old Rindy. It's little enough. It keeps the shadows separated. If I look away, everything fades. If I lose this," and Rand turned away from him, to the cool and empty fireplace, "I'll be imprisoned inside myself. You won't even need Traskar to follow me around. I think I'm frightened. That's why I didn't want to be left alone."

"I won't let that happen to you."

They stared at one another. Rand asked, his voice carrying a fine, thin edge of despair, "How can you stop it?"

The humankind needed all the truth Palaton dared to let go. "I don't know ... yet. But what you can see is partly augmented by my *bahdur*."

"By your power?"

"Yes."

Rand reached out with one fingertip, outlined the edge of the elegantly carved side table which leaned against the side of his chair. "The edges sparkle, like fool's gold or as if fairy dust touched, pale yellow, tiny pricks of light."

"Everything?"

The manling nodded.

Palaton had never seen like that. The auras he could read had come mostly from emotion, from other Choyan, though if he concentrated, he could detect faint auras from the organic, living and once alive, things about him. When he'd had his power. Now, he saw only the bleak, colored surfaces of whatever he gazed upon. "I have never seen like that," he said, "but that means little. We're all of us unique in our powers."

"And private." Rand's mouth twisted. He rubbed his arm.

"Do you hurt?"

"I ache a little."

Palaton got to his feet, glad for an action he could undertake. He opened the comline to the apartment. "Staff, I need a physician in my rooms as soon as possible. Tell them to bring ID. I've left my security armed."

Rand had closed his eyes. Slate colored bruises underscored them. Palaton crossed to the chair and put a hand on the other's shoulder. The skin, the bones underneath the loose cloth of the shirt, felt not so alien as he'd once expected. "Are my dreams so terrible?"

"No." There was faint movement of his eyes under his blue-veined lids, as if he was recalling everything. "They gave me what I want." Rand's right hand clenched. "If only I can keep it."

Palaton could feel the sudden tension in his body. This humankind, this foreigner to Cho and its people, had the drive to be a *tezar*, but it was not his to claim. It was Palaton's *bahdur* giving him the forbidden, Palaton's soul and essence, and was he going to be destined to watch it burn through Rand and be lost forever to either of them?

Palaton had to retrieve his power, whatever the cost, before it destroyed both of them. He pulled his hand away, lest the other sense his thoughts and conflict. Before he found it necessary to fill an awkward silence, the threshold filled with a Choya'i, as close as any Choya could be to being fat, her massive body pausing long enough for her to pass her security badge through the laser reader, allowing her access to the rooms. Her silvered hair cascaded down her back from a horn crown so small as to be almost nonexistent, a mere ridge upon her brow.

The physician carried a bag in her wake and pulled up. Her face twisted, and her facial jewelry swirled in its opalescent colors, the random patterns accentuating her expression. "Perhaps," she said wryly, "you should have called a vet. I have no practical experience in treating non-Choyan."

The snide remark, coming from an Earthan whose genetic drive to find balance and serenity was usually deeply ingrained, threw Palaton off-guard. Rand sat up higher in the chair, opening his eyes, pain mirrored in them.

The physician set her bag down on the small side table. "I do, however, have access to your records of treatment from the bay station and in decon, and broken bones, stress fractures in your case, seem somewhat universal." She eyed Rand with gray eyes muddied by flecks of brown. "Took your braces off, did you?"

"Yes," Rand said faintly. "I itched."

"As well you should." The Choya'i took printouts and resonance imaging copies from her bag and looked them over. She touched corresponding areas on the boy's limbs. "Here and here."

"Yes."

She deftly rolled back his sleeve and opened the trousers at the inseam. "You still have considerable bruising at the sites where we suspected stress splints. I'll prescribe a mild painkiller to keep you quiet for another few days and I would like to remind you," the physician lifted her head, looking down a prominent nose, "the absence of pain does not mean that your healing is completed. Palaton," and the physician looked fully at him. "He'll need nutritional and herbal supplements as well, to strength the bone."

"And the braces?"

"He should do well enough now with them off, as long as he stays quiet. That's about all I can do for you." She paused, and bent his arm back and forth several times. "Does this hamper you?"

Rand looked puzzled. "No. Why?"

"One elbow," she said briskly. "Looks strange. I thought it might be handicapping." She snapped her case shut and stood up. "He heals quickly. The trauma should be fine in a few more days." At the threshold, she paused long enough to add, "I'll have your prescription sent up." She left, the impact of her presence vibrating in her wake.

Rand commented, "I'm healing very quickly. Perhaps your *bahdur* has something to do with it."

"No," Palaton countered quickly. He caught himself as Rand stared. "I mean, that *bahdur* does not heal."

"It doesn't? No mind over matter?"

"Not in that sense."

"Never?" Rand frowned in puzzlement. "Are you sure?"

"I am positive," Palaton said sternly. "Never in the history of my people has there been the ability to heal in such a way."

"Oh." Rand leaned his head back in the chair. "I don't think I'll need a painkiller. Just sleep." His voice grew fainter and trailed off. The faint lines in his face relaxed and his mouth slackened. Palaton realized the boy had gone to sleep.

He stood over him for a while, listening to the rhythm of the humankind's breathing. He found himself in the guardian posture, sentry over the young, when he looked up and saw a reflection of himself from across the room. Palaton did not move for a moment, meeting the stare of his image.

"What else," he murmured, "can I do?"

Chapter 14

"Rindalan," commented the predominant Choya as he preened, "is an old fool who has asked me to continue the indulgences he committed with Panshinea and extend them to the *tezar* chosen as heir. I refuse to be a party any longer. With Congress against them, I would be stupid to do as he asks." The rooms glittered with accumulated wealth and art, different from the ancient stone walls of the palace, these newly plastered partitions, hung with heavy tapestries of great antiquity. The blazing noonday sun streaked the room with bright light and deep shadow. The speaker stood proudly, short of height for a son of the House of Star, but wiry and big-horned, his strawberry blond mane clipped close in an unsuccessful attempt to tame its curls. His large eyes blazed sapphire blue, piercing and cold.

His companion answered from a shadowed table, virtually impossible to be seen, but for the glittering of his eyes. "I'm glad to hear one of our Prelates has his senses about him, Qativar."

"I can do nothing else. Rindy has left me nothing but the dregs of his power, which he clings to like a lifeline. He should have retired long ago and left Panshinea to his own devices, to rise and fall like the Descendant on the Wheel that he is." Qativar's eyebrows rose elegantly. "Surely I can't be the only one who has seen this." He pulled on the seam of his summer jacket, having forsaken the more traditional robes of a priest. His movement might have seemed vain to those who did not know him, but to those who did, the plucking was not vanity, but pragmatism. He was undoubtedly straightening the hilt of a wrist dagger or checking the wiring of a hidden stunner. His wiry muscles moved under the sleek jacket, giving the impression of strength and bulk equal to that of a much taller Choya. Qativar was as formidable as his movements hinted.

"You know you aren't, or our unseemly alliance would never have come about." The speaking Choya rested his hands upon the small conversation table. One fingertip traced the rich, curving burl of the wood's grain. "Have you told Rindalan you intend to break from him?"

Qativar paused. He looked at his companion appraisingly. "That would be foolish, don't you think? The longer I stay in his confidence, the better I can work against him. He leaves for Sorrow soon enough, anyway."

"We are of a mind, then."

"Did you ever doubt it?"

"Doubt never entered my thoughts." The other Choya stood, cloaked by shadow, moving back closer still to the corner as if the stone wall itself would absorb his exit. "Word is that Vihtirne of Sky is trying to retrieve her water recycling patent."

Qativar gave a last pluck. His head tilted in consideration of this information. "The counties could be in turmoil if she brought that pressure to bear. But can she do it?"

"I don't know yet. The legalities of the original forfeiture are obscure. Centuries have passed. Her heirship to the patent isn't contested . . . it seem probable that the courts may not have any recourse. She is a foe to be reckoned with, Qativar, whether or not she accomplishes her desire."

"Not without Nedar. She has no one to put forth for the throne without him, and he's nowhere to be found."

"He could be on contract."

Qativar scratched his temple. "If he is, Blue Ridge will know where he is. Check the flight school for records when you have a chance. And mind your step. I want no traces coming back to us. When we move, we will be so swift neither Panshinea nor Palaton will ever see us coming."

"To that end." The other moved, shadows shifted, and the room emptied.

Qativar listened keenly. The air in the room changed pressure, ever so subtly, the slightly musky fragrance of another Choya's body drifted away, and he knew his co-conspirator had left. His fingertip brushed the collar of his jacket. "And as for you, Asten, my friend," he said under his breath, "Vihtirne of Sky will take you out for me, when she discovers you sniffing at the heels of her beloved Nedar. I have valued your support over the years, but you weary me." The Choya sniffed a little, put his shoulders back, and left the rooms of his apartment.

*   *   *

Rindalan gave a snuffling laugh. "He walks like a child," the old Choya said. "But you find pride where you will, like a newborn's parent."

Rand laughed as Palaton made an indignant noise. His dark hair ruffled in the slight summer breeze reaching the broad veranda. "It's better than limping along stiff from here to here." He took a deep breath and sat down. The view from the veranda overlooked the palace's massive gardens, floral and produce. "The air smells different. I don't know what it is or how to describe it."

"Words may never come to you." Palaton abandoned his posture of indignity. His gaze followed that of the humankind's. "I have been on many worlds, and their differences amaze and astound me, and yet the subtleties of their variations are not always easy to grasp." He took a deep breath. "I'll leave you two. Gathon has set up briefings for me, and there is still the matter of the God-blind to settle."

"What do you intend to do with Malahki?"

"What can I do? I've talked with him once. He expects something from me I cannot deliver. The streets have to be cleared. The commons have to return home. It's clear Congress will not back me nor will they suffer a continuing strike. I have to get the situation settled soon." Palaton took his hands off the veranda railing, preparing to depart, when Rindy raised a hand in entreaty.

"One or two minutes more, to meet Qativar. You promised me."

"I'll do what I can, but for a useless figurehead, they're keeping me busy." Palaton turned, as footsteps echoed behind them, and the short, vigorous figure of Qativar pushed past the draperies and into the open air.

Palaton met appraising blue eyes with a shocking coldness to them. Then Qativar turned to Rindy, grabbed him up in a hug that seemed to rattle the elderly Choya's bones. Rindy gasped with good humor and breathlessness.

"Qativar, enough, I'm too old for this."

Delight spread across the young priest's face as he released Rindalan and resumed facing them. "It's been too long, Rindy. I don't agree with what you've asked me to do. Cho needs you too much at home." His gaze came to rest on Rand. "Is this the humankind who caused so much trouble?"

"It is," answered Palaton evenly.

"He hardly looks like a danger." Qativar extended his hand. "I believe you favor an open-palmed shake, do you not?"

"I do." Rand took the other's hand carefully and they completed a familiar, yet alien handshake.

The young priest leaned back against the veranda railing. "Rindy has told me he intends to brave the vicissitudes of politics on Sorrow, to aid Panshinea however he may. I might quarrel with that, but he is my superior and I would surely lose. What I don't argue with is that you're going to need my skills to keep your balance here in Charolon."

"First we have to find a balance," said Palaton wryly.

"Indeed." Qativar smiled anew. "So I'm pleased to bring news which even Rindy hasn't heard yet."

The gaunt Choya turned, his thin hair ruffled by the fine breeze, his horn crown seeming to prickle at the sound of Qativar's voices. "What is it?"

"The Council of Prelates has asked for a cleansing. I know Palaton has little time to give for the ritual, but I've been able to sway them to let us use the Earthan temple here at Sethu, rather than forcing us to travel cross-country. Once cleansed, and backed by the Prelates, Congress can't continue to hold a grudge against you."

"A cleansing?" burst out Rindalan in surprise, while Palaton said, "Now that's a two-headed *drath*."

"*Drath?*"

The Choya looked to Rand. "Serpent, I believe the word is in Trade. A double-edged blessing." He took a chair and drummed his fingers upon the arm. "Can't this be sidestepped?"

"It probably could be, but it shouldn't," Qativar answered. "Heir Palaton, this gives the Houses the opportunity to know your power burns bright and clean, despite the lapse you suffered last year, and that the heir to the throne is a vigorous and healthy Choya. We need to know that, to feel confidence in you, to accept you as a leader in Panshinea's place. Knowing your health, the Congress cannot continue to second-guess the decisions you're making. Once you have that acceptance, you can begin to find the balance you need. Rindy," and those brilliant cerulean eyes searched out the older Choya. "Don't you agree?"

Rindy shifted inside his robes, appearing spindly within the voluminous cloth. "I'm not sure. I'm still stunned." He lifted his eyes. "There could be an advantage, I think, more than just proving yourself."

"And what might that be?"

"A subtle reminder to the Godless of what you are and they are not."

Palaton kept his face impassive. "I would have to leave Rand behind."

"Regardless, you would anyway. He has his convalescence and he's still in danger on Choyan streets." Rindy crossed his legs and covered one bony kneecap with a flap of his robe.

Palaton could not protest. He could not reveal his weakness to these two. Rand had turned his face to look down on the gardens as if afraid the new Prelate might be able to read his expression. Palaton hesitated a moment or two longer. A ritual cleansing for a *tezar* was little more than walking through the ceremonies anyway. It could not restore his *bahdur*, though that had been the intent centuries ago.

It could, however, reveal the fatal emptiness within him.

Exposed now or later. Palaton saw Rindy watching him intently. Later, he thought. Where there was life, there was hope. "All right," he said. "I'll tell Gathon to make the arrangements. When shall we do it?"

"It had better be soon," Rindy said. "I can stay with the boy if it is."

"I'll be all right," Rand protested gently, but no one paid attention to his soft voice.

"Good," said Qativar. "I'll work with the Council."

Palaton stood. "Make the arrangements," he said, his voices vibrating strongly. "But Rand stays with me."

Shock issued from Rindy, who had obviously thought the matter closed. "Palaton, this is a sacred cleansing. We have Traskar to attend him in your absence."

"I am Rand's guardian. There are forces both on Cho and in the universes who will tear him apart, given the opportunity. I've no intention of giving it to them." He met Qativar's cold stare evenly. "Do whatever has to be done."

The Prelate dropped his chin and bowed his head. "Heir Palaton."

*   *   *

"You can't leave me like this," Bevan said, grabbing at the arm of the Zarite buckling him into a webbing.

"We've brought you this far. It is for you to take yourself further," the creature told him.

"This is a life pod!"

"Inside a cruiser. We've a launch programmed. You'll be picked up, no doubt, somewhere outside the boundaries of our normal space."

"You can't know that." Bevan fought panic, both at his inability to see the world as it really was, and at the complacence of the Zarite.

"Master, we can't do anything else for you. Without a pilot, we cannot take you off-planet. This launch will take you out and release the raft before the plane self-destructs. This will carry you beyond the range of any attackers waiting for such action. Then, the life raft will bear you within tracking range of Compact rescuers. What more can we do?"

Bevan looked about at the confining capsule. "I'll die in here," he said, and felt his throat drawing tight.

"You'll get off-planet. This is all we can accomplish." The creature paused. "I'm sorry, Master Bevan. I can't promise you anything more."

Bevan felt the webbing draw tight about his chest and arms, as he was slung up in midair, so as to baffle the acceleration experienced from a planet berthing cradle rather than that of a launching from, say, a bay station. He fought the instinct to loosen the webbing, to ground himself, to get free.

The Zarite ran a soft-furred hand over the console. "We've checked. You have adequate drinking and food supplies for three weeks. Surely in that time, someone will have heard your signal and picked you up. The capsule is designed for survival."

Bevan closed his eyes tightly. When he opened them, the view was without aura and darkness. He met the light green eyes of the alien facing him. "I accept your aid," he said and swallowed tightly. "It's all we both can do."

The Zarite nodded. His whiskers fluffed a little. "Would that it were more," the native said.

A thrumming vibrated through the metal and plastics surrounding them. His round, transparent ears flicked up and then back.

"We're readying for launch," the Zarite said. "I cannot stay."

"Nor can I," answered Bevan with bitter humor. He put a hand through the safety webbing. "Thank you and all your brethren for me."

He felt rather than saw the soft yet strong grasp of the creature in response. The Zarite left and the bulkhead of the life pod closed with a firm and solid thud. Bevan shook in his harnessing. He was not the best of travelers. Coming to Arizar, it had been Rand's steady and sure temperament which had calmed him ... that and Alexa's flirtatious attention. It seemed forever and a day ago that they had been students smuggled away to a mysterious future at an alien school. Now he had no one.

He looked about the capsule interior. His vision sank into its prismatic miasma and he let out a virulent Portuguese curse, then smiled. Father Lombardi would have beaten him for that one, as tolerant as the orphanage padre had been in his time. But the man had had limits.

"What about you, Bev, old boy?" he murmured through drying lips. "What are your limits?"

His heart thumped as he sensed the movement of the berthing cradle into launch position. The capsule was set up to gyro, to stay always at a certain center of gravity regardless of the ship's movement. That, at least, gave him some comfort. He would not spend half of his brief voyage hanging upside down, though once in space, there could be no upside down.

The ship began to tremble, its thrust building. Bevan swallowed tightly. He closed his eyes, unwilling to watch through his peculiar vision.

Behind his eyelids, a bonfire built, flames burning orange red, then turning blue, and then white. When the bonfire burst across his inner eye, blazing through eye tissue and dreams, the ship launched and Bevan sank deep into his safety harnessing, his face contorting with the force of the thrust skyward. He put a hand out through his webbing as if to grab for one last piece of dirt just before he blacked out.

Chapter 15

The emperor of Cho filled the screen, his still presence even more commanding than if he had paced or gestured. He was dressed less flamboyantly for the Halls of Compact than he would be for home, Palaton thought, but he was a true son of the House of Star regardless. His light complexion balanced off the thin artistry of his gold and white-gold jewelry tracings. His eyes of pale jade which deepened to rims of forest green fixed on his watcher as if he could divine, even across subspace and through the monitor, Palaton's thoughts.

If they could have stood side by side, Panshinea would have been a little shorter and heavier. His face sagged with lines at the corner of his eyes and mouth, and his neck had begun to show his age as well. He favored the dramatic, as seen in his lavish hair of reds and yellows, graying at the temple, and the red and gold echoing of his uniform. He was no blood relation to Palaton, except by the weakest of associations through their House, nor did Palaton think that this man might be his unnamed father. He knew better, and so did Panshinea. What bound them now was thicker than the cord of parentage.

Palaton kept his silence, waiting for his emperor to speak.

When Panshinea did, the transmission thinned his voices down to a single tenor. "Perhaps," he said, "it is well the streets are full of God-blind. If not . . . the Housed might have sent their guards in, and we would have war on our hands instead of anarchy."

"You think the censureship that serious."

"It could be. I think more serious is that Devon of the Householding of Kilgalya has named Ariat the heir for the House of Earth. If we are in Descendant, as seems more surely true every day, then the Earthans have a legitimate claim to the throne. They will leave their coveted neutrality for it, I think."

Palaton had not heard of that. It was to be suspected that Panshinea's information would precede his . . . but he wondered why Gathon or Jorana had not chosen to inform him. Was the information speculation only, and Panshinea, in his usual brilliant, intuitive way, formulating his strategy as if what was speculated upon must be? "Have you *foreseen* this?"

"God, no. Common sense will tell you what the Earthans will do when they come out of their corner." Panshinea shifted before the monitor then. He had been sitting, now he stood.

"What about the flight schools?"

"What about them?"

"I have just authorized completion for three of the smallest classes ever graduated since the plague of Fangborn's century."

Panshinea's eyes narrowed. "Again?"

"Last year's was this small as well?"

"Yes." The emperor turned slightly, lifting a shoulder, and he stood as if knowing that full view of his face was blocked by the movement. "I thought it a fluke."

"We're not advancing candidates out from the Choosing among the Godless. More and more God-blind communities are not participating."

Panshinea moved again, a furtive motion not meant to be seen. "You've been busy."

"You left me little to govern but this and civil unrest from the Houses." Palaton did not let the emperor continue to hide from him. He asked for a different camera range and got it, revealing the emperor's face. He pressed for an answer. "If candidates are not forthcoming from the Choosing, what are the God-blind doing with them? Could Malahki be building a House of his own? And if he is, how long have you known about it?"

Panshinea tilted his head. His green eyes gazed directly into the monitor. "Intelligence doesn't indicate that Malahki is making such a move. The commons are not producing the candidates they used to. Neither are the Houses. Despite all our efforts, the talent appears to continue breeding out. Why else do you think I wanted a *tezar* for my heir?"

A multitude of reasons flooded into Palaton's mind: chief among them knowledge that Panshinea could siphon off *bahdur* to augment his own fading capabilities as he burned out. As if his swiftly flitting thoughts could be seen, Panshinea laughed.

"I asked for a hero. Now we have one. What will you do?"

Palaton reached up to the monitor switch, ready

to end transmission and the audience. After a moment's pause, he said, "I'll let you know when I decide."

"Do that," his emperor replied. "In the meantime, work the Houses against one another if you can. They all have their weak spots. Ask Rindy for counsel. And probe deeply through whatever course of action Gathon suggests. I sometimes feel he has his own agenda."

The screen went dark.

Palaton continued to sit there. He had heard of screen-dark transmissions, in which the subject unknowingly continued to remain on-call, revealing that which was candid and damning. He had nothing damning to reveal to Panshinea, but he would not put it past his emperor to have such a feature on the monitor screen.

He sat back at the desk, the reports from the various flight schools in front of him. He had already signed and released what he needed to. But they drew his attention, as if trying to communicate with him.

If he'd had his *bahdur*, the mystery might be revealed. Now he sat with naked eye and felt frustration roiling through him. There had been no apparent shortage of renegade *tezars* to evacuate Arizar when needed, he thought bitterly.

Palaton straightened in the chair. He ran a finger over the flight school charts. The listing here included only the results for the new cadets. He keyed open the interlink to Gathon's offices. The minister himself answered.

"Gathon here."

"Palaton. I want an analysis of *tezars* we've lost over the past twenty years or so."

"Dead?"

"No . . . lost."

"A solemn subject. The Patterns of Chaos have claimed some of our best."

"I know," answered Palaton. Even those who could master Chaos did not always keep it under control. There were maelstroms of random space which could not be navigated, like the Tangled Web, or other even more treacherous areas which they all learned to avoid. Then there were those, like Nedar, who had died off-planet and been sent home. His body, as far as Palaton could determine through discreet inquiries, had never arrived. Likely the ship sent out from Arizar had been taken out by the raiders on their way in. But there were others, legendary pilots of ability, who had simply disappeared. *Or had they?* "Have it transmitted to me as soon as you can compile it." He closed the com. He had suspected it on Arizar, and then forgotten it thanks to the strain of the last several weeks. But if the House of Flame were rebuilding itself at the expense of all Cho, it would strike first at the *tezars*, draining them away.

And it meant also, if they were quietly taking candidates out of the Houseless as well as winning over fatigued pilots ready to chance all for rejuvenation, that they already had a strong arm here on Cho.

The only way Palaton could begin to trace them was by the ashes they'd left in their wake, a trail of destruction which showed the path they had taken, but not what lay before them, which would affect all Cho. That he would have to discover for himself.

He wondered about the sudden rise of Qativar

and what might await him in the temple at Sethu. Should he go, knowing the ritual would do nothing for him, and that he might trip a trap cunningly laid for him? Should he endanger Rand?

It occurred to him that he had put Rand's safety before his own duty to Cho. It was a bittersweet knowledge. There were loyalties that sometimes conflicted between a Choya and his House and world . . . *tezar* to *tezar*, for example. Thinking of that, Palaton tired of waiting for Gathon to transmit the material he'd asked for, reached for the interlink and called Blue Ridge.

"Blue Ridge. Hathord here."

Palaton found himself grinning broadly at the image of Hat on his monitor, square, stolid, old Hat, his thick Earthan shoulders more than equal to the weight of running a flight school. "Hat!"

The Choya's eyes widened like plates. "Palaton! Your highness," and he dropped his chin in obeisance.

"Forget it, Hat. I've seen you bare-butt naked and you've seen me hanging by my chin strap, dangling at wit's end off a cliff. If I'm the heir, it's only because Panshinea found a use for me and I was foolish enough to volunteer."

The Earthan met his stare again. "Nonetheless," Hat said, "there are formalities. Congratulations."

Hat's hands were out of sight, but Palaton retained a mental image of him juggling, always juggling, a typical Earthan seeking for the balances of the various natures on Cho. "Thank you," he answered.

"And welcome home." Hat turned, looking off-screen, though he said nothing. There might have

been someone else there, but even though Palaton
asked for an adjusted camera range, nothing
showed.

"Thank you. I sent your graduation list back,
through Gathon."

"Good. The cadets are anxious." Hat's expression shone for a moment, through the wariness.
Palaton was sorry to see it settle back into place as
the Earthan asked him, "What can I do for you?"

"I'm looking for a memorial list. All the *tezars*
who've been lost."

Hat's glance flickered down, then up again. "I
haven't had time to keep one. Moameb did, but
the data would be old. Of course, the information
has been sent in to Charolon, I just don't keep it
separate here."

Hat knew, as did Palaton, that the names of
those comrades ought to be able to be recited by
heart. Palaton had been away, on contract and out
of touch, but Hathord had not. He was lying to
Palaton.

"I suppose you saw the censureship broadcast
yesterday. I'm in trouble again."

"But for all the right reasons, as usual," Hat
said impassively.

"There are greater loyalties than to one's
House," Palaton told him. He would not say it
more directly than that, for if he had to, no such
loyalty existed between him and Hat anymore.

Hat's dark eyes met his uneasily. "I'm sorry I
cannot help you."

The comradeship and bond between them had
been denied. Palaton nodded, saying, "I understand," though he did not, and then he said fare-

well. He darkened the monitor without waiting for Hat to answer.

Nedar came out of the blind corner of the study where the monitor could not perceive him. "What was he about, do you think?"

"I think," Hat said bitterly, "that he was trying to see if your body had come back."

"Ah! Do you know I had forgotten I was supposed to be dead?" The pilot laughed as he flung himself into Hat's favorite chair. "Palaton's troubles have almost made me forget mine."

Hat lowered himself to a second chair, one not built for his sturdy body. It could not take his mass and he was reduced to perching on it. "If he knew you were here," Hat said, "he would tear Blue Ridge apart to get at you."

"And he would expect you to tell on me?" Nedar arched an eyebrow. He fingered his glass of wine. "But he reminds me of something I'd forgotten. We are *tezars*. That is a kinship which runs through our veins, along with our blood." He tapped the edge of the glass against his chin. "Out of the mouths of enemies come certain, undeniable truths."

"What are you talking about?" said Hat, frustration darkening his face.

"Let me think on it a little longer. I'll let you know," answered Nedar thoughtfully. He lifted his glass and dashed the wine back.

If he could not even count on the support of his comrades, then he had to go to Sethu. If cleansing would lift the onus of the judgments he'd made, then so be it. But Jorana had not reacted well when he'd told her his decision.

"No."

Jorana shook her head a second time. Strain showed in the delicate tracings of her face, a slight pinching about her nose, the fragile translucency of her skin. "I can't advise this. I have no way to protect you inside the temple."

Palaton said only, "There should be no danger. Even the Earthans can't afford to be that obvious."

She put her hand to her brow as if a sudden pain had struck her there. "May I remind you that it was the House of Earth which sent an assassin against you the last time you resided inside these walls."

"I'm reminded. But there was no evidence then, or now, that the attack was aimed at me specifically. It could have been done to weaken Panshinea." And if he could only tell her, Palaton could list a fistful of other enemies who might wish to strike at him.

A faint glittering came from the depth of her eyes. "Circumstances remain the same today. If you were the target, you'll be putting yourself within their reach again. If Panshinea is the target, there is no better way to weaken him than by bringing you down now."

He sat back in his chair. "There should be a chink in your logic, but I don't think I can find it."

"I would be very poor at what I did if I let you do this."

"And I have no way of knowing if I can ever be good at what I hope to do if I don't do this. The

Prelates demand it of me. I've thrown enough customs in the face of the Houses by what I've done for the God-blind. I can't afford to break with any more traditions." He shuffled a report on the desktop. "Rindy seems to agree that it should be done."

"Rindalan is too close to the God-in-all now to see the face of Cho clearly." Jorana paced a step, turned and came back. "I love the old Choya dearly, but age clouds his judgment."

"What of Qativar, his second?"

"I'm not sure of him." She paused. The late afternoon sunlight caught and fired in her bronze, tousled hair. The image of her snared him, as a lantern might a moth.

He found himself staring and broke the spell by saying, "No background on him?"

"We have background. He's come a long way in the years you spent in exile. The order is desperate for young blood and he appears to have earned their trust." And she shrugged.

Palaton found himself smiling. "We, of all people, cannot discount intuition."

She smiled back. "No, we can't."

"Still," he added reluctantly, "this is a course I have to take." Another road pre-chosen for him. He felt hemmed in. He knew he took time Jorana didn't have, but he also felt reluctant to let her go. "What would Panshinea do?"

Jorana considered his question. The thoughtfulness showed in her voices as she finally said, "Panshinea would go, hoping to extract a miracle from bare rock. And if he could not produce a genuine one, he would do whatever was necessary to provide the illusion."

"Do you want me to work miracles?"

"Getting out of there alive and cleansed would qualify." Jorana paced a step or two away, then turned. "We don't even know if going will affect the censureship."

"No, we don't. But I can't sit here any longer, Jorana. I can't sit here and say, I did what I did because I have no choice. I've got a choice now, and I'm making it. If disaster follows, I'll deal with it. But what they and you and even Panshinea forget, is that as a *tezar*, I'm a damned good war commander. I won't let my wings be clipped so easily."

She smiled a little at the emotion in his voices. "All right. You're right. I did forget you're a pilot, with all that you're heir to. I'll make arrangements." She left him. Palaton watched her go before succumbing to the doubt which he had not shown in front of her.

What was a pilot without the powers which enabled him to master Chaos? What was he now? What would he be tomorrow? Did it matter what he had been and now could not be? Jorana did not know what it was she put before him.

*   *   *

Qativar radiated youth as much as Rindalan radiated wisdom. He entered Rand's chambers with a spring to his step and the boy watched him cross the room, wondering if Choyan children were like acrobats and ballerinas, touching ground only long enough to gather purchase to leap into the air again. He did not know how the Choyan reckoned age . . . he was young among his race or theirs, but what of Qativar? Old enough to have gained a position second only to Rindalan in the priesthood . . . but Rand knew from what had been left unsaid in his presence that Qativar was without equal in that respect.

"Alone again?" the priest asked, though it was obvious the quarters were empty except for Rand.

"Not now," Rand answered.

"Ah." The Choya smiled. "Then perhaps you might enjoy my company?"

Rand put aside any wariness, based on Rindy's recommendation of this vigorous Choya. With a foot, he dragged a chair close. "Have a seat. I get tired of talking to myself."

"Do you? Ah." And Qativar smiled again. "You have a quick and easy mastery of Trade, although you often use the lower form." He lowered himself into the other chair.

"Thanks, I think. I learned it at my father's knee." Rand sat back in his chair.

"From your father? What connection does he have with the Compact?"

"None. He hoped to. He was a businessman."

"I see." Qativar eyed him. The brightness of his eyes, thought Rand, was something that Rindy no longer possessed. Just as age wrinkled humans, it seemed to fade Choyan. "The Compact does not deal with Class Zed worlds on a very profitable basis."

"I know. But he wanted to be ready when we changed classification. He thought we would. He thought it was just a matter of time. He's one of those," Rand explained, "who think we have a great deal to offer."

"The enthusiasm of young races," responded

Qativar, as if that explained something. He reached into his summer jacket and pulled out a napkin, unwrapping two sticky buns. "Dinner is a long time past. Hungry?"

They shared the sweet bread, licked sugary crumbs off their fingers, and sighed in contentment at the same time.

Qativar left the sticky napkin draped across the side table. "Rindy asked me to keep an eye on you. I think he thought perhaps our age would be a bridge to one another. He knows Palaton is busy weaving himself into the pattern of the emperor's politics. That can't leave much time for you. You must have questions?"

"I don't know enough to ask." Rand licked his lips a satisfying last time. "I know Rindy was upset when Palaton insisted on bringing me tomorrow."

"That's understandable. Religion is a private matter, even among Choyan."

"Will I cause him trouble?"

Qativar shrugged. "Either the Earthan priests will accept you, or not. If they don't, this is only one way of smoothing Palaton's weaving. He needs to regain control over the commons. And he needs to prove his diplomatic ability among the Houses, which are squabbling louder and louder with Panshinea away. He has an advantage no other heir might have had: he's a *tezar*, and pilots are well thought of."

"But they wanted him cleansed for that."

"There's a reason." Qativar glanced down at the arm of his chair and idly traced a pattern in the fabric. "*Tezars* are often burned out by the work they do. It destroys them, slowly. If Cho is lucky, we have a *tezar* coming to the throne in the prime of his powers, virtually untouched by that burnout."

"If not . . ."

"It drives them mad," Qativar answered. "As evidenced by Panshinea's erratic behavior. The emperor is too far gone now to realize that he can no longer rule. It will be a struggle to replace him, peacefully or otherwise."

"Mad?" repeated Rand carefully. The other did not seem to notice his care.

"Eventual insanity is a hazard of dealing with Chaos. If we are lucky, a *tezar* has a long and fruitful life before coming to that conclusion."

He had never known. He knew that Qativar had settled a confidence on him, something those born off the planet of Cho were normally never told. *Palaton, facing insanity, as well as dishonor.* Rand felt the thought settle in him like a forewarning of doom. "And if Palaton can't pass the ceremony?"

Qativar met his look steadily. "He must. We need him on Panshinea's throne. If he's turned away . . . we might still save him."

"How?"

"A Congress of evaluation." Qativar stood up briskly. "But we'll cross that impasse when we come to it. Your presence is not a crux tomorrow, humankind. Palaton will succeed or fail on his own merits." The Prelate towered over him. "And that's the way it should be, should it not?"

Rand owed Palaton his life, and there seemed to be no way to give it back. He thought of asking Qativar for help, and hesitated. He only knew he was a stranger here. He didn't know if he was among friends or enemies. Instead, he agreed with

the priest and then let him out of the apartments,
both grateful for and disturbed by the company
Qativar had brought. Sleep took a long time
coming.

Rand was not sure if he were sleeping, dreaming, or remembering when Palaton gently shook
him. He had a vague sensation of tumbling in
darkness when his focus sharpened and he looked
into the alien face leaning over him.

Palaton said, "It's time."

Rand had a thought that he must remember
this, that when he lost his sight altogether, he
must retain the vision of looking into the proud,
strange face of the other, the large expressive eyes,
the awesome impact of the earless head sculpted
into a massive bone crown that cupped masses of
hair. Someday he would be returned and he would
be in exile, and memory would be all that he had
of this tethering with Palaton. He sat up. The
room sorted itself into the various shades of gray
dusted with illumination he had begun to grow
used to. He stood up.

"We're leaving?"

"Almost immediately. Are you ready?"

"What are we going to face?"

Palaton turned to the bank of windows. "I don't
know yet myself. Every religious ceremony is dependent upon the recipient. There are seven steps
of cleansing . . . the priests may not allow me to
continue when they discover you with me."

"It's that serious?"

Palaton nodded.

There had been nothing in the random images
of Palaton's life which occasionally flashed

through him to let Rand know what they were facing. He took a step, favoring his sore leg. "Leave me behind then. I can wait another day or two to get out."

"It's not a matter of that. I need you with me."

Rand thought of what Qativar had told him. "They'll be testing your powers?"

"No . . . but the absence of them may become quite visible. I've never gone through this before . . . empty."

Palaton's voices were so bereft that grief clutched at Rand's throat, stopping his reply. He clenched a fist. "I'd give them back," he got out, and stopped yet again.

"I know. And if I had the ability, I'd take them back, so long as it didn't harm you."

Rand leaned back against a chair for strength. "What if I were dead," he asked suddenly.

"Then all hope would leave."

"Are you so sure?"

"I am not willing to find out." Palaton put his hand out and brought Rand back to his feet. "There are Gods on your world, are there not? Then why are you so afraid to meet One?"

" 'Because' strikes me as the only answer I have," Rand said.

Palaton began to laugh as he escorted the other to the apartment doors. He paused long enough to pick up a light, Choyan summer jacket from the back of a door hook and to disarm the security system.

As far away as home seemed, nothing had prepared him for Cho. A leaden summer sky hung close over the city, waiting for the crack of light-

ning and the drum of thunder to loosen its tears.
The street smelled of baking dirt and tar. Birds
darted here and there after bugs which he could
only catch glimpses of before they were snatched
eagerly out of midair. He saw a small, scruffy
looking animal race away from the tires of the
conveyance, but it had gone before he could point
it out to Palaton and ask what it had been.

Age hung as close over the city as the threatening storm. It curtained every major building, op-
pressive and dark. He saw walls so solid nothing
might bring them down. Palaton caught the object
of his interest.

"We build," the Choya said wryly, "for
longevity."

"Nothing new?"

"Not in this sector. We build new for the commons. They're hardest on our resources. We have
Housesteadings going back thousands of years."

"And where is yours?"

"I haven't one, now. My grandfather lost it to
debts."

"What happened to it? It must still be there,
right?"

"It's still there, but it's not available to any of
my family. Someone took it over. Probably another Star, but possibly a Sky. Skies love to see
another House fail. If you want to know what I
call home, it's Blue Ridge."

"Blue Ridge?" Rand savored the name. He knew
it from the overflow from Palaton. Cadets and barracks and steaming *bren* on deathly cold morn-
ings, the wind screaming down off a blue
mountain plateau, *thara* trees in bloom . . . yes, it
had the feel of home to it. It reminded Rand most

nearly of the New Mexico mountains where he'd spent part of his youth. Never mind that he'd never actually seen a frail, fernlike *thara* tree outside of his mind.

"Both the Householding of Volan and Blue Ridge are half a planet away," murmured Palaton.

"But not lost."

The other looked at him silently and Rand wondered if his stolen memories had left the other barren, if he had taken that away as well. His lips parted for a reply when the sight of a dark cloud of flitting, squealing shapes swooped over the dome of the conveyance, their passage rattling the windows.

Their wings thundered against the sullen air. He could see piercing beaks and bright quick eyes, watching him, watching them, as the flock passed over, wheeled in midair and turned into the climbing sun.

Rand turned his astonishment aside to see Palaton smiling. "Nightchasers," he said. "Noisy and spectacular. There must be a rookery close by. Perhaps in one of the parks." He settled back into his chair and closed his eyes, inviting no further comment and leaving Rand to soak in the sights of the fortress city.

The technology he'd expected was not to be seen though he knew it had to be there, layered underneath. When the clouds occasionally parted, what sky could be seen was a brilliant cerulean. If fires burned, they must burn cleanly. He watched out the side windows avidly, trying to catch sight of what this city took for granted.

The city sights had thinned considerably when Palaton roused from his meditation and opened his eyes. Rand was appreciating the wildflowers that dotted the empty lots and ran along the roadside, their faces mosaicking the countryside.

"What interests you?" asked Palaton, leaning forward.

"The flowers."

The other looked. "Daybrights," he named them. "They grow wild, like the weeds. By midday they will have faded, their blossoms as brittle as straw by nightfall, and their crumbled heads on the ground by midnight. But tomorrow morning, the new buds will be ready to open."

"They're strong."

"Strong?" Palaton's eyebrows arched. "They barely last a day."

"The bloom might, but the plant is everywhere. Think of the roots it must have. You don't irrigate out here . . . it catches water when it can. But still it grows. I bet if you stopped maintaining the roadway, it could push it aside, crumble it to pieces."

Palaton looked past him in silence for a moment, then said, "There are ways to measure strength. I was not aware of this one."

A hangar loomed along the roadway. Rand could see a skimcraft being readied, crew walking up and down the runway to fuel it and clear the area.

He glanced at Palaton. "You piloting?"

The other's skin darkened to a rosy hue. "Not this time," he answered. "And we haven't far to go."

Rufeen waited for them, her uniformed figure partially obscured by the squat tail fin of the skimcraft. It hadn't been built for speed, but for comfort. The Choya'i smiled broadly as she caught sight of them.

"Well, manling. You look a good deal healthier than when I saw you last."

"And you look . . . more uniformed."

Rufeen looked down. "Indeed, I do. This is what's expected of an imperial pilot. I think the colors suit me. Choya, shall we be seated? I'm told that commoners have found out we have flight plans and there is a demonstration march en route. We need to grab some sky."

Palaton muffled a sound, following Rufeen as she ducked her head and entered the skimcraft. Rand wasn't entirely sure what kind of sound it was that Palaton choked back, but the Choya's reaction had been interesting.

They followed the sun. It was still bright noon when they landed, and another conveyance awaited them. They had outrun the storm and the city. Here was country that was almost entirely barren, a near-desert ecology, open space running as far as the eye could see. There were no daybrights edging the runways, but Palaton took the time to point out the shrubbery laden with a star-shaped yellow flower. "Tinley," he said.

Rufeen gave them an amused glance. "Starting with the birds and the bees, Palaton?" she asked.

"The boy has an interest."

"The boy has a thirst," she corrected mildly. She looked to Rand. "Take the throttle for me on the way back?"

"What?"

The Choya'i shrugged. "Piloting a skimcraft takes little skill. Want to try it?"

"Yes."

She ignored Palaton's hard look. "I'll expect you then," she said. "Don't let the Earthans make a convert of you."

Rand met her teasing glance. "They wouldn't try," he said, fairly sure of his welcome from what Palaton had said earlier.

"Perhaps. There is that about you which does not feel alien. Who knows what an Earthan would try?"

Rand watched her turn her mocking stare aside and grow quiet. He looked at Palaton. "Are they so different?"

"Yes, and no. There are three major branches of Choyan: Earth, Sky, and Star. We're Stars. The Earthans are less technological, more empathetic with nature. Their skills run to agriculture and animal management. They're also used to being a buffer between the Stars and Skies. They're always searching for the equilibrium of things. Making an alien a religious acolyte might appeal to that search and balance. I don't recommend you do it, however."

It took Rand a bare second to realize that Palaton teased him a little, as well. "Rufeen," he asked, "what about letting me try a landing, too?"

Palaton's head snapped back to study him while Rand kept his face bland and Rufeen burst out in laughter. It took a moment for the tension to fade from Palaton's jawline, and he gave a tiny nod of concession to the human. Rufeen put a hand to Rand's wrist.

"Look, there," she said. "Over the next rise."

Rises gave way to foothills and foothills to cobalt mountains, shadowing even the sun in their vastness, growing not distant but formidably close, and before them he saw the building.

It had been a mountain once, before being sculpted down and tunneled through to become a temple. Rand saw it rise on the horizon, intricate, commanding, graven in blue and white stone. The sheer beauty of it stung his eyes as the conveyance pulled closer.

Spires pierced the skyline, and the foundation straddled the earth solidly. Archways and gateways offered a maze of an entrance. The windows were open to the elements and a faint wind whistled through their shutterless hollows. It would be as tall as a New York skyscraper and as vast as a city block when they reached it. Rand looked at it and realized that anywhere else he would ever journey, this temple would remain forever in his memory as one of the wonders of civilization. As they drew nearer, he marveled at the stonework.

He had never seen rock or marble like it. It reminded him of the only time he'd ever seen the Atlantic Ocean, stormy blue laced with gray and creamy foam. As he looked at the temple, it seemed to him that the very sky above, clear and far from the storm which had threatened Charolon—and even the white diamond of the stars in it—was being drained away, funneled down into this temple, and forced to root in the earth.

He found his breath. "Do they know what they did?" he asked of no one in particular.

"Yes," responded Palaton's low, rich voices. "We believe they did, as ancient as it is. They tied the sky to the earth and even the stars did not escape them."

As Rand dropped his gaze, he saw the robed Choyan pushing out to meet them. The conveyance huffed to a halt and settled on the valley floor.

Palaton ducked his head and got out. He reached back for Rand, saying, "One battle at a time, the war will be won."

Rand felt his heart thump in response. How difficult would it be to fight a people who could see God?

Chapter 16

Qativar threaded his way across the darkened bar, pausing now and then to cast a harsh glare at any Choya who dared to lift a hand to him, his face bleak and scowling in the dim lamplight. He saw his quarry on the diagonal and his scowl deepened. He joined the bulky, broad-shouldered Choya, his voices lowered and pitched so only the two of them could hear what was said.

"I told you I never wished to meet with you in public."

"Public?" Malahki pitched his voices in a like manner, difficult for him, and the gold in his eyes sparkled like ore in a deep, dark mine. "The scum of the earth drink in here. If any were sober enough to see you, I doubt they'd know or remember you."

"I did not," Qativar answered as he seated himself in the booth, "get where I am trusting to chance."

"Nor I." Malahki put a hand out and pinned the other's wrist to the tabletop. Underneath the transparent top, a child's game of illuminating patterns was inlaid. Most of those patterns could no longer be lit by the dwindling psionic power of their race . . . but one or two of them now flickered briefly under the onslaught of Malahki's barely contained rage.

Qativar let himself be held for a fraction of a second, then he twisted his wrist free of the hold. Malahki's empty hand fell to its back, palm upward, fingers still grasping, and Malahki left it in that position.

"Have you what I asked for?"

"I have," answered Qativar evenly.

"Then give it here." Malahki twitched his fingers.

"I might ask what you intend to do with it first. *Ruhl* is difficult to procure."

"Not by you it seems, and I might ask the same of you."

Qativar slipped his hand inside his summer jacket and produced a minute vial, liquid gleaming inside. "I doubt if my uses for it are the same as yours." He pressed the object into Malahki's callused palm.

Malahki's hand sprang shut like a trap. He pulled the object to him and secreted it inside his waistband. "An aphrodisiac has but one or two qualities."

"*Ruhl* is powerful enough to make any of the Housed lose their minds for a cycle or two." Qativar was rewarded by surprise in the other's face.

"Not unless used in nearly toxic quantities."

Qativar shrugged. "You have your weapons, I have mine. Either way, the commons will be free some day."

Malahki rocked back in his chair, feigning nonchalance. "You and Chirek have your ways. Both of you think I know nothing of either . . ."

"We're on the same side by chance," Qativar

interrupted, his blue eyes hard and cold in the corner's dim light.

"But with the same end in mind."

"I do not speak for Chirek. He goes among the commons, ministering to them. I go among the Housed, lying to and cheating my enemies. I think my method may prove to be the more valuable."

Malahki stood. He patted his waistband to reassure himself the vial was still there. "Regardless. Thank you, Qa—"

The priest stopped him with a slice of his hand through the air. Malahki halted with his head up, for a moment looking for all the world like a wild animal caught in a sudden, blinding beam of light. He blinked once or twice and then pursed his lips.

"I stand corrected," he said with irony. He gave a half-bow and left.

His order of wine came to the table and Qativar sat looking at its golden hue. After a moment, certain that no one followed after, the Prelate raised the glass to his own lips and drank.

Ruhl muddied the senses. It would so disturb the *bahdur* of a Choya that it was like an extreme intoxicant. Impregnation among the Choyan was a choice of both sexes, and both must cooperate, to be fertile. But *ruhl* changed the rules of that choice ever so slightly. Qativar wondered whom Malahki intended to drug, and why. It would be interesting to know.

As for himself, he had an entirely different use for *ruhl*. In his laboratory experiments, he had almost standardized the dosage, to thin out that threshold between intoxication and toxicity. He had succeeded in reducing *bahdur* to a minimal level . . . a level every Choya, even a commons, could achieve. If he could make it permanent or even stretch the effect to a considerable amount of time, say twenty cycles, he could homogenize his people. Genetic superiority which was kept closed by the Housed would be no more.

And if *bahdur* could be reduced by drug dosages, then it stood to reason it could also be enhanced, under controlled circumstances . . . anyone could then become a *tezar* . . . drink the right drug at the correct dosage and any Choya could master Chaos.

And he would have the key to doing so.

There would be no more burnout . . . and no more Houses trading on inherited superiority. There would be a world of commons, with access to excellence if and when it suited the common good. The Choya who would be emperor, then, would be the Choya who had brought this profound change to their world.

Oh, he and Chirek were on the same side, all right, but Qativar sincerely doubted if they had the same motives. Chirek believed that the Being of Change who would someday move among them might be a Choya who would bring the barriers of the Houses down, allowing intermarriage and commingling of the powers which had kept them so separated. Qativar also doubted that one individual would have the power to so collapse the Houses. That would be a matter for revolution, and revolution would destabilize the planet enough that the Abdreliks, the Ronins, perhaps even the Ivrians and Nortons would come swooping in like scavengers to pick them apart.

Besides, though rare and seldom acknowledged, there were Housed who strayed and sired offspring with the God-blind. It was this constant interflow which kept power springing up among the commons, sometimes even input strong enough to make a child talented enough for a Choosing. But no Being of Change had come among them yet, no one Choya powerful enough to turn the class structure of Cho inside out. Not yet. Unlike Chirek, Qativar had no desire to wait for a miracle of birth. He trusted to scientific progress for his hopes. He had thousands of commons willing to volunteer, in exchange for the future. It mattered not to him whom he might sacrifice in attaining his goal.

He put down his empty wine glass, concentrated on dimming the light in the bar even more, then left.

* * *

Rufeen took a look at the committee of Prelates gathering on the pink and beige sands, with communicators orbiting their ranks like scavengers, and said only, "I'm staying with the ship." She rocked back on her heels, with a stubborn twist to her lips.

Palaton answered mildly, "As a *tezar* should."

She looked at Rand, crossed one eye in mocking solemnity, and disappeared back into the cockpit of the ship.

Her levity had struck through the shell of nervousness beginning to wrap around Rand. He gave a quavering laugh. Palaton looked down at him.

"Ready?"

"I don't know yet."

"Remember to shield your mind. Remember who and what we're among. Those who join the priesthood are among the most sensitive of the Choya. They will be able to divine what you are."

"And what you're not," Rand answered.

A look not unlike fear passed quickly over Palaton's features. He nodded then. "That is a possibility. I'll face it if I have to." He took a deep breath. "Sethu is ancient, even among my people. *Bahdur* is probably ingrained in its very rocks." He looked down the ramp. "They're waiting."

A Choya'i stood to the fore. She was Earthan, of course, her mane braided back where the sun put chestnut streaks in the sable tresses. She did not have Jorana's sleekly elegant form, but she did carry beauty and power only partially hidden under blue robes so dark they appeared to be black at first glance. Her eyes of purest brown took a steady, even measure of Rand even as the priests gathered behind her shifted nervously and would not meet his curious gaze. They were all dark-maned and dark-eyed, similar to the Skies although the Skies generally had light colored eyes and even darker hair. But the Earthans had not the slim, tall lines of the Skies whom Rand had met; they were a solid people, like the rocks and dirt of their world. Earth, Sky, and Star, Rand realized, all had distinctive body characteristics and coloring, while the commons were a muddied pool of all and none.

The Choya'i extended a hand to Palaton. "I am High Priest Tela," she said, her voices an incredibly beautiful soprano, one an echo of the other. To hear her made Rand shiver. What a singer she could have been.

He put out his own hand for the Choyan touch

of welcome. The High Priest looked at him and
hesitated just a moment before touching upward
palms with him.

It was not fear he felt or saw, but a lightning
moment of distaste. "Thank you," he said, "for
welcoming me."

There was no reaction on Tela's broad face. She
either did not hear the irony in his voice or did
not condescend to react to it, although Palaton
flicked a quick look at him. Tela dropped her
hands and folded them. Rand watched her, wondering if she fought an impulse to wipe them on
her robes.

"Your acknowledgment of welcome is prema-
ture," she said to Palaton. "We do not know if we
will accept the humankind. We have not yet decided if the sacrament will be breached."

"And I have had such poor manners as to have
forced him upon you," responded Palaton. "But he
is my ward, Prelate, and as such, I was loath to
leave him behind."

"We have a life," Tela told him, "that does not
bear off-world scrutiny."

"As I am well aware, having been off-world
most of my adult life." Palaton's jawline stayed
tense and Rand realized that they fought with
words, as if in hand-to-hand combat.

Tela's right eyebrow arched. "And I am reminded that I, as a simple priest, have not." She
looked at Rand. "We believe as we do for our own
survival," she said. "The plague of Fangborn's
Century, among other reasons."

"As we reach out to others, for our own survival," Rand answered.

"Yes. Your world has many problems it has not

solved. It would be well to know that some problems are never solved, that the process is an ongoing attempt, and that one can never cease."

"But some ideas are better than others," Rand came back, "and some avenues ought to be taken. We only want advice from those who have experience. We can't afford to make a wrong choice."

"Perhaps," suggested Tela mildly, "you've already done so."

"Then," Rand said, "tell me and I'll try to do better."

"Do you speak for all?"

"No. I don't have that right. But I can be a messenger."

"Interesting." Tela raised her rich, brown eyes to Palaton. "He does not retreat, does he?"

"No. Just because he needs my protection doesn't mean he's craven." Palaton put his hand on the back of Rand's neck where it appeared to rest casually, but the index and thumb pinched ever so slightly into Rand's muscles. He stood very still.

The High Priest looked back to Rand. "You're aware, are you not, that you've chosen a hero for your guardian?"

Palaton's fingers pinched slightly deeper. Rand swallowed before answering, "If honesty and integrity are heroic, yes."

"Ah! He's not aware of your exploits as a *tezar*?"

"No," said Palaton evenly. "He's not been enlightened."

The priest smiled. "Perhaps he should be." She turned on her heel. As if suddenly aware of the communicators and all those third eyes watching her closely, she put her shoulders back and held her horn-crowned head a little higher. "I am not convinced that it is necessary the manling accompany you."

"I was not aware I had to convince you," answered Palaton. "Nor do I know of any argument which I could use. Either you do, High Priest, or you do not make this allowance. If you do not, I will return to Charolon. If you do, I will return to Charolon. How important and successful the interlude, is up to you."

"Yet you came to Sethu."

"Yes. I came because I've been away from Cho for many years, and my soul hungers."

She looked back over her shoulder as if struck. Rand felt Palaton's hand close tighter. The Prelate asked, "And does the manling also have a soul?"

Rand answered for himself. "We think we do."

"Thinking so is an important step." She turned around again. "We have much to consider, my Prelates and I." With another glance at the communicators who seemed to obey an invisible borderline of how close they could approach, she drew aside the group of priests and acolytes who had accompanied her though all had remained silent throughout the exchange.

Palaton dropped his hand from Rand's neck. He shrugged to relax his own suddenly cramped muscles.

"How successful were we?"

"I don't know," Palaton said quietly. "She and the others undoubtedly had their minds set before they came to greet us. Having made the offer to me, they could scarcely refuse the sacrament out of hand when I appeared with you." He turned his back on the group. "Sethu is isolated now. At one time, these sparse foothills were a forested country. Rivers abounded. The Earthans led a full and bountiful life here."

Rand looked toward the horizon, a high desert profile, which was difficult to imagine forested. "What happened?"

"We logged it down. But before that, we were so populous here that we even changed the weather patterns. Our technology, our very presence built up a huge thermal dome of air, changing the jet stream permanently. We lost the rain. When we lost the forests as well, with the watershed, we lost everything. We could terraform it now . . . we know how to do so, but it makes little difference. Over the thousands of years, it has adapted permanently to its climate, and though you can make the desert fertile to some extent, you can't maintain it unless you change the weather pattern again. That we cannot do without affecting other areas. So we balance. We only balance."

"No permanent solution?"

Palaton came around to face him. "The only permanent solution to life," he remarked, "is death."

Rand felt cold even in the heat of the sun. He shifted uncomfortably. "Tell me what Fangborn's Century is."

"Fangborn was an emperor. The last of the Skies. They gave us space, you know," mused Palaton. "We Stars took it from them after Fangborn, and kept it."

"He brought plague to Cho?"

"Unwittingly. With the first trade between other species. We were hard hit, and at first, our epidemiologists didn't know it was an alien infiltration. It's a convenient excuse to remain xenophobic. My people hide behind it, thinking to protect what they are." Palaton spoke softly, so as not to let his voices carry.

Tela came away from her group. She set her chin. "I cannot force my priests to work with you," she said. "But they have volunteered to accept your presence, citing that your affiliation alone with the humankind is a symptom of your need. We do not know if the . . . other . . . has a soul or not. Perhaps this would be an opportune time to observe and decide, if Cho is to be drawn into conflict with the Compact over such a species. Therefore, we have decided to take both of you in." Her eyes glittered at Rand. "Fair warning, manling. We *will* search for that soul of yours."

"Good news," muttered Rand, "you're in. Bad news . . . they intend to dissect you."

"What was that?" asked Palaton, bemused.

"Nothing. I hope."

Chapter 17

"It's blasphemous," Hat said, clearly disturbed. "The communicators only have reports, but it's said the priests took them both in, the humankind as well."

Nedar studied his boots, crossed at the ankles, as they rested on the priceless *giata* wood table in Hat's private quarters. "What could they do but rely on reporters," he countered. "Communicators aren't allowed on temple grounds. They can only get so close." The great unshriven of their society, media manipulators had centuries ago been excommunicated from the temples of every House.

"It's not that." Hat perched on the edge of a great study table. Its slab of gray marbling, and the heavy-bodied Choya's shadow in its reflection was just another dappling of its smooth surface. "He took the other with him."

"He only pulls his burial shroud closer around him," Nedar said, dropping his feet to the floor and sitting up. "It's getting late. You have cadets to chaperone. They did well today?"

"Well enough." Hat rubbed red-rimmed eyes. "Our numbers dwindle, Nedar, and there seems to be little I can do about it. To fail at becoming a *tezar* often means dying in the attempt—and yet, those who perish have *bahdur* bright enough to bring them here. If not lost to death, what might those lives do for Cho? Why should we lose them to death if they're not good enough to fly?"

"You would change the qualifications to pilot?" Nedar's voices sharpened, but the weary schoolmaster did not seem to notice his tone.

"Oh, no. No. It just seems a waste. Failure ought not to bring death. We're losing our *bahdur* generation by generation."

Sometime during Nedar's absence from Blue Ridge, Hat had obviously been influenced by some of the radical philosophers who were part of the Choyan fringe. The pilot did not believe in such philosophies, but it was obvious that fatigue, like wine, brought Hat's melancholia bobbing to the surface. He cupped a hand about the other's shoulder. "You worry too much when you're tired."

Hat lifted his head. "The glider trials start tomorrow."

Nedar had not been paying much attention to Hat or the cadets. The information startled him. Tomorrow would bring death close, without a doubt. There were always cadets who could not fly blind. "I hadn't realized. Hat, it's for the best. We both went through it. It's our first law: nature selects for survival. A *tezar* cannot master Chaos unless he can fly blind, dependent only upon his *bahdur*. Everything happens for the best."

Hat looked at him steadily. "I wish I had your confidence."

Nedar gripped the other's beefy shoulder tighter. The brief thought that Hathord was out of flying shape, out of his prime, went through his head before other, more powerful thoughts flooded in. "You forget your House, my friend. You were born to worry and nursemaid, as well as to fly. The cadets don't know how lucky they are to have you as flightmaster. Tomorrow will take care of itself, and we *tezars* will take care of Cho, as we've always done." He released Hat. "Are the corridors empty? I have a hankering to sleep in my old quarters tonight."

"No one dares venture in that wing anyway. You know the superstition . . . they fear treading in a pilot's footsteps until they themselves have their wings. I'll have a breakfast tray left here waiting for you in the morning. We'll be at the plateau early."

Hat took far greater care than Nedar did at hiding the other's presence in the school. But that was the difference between the two of them. Hat did not know what he could do to undo a sighting if Nedar were found by one of the cadets, so he used all the caution he could to avoid the problem. Nedar had already decided upon a permanent solution if the problem arose.

"Tomorrow will take care of itself," Nedar said. He left Hat leaning upon the *giata* table, musing at the shadows about him.

It was a cold, brisk night at Blue Ridge. He pulled his jacket closer about his shoulders as the weather permeated even the enclosed corridors between the wings of the various barracks and halls. He took care to muffle his steps as he walked, not from caution, but to keep his thoughts clear, for there was a torrent of them, a flood, set off by word of Palaton.

Palaton did not hide in disgrace. No. He'd had Cleansing offered him on a silvered platter by the damnable order of priests, a hierarchy which defied even the boundaries of the Houses. To be sure, each House had its order, but they wielded power regardless of their House and Householding and well the smug bastards knew it. So why this concession to Palaton, who had brought the commons thronging into the streets and seemed unable now to disperse them? Who had brought the tainting footsteps of a Class Zed being to Choyan soil? Why?

Because Palaton was favored and he was not. Despite all that he had risked and lost for Cho, he was outcast. Burned out. Forsaken by all but Hat.

It would not be so if he had his soulfire. That possibility among all others leapt high in his frenzied mind. It would not be so if he had *bahdur*.

And despite Hat's fear of the morning, if the cadets slept lightly, they didn't do so out of worry. They would be pumped, waiting, agonizing over the first break of light, primed to do that for which they had been trained their whole young lives . . . to fly! To cast themselves into the wind and control a winged machine to keep themselves aloft. Their zest would blaze tonight. He could almost taste the sparks spilling out, fizzing along the stone corridors, bouncing like drops of water in a searing hot pan.

A gnawing hunger opened inside of him and Nedar came to a halt in the empty corridor. He rubbed a hand across his brow as if he could brush away the blurred thoughts and concentrate on the keener ones. They came in a crystalline rush. For a moment, he stood appalled, and then his old arrogance cloaked him.

Whatever morals bound him, he tossed them

aside. He deserved it more, and without further rationalization, he turned abruptly and made his way to the wings where the young cadets were housed.

He made his way outside and stood in the gloaming where they could not see him, and heard them from their windows. Hat must sleep the sleep of the deaf and dead, if he thought his students safely abed. They sparred and gibed at one another and, for a moment, Nedar fondly remembered his old days.

The glow of memory sped away. As he had thought, he could taste the spillage of their power, wasteful, sparking and fountaining with no purpose or even a care to its usage. He stood, and his lips opened greedily as if he could sip the *bahdur* from the cold night air. His nostrils flared as if he could gulp it down. His heart pounded as if it, too, sensed the nearness of that which was more than life to him.

Bound in that temporary ecstasy, he thought more of what he intended to do and why he should and should not do it. He hesitated, and then shrank back against the walls as a cadet leapt out of a window with a crow of triumph.

They'd wrapped his head with a scarf, blinding his eyes, and pushed him from the high-ledged window. He landed deftly enough and, with an arch of his back, flung his hands into the air in triumph.

"I've landed!"

Fog puffed into the air with his bellow. A Choya'i leaned out above him. "See! I told you he would land heads up."

"It takes more than that to make a pilot!" Two

windows down, a volley of protests and good-
natured teasing.

The blindfolded cadet tore his scarf off with a
flourish. "Have I won the bet?"

"No! No!"

"What? You want me to fly higher? Very well."
The student stuffed his scarf into a pocket and
began to scale the building, climbing to the third
floor roof.

The windows sprouted Choya, all looking and
hollering at the cadet. They lay on their backs to
look upward, half-in and half-out of their rooms,
their warm voices issuing wisps of lace upon the
midnight air. Some coaxed him down, others
called for peace and quiet, and some urged him
on.

Nedar watched, his own breath caught in his
throat, for the cadet reminded him of himself,
brash, daring, talented. He saw the Choya wrap
another blindfold about his eyes.

A last jeer. "No fair levitating!"

The cadet snorted back a disdainful reply and
then inched forward until his booted toes hung
over the edge of the roof. He bounced a little on
the balls of his feet. Then all grew still.

The night breeze teased the end of his blindfold,
snapping it behind him. He poised on the brink
and Nedar wondered what doubts might be running through his mind. Would his power guide
him to a safe landing? Would he twist an ankle,
break a leg . . . or tumble in sudden panic and fall
to an unexpected death?

The Choya snapped upward and leapt outward,
his arms extended, and he threw his body into a
gravity-bemusing somersault. The scarf streamed

behind him, a white streak against his face that cut into the dark envelope as he plunged. His body rolled and twisted slowly, seeking centering and ground. If he fell on his neck, paralysis would be the least of his worries.

He came down feet first and his knees gave to take the shock, but he stayed upright. The Choya took a deep breath and then straightened once again. Nedar saw the tremble of his hands as he threw them into the air.

The roar of approval cut off abruptly. Heads popped back into the windows in sudden silence. A lone voice called out, "Threlka! The proctor's coming through. Take the back door in."

Lights went out and the bank of windows fell into moon-scored darkness. Threlka unwound his blindfold, made a bow to the now nonexistent audience, and took a staggering step. He winced a little.

"Idiot," he said under his breath. He stuffed the blindfold back into his pocket and, hugging the wall so as not to be seen from the windows, made his way toward the back entrance, where Nedar waited.

The pilot could smell the spent *bahdur*. He could taste it. He could almost see the rippling aura about the weary cadet whose brash mood had been snuffed out so abruptly. He could hear the crackle, like summer lightning, of the power surrounding the other.

Through half-open lips, Nedar gulped down a whistling breath. The cadet heard it. He came to a stop and, eyes narrowed, peered toward the corner.

"Who's there?"

Their gazes met. Nedar, used to the dark, un-doubtedly saw him better than Threlka saw Nedar. In that split second their eyes held, Nedar decided on his course and lunged. Hunger spurred him. Need closed the gap before their bodies met. The Choya shuddered in his grasp just before the cadet's neck twisted and gave with an ugly sound and the *bahdur* flowed out of him like water from a broken pitcher.

Nedar drank all that he could. It would not stay with him. It would run out of him just as it had run out of the dead cadet. He could not bond the *bahdur* to stay within him, bank its fires, use it sparingly. He did not care.

For the moment, he was full.

The deed over, he stayed in the shadows, the cadet's sagging weight in his arms. Then Nedar looked up to the roof. He took the body with him, affixed the blindfold and kicked it off. In the morn-ing, cadets who'd drunk too much would swear that Threlka had made the jump safely, but with the body before them, with the overwhelming evi-dence in front of them, it would be obvious they'd been wrong. Or, perhaps, that Threlka had made a second jump, unseen.

It would not matter. The cadet would be dead.

It did not matter. Nedar moved quietly across the roof and marveled at the auras rippling in the nighttime sky. He'd forgotten how bountiful the power could be. He vowed he would never again be empty for long enough to forget.

Chapter 18

Bevan woke, for the fourth or fifth time in his re-cent memory, which, like the universe about him, seemed to be expanding and collapsing. He sat sullenly for a moment in the near perfect darkness of the eggshell raft, for waking was little different from being unconscious. His stomach roiled, pro-testing the lack of gravity as well as the need for food. He reached out blindly, found the water hose, pulled it to him, and took a sip to wet his mouth. The water tasted stagnant. He wondered how many days had passed. Three, perhaps, or four. Maybe only one, but long enough for the ship to have obtained FTL and then cast him off. He had been awake when that had happened.

Now he sat, catching glimpses of Chaos despite the shielded windows. His mind saw what his eyes had not been meant to. He could not shut out the random visions any more than he could control them. Helplessness flooded him. Never in his whole life had Bevan settled for being a victim. Not on the streets of Sao Paulo, where human life was less precious than garbage, which at least could be recycled. Not in the orphanage where his soul was one of many being harvested by the Theresites.

Illumination seared the darkness. Bevan put his hands to his head, clawlike, as if he could keep his brain from exploding. Chaos speared its way inward, frying his eyes from the inside out. He sat and rocked, moaning, his voice thin and distant until the vision fled, driven away by his frantic efforts. He dropped his shaking hands to his lap.

Impulsively, he reached out and opened the portal shield. The turmoil of Chaos boiled in front of him. His senses churned, keyed to the miasma, and he reeled back in the safety web.

But he could not turn his gaze aside, as the metal and plastic of the life pod melted away and it felt as though he hung in the midst of all eternity. If there were a hell, this was indeed it.

But this could not be hell, for he rode the heavens, did he not, the starry firmament which ruled over earth and hell alike? Bevan writhed in his webbing, caught and dangling over an abyss of midnight and rainbow. His eyes watered at the brilliance despite the portal screening.

He cuffed tears away. He hung so long he became aware of the straps cutting into his limp form, and of the stale smell of his clothing, stiff with old sweat. There was a center to this Chaos and he had become it and, once having found a center, not all was as chaotic as he thought. He looked and saw a magenta river flow by. It curved across his vision, then plunged over a sudden cliff, dropping in a veil-spreading waterfall that boiled at its termination.

Bevan watched the river flow by again and again, to the same destination, until his mouth grew dry and he realized he'd been watching the phenomenon with his jaws agape, stunned at the sight. Fraction by fraction, he forced his head to turn, painstakingly seeking another pattern in the churning heavens.

He found a weeping willow tree, its leaves cascading to eternity like a shower of sparks from fireworks. Beyond, a cup spun alone. Then an immense butterfly swooped through.

Bevan grasped at that as if someone had thrown him a lifeline. The butterfly pattern was indicative of a random attractor . . . a planet or a sun, perhaps, for although the pattern seemed stable, it wasn't, but it was stable enough that something with an extreme gravity pulled at it and shaped it.

How had he seen such a thing? And, if seeing it were true, what did it mean to him?

Nothing. He was held in its grip, not it in his. And yet . . . Bevan clung to the hope, as he clung to his webbing, that if the butterfly held true, there was a chance of finding his way out.

He put his hand out. He touched barriers that his vision no longer illuminated for him. He was caged though he did not see the walls. His fingers played over the crude instrument panel of the life raft. There was little he could do to manipulate himself. But if there were a way. . . .

His sight abruptly failed him. He plunged into the abyss. His hearing picked up the thud as the portal shield came back into place, curtaining him away. The abrupt loss sickened him, disorienting him beyond caring, and he twirled in the webbing, sick and vomiting, his senses so distorted he could not control either them or himself. Mercifully, he lost consciousness again.

* * *

"The counties are restless," Vihtirne said. She sat by her monitor, nails tapping on the desktop. "I want a vote called."

The transmission from Charolon came in, streaked and faint. Sunspot activity, she thought, but narrowed her eyes anyway. "With Palaton gone for several days, now is the time to force the issue."

Asten was not within full focus range of the monitor. She caught only a glimpse of his three-quarter profile, and his glossy dark hair. The Choya, as was his duty, was intent on the activities within the Congress. She missed his sweet attentiveness, she thought, and tapped a nail on the mike and watched him start as the brittle sound of it reached him.

"I heard you," he said smoothly, and looked back at the camera. "I've brought some pressure to bear on Caldean. Let's see if he can withstand it. . . ."

Havoc reigned on the floor of the Choyan Congress for moments longer. Then a strong voice called out, "I question the placement of the contract."

Vihtirne listened with pleasure, her lips parting. Those strong tones belonged to Caldean, all right, and whatever Asten had done had lit a fire under the frizzy-headed statesman. He stood to the fore of the chambers.

"I have here financial statements which suggest that the Householding of Trenalle has overestimated its worth and ability to complete the aerospace contract as given. We all know that Trenalle is a venerable Householding of the Stars, but where is it written in stone that those who pilot for us must also build the cruisers? These figures tell me that the contract will be a burden for Trenalle and that the chances of the project being finished on time, on budget, are slim."

An elder Choya'i's reedy, thin voice cut through the sudden swell of sound. "Shut up and sit down, Caldean. The contract's been awarded. This discussion is moot."

All cameras, from Vihtirne's several monitors' viewing, focused on Caldean. He hunched his shoulders, bunching his body, and a stubborn look etched itself into his brow. "The contract is not placed if there is a question. And I question it, dear Sopher, and so should you."

The camera view swung to Sopher, a tiny bit of a Choya'i who looked as though all life's juices had long ago been sucked out of her and her carcass left to dry in the sun. True to the style of the last century, her horn crown had been shaved to the skull. Nothing gathered and bolstered her mane of hair, which age had thinned until little remained but singular long, silver strands. But her eyes did not know defeat. She put a hand to her throat, upping the volume on her broadcaster.

"I question the whole propriety of these proceedings. We have an heir to the throne. Why do we sit in session without him?"

"Because," and Caldean gave an exaggerated bow in the direction of his Congressional opponent, "these are urgent matters which cannot wait for the discretionary appearance of the heir. His vote is only good as a tie-breaker. This contract must be implemented as soon as possible, or Cho will lose the bid, and I'm told the Ivrians are waiting, beaks clacking, to take up the slack. I don't want to see this production go off-world any more than you do! We can produce these cruisers. But I strongly question the good judgment of handing them over to a Householding which teeters on the brink of bankruptcy. This contract will not save them, but rather will break their back. There is no wisdom in favoritism of this sort."

Sopher showed a tooth. "Financial attacks are even more insidious than moral attacks. Does Trenalle not get a chance to defend itself?"

The camera shot panned wildly as a weary Choya got to his feet. "The Householding of Trenalle," the speaker got out, "cannot dispute the facts on record. We do, however, dispute the conclusion. We need this contract. We can do the work on time." But the look on his face was one of defeat, as if knowing that the matter had already been settled.

Sopher, on her desk monitor, no doubt caught the same look. Vihtirne switched her camera selection to view the Choya'i as she pondered the Choya across the Congressional floor. Asten came on as an over-voice, "He knows he's beat and so does Sopher."

The Householding of Trenalle had always been shy of *forecasters*. They could not *see* the consequences of the contract, but could only hope. Caldean's objection, however, must have raised new doubts in a family already plagued with too much doubt.

"Now," said Vihtirne eagerly, "it remains only

to place the contract." She went back to her main monitor to catch Asten's confident nod.

Sopher said, "I yield to Caldean. The contract must be placed with another facility." She consulted an electronic log. "An underwriting bid was presented by Householding Depner, of Sky. Does that meet with your approval?"

Another din of noise resolved itself in a call to vote, and when the voices had done rolling out, Vihtirne sat back in absolute triumph. Not only had the contract been snatched from the House of Star, but now it rested within the grasp of her own family of Sky, for Depner was a cousin. She had hoped for such results.

Asten murmured, lips barely moving, "I trust you are pleased."

"Beyond that, my love. The sooner your business is finished, the sooner you can come back to me."

The corner of Asten's mouth twitched and he moved his head quickly, out of camera focus, as if to avoid revealing more. The movement happened extremely rapidly, but Vihtirne noticed. May the seven steps be denied him forever, for thinking she might not. That he feared her, she knew. That he might loathe as well as love her, she had just seen revealed.

Vihtirne shut off her monitors and closed down the broadcast. She threw her mike across the room. Then, after a moment, a smile creased her face. What was such a tiny flaw in the face of such triumph, after all? And Asten dared not fail to return to her. Not yet, anyway.

She moved to thrust herself from the chair when a tiny noise echoed in the sound chamber. Vihtirne turned to face it, chin up, back stiff, not knowing if she faced a clumsy retainer or skilled assassins.

Nedar took three steps across the tiled floor. His handsome sharp-edged face showed more years than it had the last time he'd graced her with a visit, but the delineation only increased his good looks. He wore the black leather jacket of Blue Ridge and she wondered if he'd been hiding there, gathering himself and information, before answering her call. "He is too young to appreciate what he might be throwing away."

Those voices melted something hard inside of her. With Nedar, she could be all Choya'i, all curves and no edges. She had picked him to rule her, as, indeed, she had picked him to rule all Cho.

"Where have you been?" she demanded.

"On Palaton's heels, trying to catch the scraps. I wasn't fast enough with Panshinea. It seemed wise to give up the chase for a while. Palaton appears to be doing himself more damage than I could." Nedar stripped off his gloves. It appeared he had flown himself to her private airstrip on the Householding grounds. "Am I intruding?"

"Never." Vihtirne got up and closed the distance between them. Tall herself, Nedar was yet taller. She had to tilt her head back to meet his expression. "I missed you. And no one asked you to chase Palaton alone. That is what the House of Sky is for. That is what I am for."

He put his hand on the curve of her throat, caressing it, and then he rotated his hand about so his fingers rested on the back of her neck and he pulled her closer yet, so that their lips might touch. He said quietly, "I won't give the kill to anyone but you . . . when I have Palaton cornered, you will get first blood, my mistress." And he sealed that vow with a kiss which burned with his fervor and his *bahdur*.

She succumbed willingly and let him overflow her with his power. Of all the Skies, she thought, he was the most like her, twin to her in ambition and talent. He would not fail her. And as she gave in to his embrace, there was a tinge of fear which sweetened the eroticism. Nedar was more powerful than she. There was danger in this liaison. The knowledge made her blood run hotter. She had no choice but to surrender to these moments.

Chapter 19

The Prelate guiding Rand to his quarters stopped and opened a door. A sun-fresh smell flooded them. Rand put his head inside the doorway and saw a small but cheerful room. The priest pulled a flask from his belt. In Trade which Rand could barely understand, the Choya said, "Bathe. Rinse with this, for bathing." He let go of the flask hastily as if fearing their hands might touch.

Nonetheless, as the object bridged their hands, Rand caught a fleeting sense of loathing along with the fear. He gave a nod to show he understood and the Prelate took to his heels down the temple corridor.

Rand shut the door behind him. The doorway had arched overhead so high it might even dwarf Palaton's lofty height. Rand craned his neck to look up at it. Had Choyans grown smaller . . . or was this merely an architectural style? He did not remember the doorways of Charolon being so high.

The temple carried a sense of antiquity, like Charolon, but the room was also filled with objects that spoke of the kind of technology he'd missed at the imperial palace. Rand touched a light panel, and the sunlight flooding the room

instantly dimmed ... yet he was within rock.
Looking about, he saw a chimney, its flue-opening
actually a reflective panel. He touched the light
again and the room brightened. Simple ... if the
roof were just over him. Interesting, buried in
rock, just how might it be done to several hundred
rooms and corridors? He dimmed the light down
to an acceptable degree and left it.

His bag had preceded him. It lay on the Choyan-
long cot as if tossed there. He pulled out shirt and
trousers, modified gear to fit his height and
weight, the fabric tough yet soft to his touch. At
the desk next to the cot, there were several appliances which did not respond to any attempt to
operate them. Rand sat for a moment, arms on his
knees, each hand filled with a recalcitrant object
which did not seem to have an activation pad or
switch. Yet they looked utilitarian enough. One he
guessed to be a horn groomer of some sort, and
the other a portable lamp which could be attached
anywhere it was needed, moving the light source
around the room. Yet he could not activate it as
he had done the main system.

Rand tossed the appliances back on the desk. He
shed his uniform and searched out the washroom.
The shower was a light mist, easily adjustable by
voice, though it was a bit slow to respond as if
unused to Trade or his accent. He had thought
himself grown fairly proficient in the language,
particularly since his association with Palaton.
Could it be they both spoke atrociously?

He opened the flask. A noxious smell made him
jerk his head back. The waft of disinfectant nearly
gagged him. Bits of stems and ground leaves
flooded the liquid in his palm ... made herbally,

whatever it was. Almost reluctantly, he palmed his skin with the fluid. The misty shower foamed it up and as he washed and it foamed, the smell grew more pleasant until it was bearable. He scrubbed every inch of himself thinking that this procedure was at least easier and less humiliating than the decon he'd undergone at landing.

Scrubbed and dressed, he left his room in search of Palaton. He knew where the other had turned off, but went past the hall, for he found himself in a curvature of corridor he didn't remember. Rand retraced his steps to his room and opened the door. Yes, his worn clothes lay spread where he'd dropped them.

He'd seen no intercom. Rand closed his door and stood for a moment, thinking. There was a whisper of cloth on stone.

He turned. A tall Choya in a hooded cloak approached. The Choya paused, as though as uncertain as Rand felt.

"Prelate," Rand ventured.

The being drew close enough for Rand to see a heavily cheekboned face, eyes of gray and brown, and a wide, thick-lipped mouth stretched in an uncertain expression.

"Humankind," the Choya responded after a moment.

"Perhaps you could direct me. I'm looking for heir Palaton's rooms."

"Your guide?"

"Has not returned."

The Choya's nostrils flared as if sniffing Rand's scent. He felt the color rush to his cheeks. Was this being not going to pass him on unless certain he'd been disinfected? The Choya's face relaxed.

He lifted a hand. "Follow the corridor at the third door. The door was open when you came through before. Now it is closed. You will have missed the corridor. Heir Palaton is occupying the room marked with the crescent moon and star."

"Thank you."

The Choya bowed with a rustle of cloak and hood. "It is nothing." He passed by Rand, moving with that same swift, long-legged stride of Palaton's that Rand could not keep up with.

Rand counted the doors down and found the closed corridor, as told. He entered it.

A chill hung here that he did not remember. The walls were bare, he thought he remembered friezes. His still drying hair clung damply to his skull and the back of his head, cold and stringy. He held little sense of direction since entering the temple, but his *bahdur* gilt sight seemed to be reacting oddly. It flickered as if being masked or drained as he went deeper down the corridor. At last he found the door marked with the crescent and star symbol and put his hand on the latch.

"Rand!"

Palaton called Rand's rooms and got nothing but silence. He toweled his mane off thoughtfully, wondering if the manling were still in the shower, although the water restrictions in use here scarcely made for luxurious bathing. He did not mind ... bathing was one of the first rituals of cleansing he would face, and the underground springs here were legendary.

He did not like being separated from the humankind, but he knew he dared not make waves, at least not yet. High Priest Tela had been more cordial than he had expected, though he knew Rand walked a dangerous line between guest and prisoner. With Choyan courtesy, they waited for Rand to condemn himself. When that happened, they would act, but not before.

Yet even what the Earthan priesthood would do then, he could not predict. If this had been a Star temple, under Rindalan's influence, Rand would simply have been removed and returned to Charolon to Traskar's and Jorana's watchful care. Here, although not in the hostile territory they would have been in if they had gone to a shrine of the Skies, he had only his past history with the Earthan House to worry him.

If removing Rand would bring harmony and balance back to Cho, it might be conceivable Tela would order it. More than removal might be in order if the Earthans thought to strengthen their claim as a House Ascendant on the Wheel, whose time had come to occupy the throne.

Yet without Rand, he had no hope of completing this cleansing without being revealed. It was a calculated risk which Palaton would have taken willingly with his own life, but hesitated to do with another's, even a humankind's.

Palaton finished dressing and called again. There was still no response. He did not like the implications and, without waiting for the Prelate whose duty it was to guide them into the cleansing, he left his rooms in search of Rand.

He found the manling's rooms easily enough. As he opened the door, he could smell the herbal disinfectant's lingering aroma. He looked around and saw the room had been stripped of many of its amenities, most of them triggered psionically. *Keeping secrets,* he thought in amusement.

But Rand was not here. Palaton stepped back. He shut the door. He waited until the aroma which had flooded through the doorway had dissipated, then stepped several paces back the way he had come.

Yes. The aroma hung in the still air of the corridor. He hadn't noticed it before. The fragrance thinned as his body moved through it, dissipating the herbal scent. It took him to a closed corridor entrance.

There were symbols on the high arched doorway. Palaton saw them in alarm. If Rand had gone this way, he had blundered into part of the inner sanctum, where even Palaton hesitated to go.

He opened the corridor. Yes, sharper here, the herbal aroma. Palaton strode inward, hurrying, hoping that Rand had not gone where those not of the priesthood weren't allowed. There were chambers called the Ear of God carved deep in this part of the mountain. The corridor should have been locked and shut against any intruder. He could not begin to guess how Rand had opened, or even found, this hidden way. He removed his boots so they could not mar the hidden way, tucked them in his belt and entered hurriedly.

The corridor swallowed the sound of his running steps. It curved before him like the crescent moon of its birthing, and Palaton ran a good distance of it before he saw its end, shadowed and dim, and Rand standing there. The humankind had his hand upon a door of mysteries. Palaton recognized the sanctum with a gut-jolt of fear and cried out to stop the humankind from opening it.

"I'd like to know who directed you there," Palaton said, sitting on his cot and pulling his boots back on.

"I might recognize his eyes," Rand answered. "They were fairly distinctive. But as to the rest, his crown and such . . . no."

Palaton stamped his feet deeper into his boots before looking up solemnly. "They could have executed you if you had entered."

"Or you." Rand took advantage of Palaton's extra towels to dry his hair, which felt cold and clammy as though the corridor had been a tomb.

The pilot shook his head. "I know better. I wouldn't even have entered the corridor if I hadn't been looking for you."

"They separated us on either side on purpose."

Palaton nodded. "That is likely."

"Do you think Tela set me up?"

"I don't know. If she had, as High Priest, it's likely she's the one who would have directed you, to ensure the working of her plan."

"So someone else took advantage of an opportunity."

Palaton shrugged. "Speculation."

"They don't really want to kill me, but they wouldn't miss the chance if it came up."

"I think," Palaton said, "that you have the core of it. It would be wise to remember that next time you wander off."

Rand shuddered. He ran his fingers through his hair, combing it into obedience. "You shouldn't have brought me here."

"I was hoping . . ." Palaton paused. "I am a religious being, Rand. I have faith in the rituals I grew up with, although they can't cure a *tezar* with neuropathy. I had hopes, if you were with me, we might accomplish that which we need to do."

Rand's turquoise eyes watched him closely. "Do you think so?"

"I hope so. This is not an area of rational thought." And Palaton gave a slight smile.

Rand thought of Qativar's soft advice. How far would Palaton go in endangering Rand simply to regain his *bahdur*, fresh and burning brightly once more? He looked at the other and for a moment, another vision blinded his eyes, that of Palaton pulling him from bombed out rubble on Arizar, saving him, embracing him in relief with the fervor of a mother for her child.

Choyan do not befriend humans, but he had thought that he and Palaton had that bond, and that he could rely on it. Now he did not know.

A soft knock on the door interrupted his hesitancy. It was the Prelate come to guide them.

*   *   *

The vibrations of environment-maintenance machinery hummed in his ears. The Abdrelik-comfortable air of the bay station sank into his lungs, humid and odiferous. John Taylor Thomas shrugged under the surveillance monitoring, uncomfortable and ill at ease, his stomach rebelling against the tranquilizers given him for a hasty FTL flight, and his inner ear telling him he was still not on solid ground. The Abdrelik scanning him made a smacking, growling noise in his ear and Thomas refrained from looking to see if the alien had drooled upon his shoulder. He had little else he could control here but himself and as for that, he clamped down rigidly. The Abdrelik finished his scanning and moved away with another barking grunt and began to scan the two men the ambassador had brought with him.

Something clanked within the staging bay. Thomas flinched, looked up, and heard metal groan. The artificial gravity of the satellite did little to quell his sense of being off-balance and he wondered if GNask had done this, too, on purpose. Another clank vibrated through the metal beams of the bay and then a portal began to blossom across the bay from him.

Thomas felt his stomach clench. His daughter should be with GNask. He had been promised and thus taken from the secure neutrality of Sorrow of his own free will. He did not think that GNask had chosen now and by this method to end their partnership, though it was inevitable that one day the Abdrelik would do so. The ambassador had little illusions about the conclusion of their association, and, not having them, hoped to avoid it. But today he'd chosen not to avoid because he'd not seen Alexa in nearly three years and at this moment he could not surrender to fear.

But all the same the palms of his hands grew damp and he could not contain the tic along his jawline which deepened as two shadowy figures, one immense and the other like a tiny, glimmering comet caught in its orbit, approached. The Abdrelik wore only belted shorts and grip-boots, his vast fleshed bulk like that of a hippo brought to shore. The symbiont of the Abdrelik rested on his shoulder as if it were a pet, stalked eyes watching Thomas inquiringly.

"A happiness," said the Abdrelik, "which I promised you." He hunkered down on his squat hindquarters and let the comet shimmer past him, though the girl stopped of her own accord within arm's reach of GNask.

"Alexa!"

She looked up, her pale face framed with lustrous dark curls, her eyes deep within the planes of her expression, their color lost to him momentarily. "Father," she answered softly, but came no closer.

Thomas went cold. "What have you done to her?"

"I?" murmured GNask. "Nothing. Ask the Choyan when we face them in court. If they will answer us."

Alexa brought her chin up. "Come as close as you please, Father."

Her tone was chill, menacing and yet teasing, as if she mocked his love and concern . . . and fear. Her eyes glittered in the shadows of her face. She held out a hand.

Thomas swallowed. He turned on one heel and snapped his fingers. The second man in his employ came to abrupt attention and strode forward, carrying case in his hand, and before he reached Alexa, he already had a syringe in his fingers.

"You guaranteed her health and safety," the ambassador said as the man caught his daughter up and she let out a squeal of protest. "If you don't mind, I will prove it to myself."

GNask shrugged, an elephantine ripple proceeding down his bulk. "As you wish."

Alexa hissed with pain as the physician drew blood and skin samples. She fastened her gaze on her father and said nothing further as the physician proceeded with a cursory exam, hair, nails, scrapings and what other evidence he could take.

As the physician freed her, Alexa pulled back with a snap. "Happy, Father?"

"Not yet. But I will be." Thomas watched as the physician retreated across the bay, until the man was sandwiched between himself and the remaining man, a security enforcer. He pushed back memories of his child, his chortling toddler with a bold and lively sense of humor and adventure, shoved them down along with the gorge which had risen in his throat. The cold and capricious creature facing him bore little resemblance to the daughter he'd lost. "Are you well, Alexa?"

"Before you assaulted me? Passably. Lonely. I get very lonely among the Abdreliks." She ran her hand through her tangled curls and gave her head a little toss, actions at odds with her words.

GNask shifted his weight. She jumped a little at that and gave a slight, nervous laugh as she resettled.

"Is there anything I can bring you?"

Alexa looked at him in solemn thought. "Peanut butter," she said, finally. "I miss it. And coffee, perhaps."

"Books? Disks?"

"No. I have ... no interests there." She looked over her shoulder as if to catch a signal from GNask, but none that Thomas could see had been given.

"I want you to come home with me."

This time GNask did move, his face rumpling up and then smoothing out, but Alexa had not turned to catch the expression. She only tilted her head again, eyes like deep coals, and said, "Someday."

GNask cleared his throat. "Our time has run out."

Unable to bear another second of the interview anyway, Thomas strode back, dropping into the brace of his escort. Alexa pitched forward and impulsively embraced him. She whispered, "Daddy," in his ear and then was gone before he could hug her back. The Abdrelik guard muscled Thomas and his two men into the outer staging area. The ambassador stumbled through as the portal clanged shut at his heels. He gathered himself and gained the boarding ramp of the cruiser waiting for him, the staging dock floor littered with fuel and power lines like webs trying to ensnare him. He made the cruiser just in time to be horribly, desperately ill.

His physician knelt by him in the narrow bathroom and passed a cold, damp cloth over his forehead, steadied his jaw, and wiped his mouth as well. "Better?"

Thomas gulped and rocked back on his heels, unable to get up from the flooring. He looked at the physician. "Did you get enough blood?"

"I think so."

Thomas squeezed his eyes shut as another wave of nausea ripped over him. "I pray to God so," he said and gritted his teeth.

"We'll know soon enough," the research physician answered with a great deal of satisfaction. He reached across the cruiser's toilet and mopped at Thomas' forehead again. "Now let's get you ready to go home."

Thomas turned and looked out the facility doorway, as if he could see through the cruiser's walls and across the docking bay, to where his daughter remained. "Not yet," he murmured. "I'll go home when my daughter does. Take me back to Sorrow."

The physician had no reply to that.

Chapter 20

"There are seven steps," Palaton said, his voices lowered to nearly inaudible, but he knew that Rand could hear him and, more importantly, that the other was listening. "Seven steps of contrition."

"I've lost count." Rand spoke as if he could not imagine the Choyan sinning, and Palaton smiled faintly in reaction to the tone of the other's voice. "How many do we have left?"

A pause came out of the darkness which enveloped the two of them inside the stone walls of the temple. Then Palaton answered, "For some, the bathing is enough. For others, nothing suffices." Palaton let out a heavy sigh. "The only cleansing I will find here will be for my diplomatic career." As to that, he expected limited success. The Earthans had shown their prejudice in quiet, subtle ways. The Prelate assigned to Palaton's cleansing spoke abominably bad Trade. Palaton had not known whether to take offense, for Trade was the second language of Cho and all generally spoke it passing well, but among the priesthood, there should be no need for use of a language not born on Cho. Therefore a priest might not have the language mastery a merchant did. Had it been a re-

luctant concession of the temple-mates or had it
been an oblique insult to the presence of an alien?
And then there had been the intentional misdirec-
tion of Rand into sacred areas where trespass
often meant death. Two quiet days had gone by
since, if he could still reason time correctly and
nothing further had happened overtly.

Now they sat in darkness, cleansing the sense
of sight, somewhere within the labyrinth of the
mountain temple, deep in the roots of the building, where building and sculpture ended and nature began. Rand had kept quiet until they were
isolated here, cleansing their sight, so shut off by
walls of solid stone that he'd felt free to speak.

"You must have a sense or two that I missed,"
Rand answered, finally, softly.

"Well, of course, there are the five of the physical body. Then there is the spiritual sense."

"That's six."

Palaton stirred uneasily on the rock which cra-
dled him. For Rand to know of *bahdur*, to be carrying it, was enough of a betrayal of his people.
To delineate the many ways in which it enriched
the Housed, in which it was used in everyday life,
went a step further, a step which Palaton was not
willing to take. He said only, "And then there's
bahdur."

"It's not the same?"

"No. The God-blind can sense God the way you
and I can sense and detect the wind. They know
the God-in-all exists because they see His works.
But they cannot know Him directly."

"Yet all Choyan go through this."

"Yes."

"But how can it help the commons?"

The Choya absorbed for the barest moment how quickly Rand was taking in the world he'd come to. How quickly he'd referred to the God-blind as the commons. "Religious philosophy," answered Palaton, "abounded everywhere, but it was the Houses which organized it, and to be one of the Housed, one had to have *bahdur*. The Godless were administered to, to be kept in their place, to remind them what they lacked, to inspire them to achieve positions within Householdings if they could." *As if wishing to have* bahdur *might light its fire within their breasts*, he thought wearily to himself. *As if it might be something anyone could aspire to.*

"Why cleanse the senses?"

"Because any purification is a rebirth. You and I cannot be reborn, and neither can our worlds, but it became decided and known among our Prelates that the senses with which we perceive ourselves and our world *can* be reborn, cleansed, purified. And since most of the way we react is based upon our perception of the situation, change can be more effectively initiated if the perception is altered."

"It doesn't work for *tezars*."

"No." Palaton shifted again on the bed of rock. The sound he made was muted by the depths of the temple. "Not strictly speaking. In theory, each Choya is born with a bonfire, a soulfire, within him. It lights his soul, illuminates the way for him. When it is burned out, it is burned out. There is nothing left but ashes."

"Then how could I have helped you on Arizar?"

Palaton could sense Rand moving, sitting up, reaching for him across the cave darkness. "I don't know," he answered simply. "And those who could tell us are either destroyed or fled."

Gravel crunched underfoot. He smelled Rand before he felt his touch. The humankind crouched by the carved rock he lay on and took up Palaton's hand. The feel of the other's hand became intense . . . warm, strong, uncallused young fingers holding Palaton's fingers. He could feel the sparks of *bahdur* crossing the boundary of mortal flesh and striking him, as if seeking to come home. He welcomed the shock.

"What is the worst thing a *tezar* can do?"

"Take a contract to attack other Choyan, I suppose."

"Has it ever been done?"

"Not before Arizar . . . and I can only think that those who piloted thought they were attacking renegades."

"Were they?"

"I don't know . . . yet. But I intend to find out."

Rand's hands seemed to cool in his. "What else?"

"Choyan who steal the *bahdur* from other Choyan."

"Steal it? Is that possible?"

"Rarely, but yes. It is a futile, horrible, parasitic crime." Palaton thought of Panshinea, who practiced it from time to time in a vain effort to keep his own power. He thought of *tezar* candidates he'd known when a cadet who fed off others only to fail themselves as well. "It is like pouring wine into a glass which cannot hold it. It will slowly drain away and it will take another death to fill it again."

"Taking *bahdur* causes death?"

"Generally. Do you see, Rand, how we took hope from Arizar? As Brethren, you seemed to be able to do what we could not do for ourselves. And we did not die relinquishing it—we only had to protect you from what you carried. The neural blockers the College developed ... blinded and deafened, the enormous sensory input you would have received otherwise became manageable."

"No." Palaton could sense Rand's shaking head. "Not all Brethren can carry *bahdur*. There were those who became insane on the upper campus. Bevan, Alexa, and I *saw* them. And there was a crematorium there, too.

"Then their sins are compounded. When I find them ..."

They lapsed into silence and sat, waiting for the priest who could barely speak Trade to come and take them to the next step.

The solar of the temple was crowded with the priests and acolytes taking their late lunch. Sun streaked through the curved paned windows, striking the tables and diners below with hammers of light and heat. High Priest Tela paused in mid-step, then made a clucking noise and, tray still in hand, bypassed the solar and went instead to the eating nooks in the winter garden. She and the Prelate shuffling at her heels were the only diners there.

The Prelate, a thin, emaciated, nervous young Earthan did not sit comfortably opposite her, but perched, his face furrowed with anxiety as he began to pick at the meal he'd gathered on his tray. Tela watched him. He'd taken a buffet of every item set out for lunch and arranged it on his tray, but if he ate a tenth of what was before him, she'd be astonished.

"Kale, you waste food. Or perhaps I should say that food is wasted upon you. Either statement would be correct."

The Prelate paused, spoon trembling in his hand. His face paled. Like most of the priesthood, he shunned the facial jewelry of the Housed. To Tela, he looked like a blank canvas upon which nothing, not even life, had yet made an impression. Why, then, so much fear? So much anxiety?

Kale's lips worked before he said bitterly, "Do I have to take your insults as well? Was it not bad enough to give the heir and his foreign dirt to me?"

"You bear the burden remarkably well," Tela murmured and picked up her drink to sip it.

"More insults. I bear what I have to." He looked away from her, down at the neat mounds of food and began to pick at each, a morsel here, a morsel there. One or two he began to actually chew and then spit discreetly into his napkin.

"They seem to be courteous guests. Palaton, I would even venture to say, is among the more devoted of the *tezars* I've seen. As for the other . . . he keeps quiet and does as he's told . . . I don't think we could expect more of him."

Kale's gaze flickered up at her. "I don't know why you allowed it here."

"There is enough controversy stirring on Cho without adding to it." Tela picked up a greenfruit and crunched it. "Besides, no matter what we did, it would have caused comment. Beyond politics, Kale, our duty is to see to the spiritual well-being of our fellows." She paused to chase a bit of seed around her teeth. "How goes their progress?"

"We're nearly finished."

"So quickly? It's only been a few days."

"They cannot count time in the caverns, and I do not care to. A cleansing is not metered in daylight or nighttime hours."

"Of course not." The High Priest smiled encouragingly. "You placed them last with the sightless?"

"Didn't I just say so?" Kale picked a forkful from a mound, tasted, then bolted down the helping as if starved.

"Actually, no." She picked up a slab of bread and mopped gravy with it. "Do you think Palaton gives full weight to the ceremony?"

Something stirred in the corridors behind her. She thought of Choyan leaving the solar and did not worry more. But Kale looked up, paled further, and gulped down an empty mouthful.

"What is it?" She swiveled about in her chair, to see a wing of Choyan enter, robed as acolytes, faceless within the depths of their cowls, weapons in their hands. The nearest one grabbed her shoulder with a hand of iron and the other following came forward with a scarf to muffle her cry of protest.

"It is nothing," Kale answered, as the Choya to the fore plunged his knife deep into the High Priest's breast and dropped her lifeless body to the slate flooring of the winter garden. "Not any more." He slashed a hand through the air. "You know where they are. Go. Go. I will not know further what you do!" He sat down and began to devour every bit of food upon his tray, heedless of the body beside him. Or perhaps the murder gave him an appetite. He did not look up as the assassins left the winter garden and made a fleet-footed run toward the temple's labyrinth.

The stone drummed. He could hear its tonality in the very bones of his body, thrumming in his skull.

"What is that?"

Rand stirred. He let go of Palaton's hand and flexed stiff fingers. "What's what?"

"Noise. Quiet. Let me listen."

Rand had grown used to the startling idea that an earless people heard far better than he did. Perhaps the bone caught vibration and translated it. He listened, but heard nothing. He held his breath lest he disrupt Palaton's concentration.

"Runners," the Choya said. "Through the temple." He got to his feet and, searching through the darkness, gathered up Rand and got him on his feet. "No one runs in the temple."

"Urgent business?"

"If the business is that urgent, I don't want to be here to see what it is." He began to move, taking Rand with him. "Jorana will have my head for this, if I have one left for her to harvest!"

"What is it?"

"Death."

Rand stumbled. Palaton hoisted him up again, saying, "Use your senses."

"I'm blinded in this murk." Panic jangled his insides, but there was nowhere to go.

"No, you're not. Concentrate. You'll have to guide us both."

Rand had long since succumbed to the black-

ness of their voluntary tomb. He had spent half
his time with his eyes closed, merely listening to
the sound of his breathing and the Choya's breathing. Choyan breathed differently, a little longer,
and a little further apart. Now he braced himself,
with Palaton's hands hard upon his elbow.

"I need *some* light to see."

"There isn't any, not here. You're filled with the
ability to see what's beyond your eyes. Let it spill
over or we'll both die here."

Rand tensed. "What if this is part of the
cleansing?"

"It isn't." Palaton urged him a step forward.
"We've got to get out of this chamber. When they
bring light in with them, we'll be blinded. It will
overwhelm us. We'll never see who struck us."

Pixie dust flowed from him as he squeezed his
eyes tight and then tried to open them wide, to
see what was unseeable within the inky atmosphere. Like sugar sprinklings, tiny points of illumination dotted faint outlines of rock and boulder.
Rand began to move forward, hesitantly, gaining
speed as his feet proved his vision sound. He drew
Palaton with him.

"Which way," he said, and his voice sounded
unnaturally loud.

"Through a door, preferably." Palaton's voices,
dry with irony.

Rand turned on his heel. There was a door back
the way they had come. Palaton tugged on him.
"Not that way," he said. "They'll be in the
corridors."

"Then this way." He found another door, barely
etched in the rock, a passageway confounded by

the stonework itself, but his eerie vision found it and sparkled its outlines clearly to Rand.

The door would not yield to him. He ran his hands over the stonework, grit tearing at his nails and rasping the tender flesh. A nail tore to the quick and he swore at the sudden, raw pain. Then the door moved. Palaton stood with him, running his hands alongside Rand's, and it was the pilot who said, "It's balanced in the middle, not hinged to the side. It should be coming open now."

And it did, though the passageway was narrow and short. Rand put his hand up to Palaton's shoulders, saying, "You'll have to bend far over. It won't take your height."

Palaton's response, as Rand pulled him over and shoved him through, was too muffled to understand. The boy thought only that he muttered "Ancient." He waited until Palaton said clearly, "I'm through," before pushing in himself.

They shoved the thick and heavy door back into position behind them. The corridor beyond felt labeled with time and dust, like a shroud or curtain draping itself down upon them. Palaton shuddered.

"I haven't the sight to look at it," he said, "but I don't envy you."

"It doesn't look much different. This way." He put his arm about Palaton's waist, taking the other's arm and wrapping it about his shoulders, so they could walk in tandem, though it had to be uncomfortable for Palaton who had to stoop to Rand's height.

The other felt stiff in his embrace. Rand could feel the tension in the Choya's body. Palaton looked down at him. Rand saw a flicker of expres-

sion through his *bahdur* enhanced vision. There
was conflict in that face. Did he not trust Rand?
He unbent and leaned back down, gathering up
Rand. Side by side, they fled down the tunnel.

They made good time shuffling through the fine,
siltlike dust and age which layered the corridor.

No one and nothing had been through here in
many a year. More than that, Rand could not
clearly tell. "What if this is a dead end?"

"A possibility against a certainty? We'll take the
possibility," Palaton said, his breath warm against
Rand's ear. "Keep going. They have to be following. There are ways of tracking us."

They found a kind of lumbering speed and kept
at it forever, until Rand's ears rang and he realized his heart raced, and the air he panted down
seemed too thin and insubstantial to breathe. He
staggered to a halt. Palaton let go of him and
breathed heavily as well.

The Choya turned in the passageway. As Rand
watched through weakening eyes, he paced a step
or two forward, palms over the rock face.

"This tunnel is not hewed by craftsmen. We're
in the belly of the mountain itself."

"Are we?"

"By the feel of it." Palaton straightened.
"Though you can tell better than I." He rubbed
his nose as if the dust tickled him. "Come my way.
I can feel the air stirring. I think the passageway
opens up again. Can you see?"

The flat, one-dimensional sprinkling of dust
swirled into a diffuse cloud and for a moment
Rand could see nothing ahead. Then he sensed
that what he "saw" was open space. "Enough to

think you're right. I can't see the floor well, though. It could be a pit."

Palaton strode forward, dragging his boots. He said diffidently, "Catch up when you have your breath."

Rand tried to reach out and snag him, but the other was gone, out of reach, enveloped by that swirling cloud of dark and golden sparks.

Chapter 21

Bevan woke, and knew it could be his last time waking, felt the feebleness of his heart rate and heard the shallowness of his breathing in his ears. *I'm little more than dead*, he thought, and added bitterly, *even the peace of dreaming is being taken from me.* His crusted eyes began to water, but whether they were tears or simply the effort of raw flesh to soothe itself, he did not know. He blinked but his eyes, so blistered by the sight of Chaos, took little comfort from the salty tears bathing them.

He hung in the safety webbing, his bones gone paper thin and brittle. His teeth wobbled in their sockets, so it was just as well the pod's solid food had long since run out. Better for his body, too. He was no longer strong enough to flush the excrement from the raft. He hungered though, and that was pain enough.

He reached for the sipping straw and let brackish water soothe his swollen tongue. He probed at the teeth he deemed most loose. They gave way before his examination, but stayed in their sockets though unsettled. Loss of calcium? Massive loss of mass? Bevan giggled at the thought. Perhaps his teeth were rooted solidly enough in his jaw and it was his brain which had grown loose.

Sleep still clouded his vision, for it appeared the life raft walls were solid again, between him and the warp of space they traveled. He knew better and when he was done gripping the straw with lips which felt like ground meat, and drinking water gone stale and hot, he spat the last swallow of water across the life raft. Gravityless, it splattered as it sprayed and droplets floated about. The recycled air was not humid enough, drying him out, and the spray would be absorbed soon enough.

Bevan narrowed his eyes and the solid walls faded until he hung, suspended in black velvet, twirling like a emaciated and mummified spider in its web. He put out the hand of his mind, something he'd invented over the past many days, a projection only, he thought, and stirred the soup of Chaos. It roiled to his touch. The feel of it brought a certain satisfaction with it, rather like playing with mud as a child and squelching it through his fingers. Yet if Chaos were mud, then he could build with it, and this fabric was more elastic. He could trouble it for a while and then it would sluggishly slip back into its patterns as though it had rules and shape and conformity, which Bevan knew it could not. Nothing was as it seemed.

Yet it amused him to dip into the stew pot and stir it about. He did so again, stringing the substance like taffy not cooked long enough to hold and watched it drip and dribble off his immense imaginary hand.

The life raft shuddered. Bevan felt its jolting

movement and stopped in his play. He licked his lips. The pod steadied and he hung very still in his webbing, as though his movement had rocked the tiny ship. He heard nothing, felt nothing more. Bevan laughed. He was ineffectual inside the raft, he could do nothing to alter his course nor save himself. The retros to bring them out of FTL drive would fire when the computer, if it still worked, had been set by the Zarites to do so. He could not signal for aid. In a matter of days, perhaps hours, he would no longer be able to drink or breathe, for the resources of the pod had nearly run out.

He stirred the slime of Chaos once again.

The life raft began a counter-rotation. He felt it slowly accelerate into a spin. And down, it was dropping down, he felt it in the sink of his gut. Bevan's forehead popped out in sweat, dehydrated though he was.

Yet a jolt of triumph shoved away the fear. It pierced him with revelation. The sweat dried upon his face as if it had never been, the air as thirsty as he had been.

"Son of a bitch," he murmured aloud through cracked and swollen lips. "I know their secret!" And he began to laugh at the simplicity of the revelation, never caring that the life raft was dropping like a stone down an empty elevator shaft, that his ears had begun to buzz with the heart rate of a racing engine, that his life was precariously on the line.

He reached out with his imaginary hand and *pushed*, shoving himself and the life raft into real space. The vehicle shuddered as it answered his call.

There was a moment of dead silence. Bevan clutched his webbing. The swirl of Chaos faded

and the too solid walls of the raft returned, surrounding him, pinning him down, encasing him,
a death egg.

The life raft came out of the dead quiet with a
cacophony of whistles, bleeps, and shrills as the
tiny console erupted with signals, the pod eddying
into known space, sending and receiving.

Bevan began to cry, his eyes burning to issue
tears, his chest caving to breathe sobs. Now if only
he were *somewhere* and someone was listening.

He could still come out of this alive. Perhaps
even sane.

Perhaps.

He waited, half-holding his breath, until the life
pod began to jar and thud and he knew he'd been
pulled into a hold. A teeth-rattling clunk made
him gasp, and tears brimmed in his eyes from the
realization that he'd been found and docked.

The stale air of the pod exploded with a whoosh
outward as they cracked the pod and Bevan sat,
dazed and blinking.

A smooth-quilled Ronin leaned in. He looked
about and saw Bevan dangling in the safety webbing. A broad grin streaked the ugly alien's face.

The irony of having come all this way only to
fall into the hands of the Ronins struck Bevan and
he began to laugh. But he could not stop, as his
heart began to race and his head to pound with
the laughter which sobbed in and out of him as if
he were nothing more than a fleshly bellows.

*   *   *

Jorana entered security. The commons on the
streets had calmed. Many of them had acquired

day work permits over the last several days and
thronged only at night, clamoring impatiently for
Palaton's return. Things appeared to be settling
down, but the nerves in her fingers pricked at her,
and her horn crown ached with worry that she
had decided to assuage. "I want an update at
Sethu." She narrowed her eyes to accustom herself to the slightly darker aspect of the room. Monitors of every size and shape lined the walls,
viewing not only Charolon, but all of the counties.
Security workers looked up, saw that she had arrived, and dipped their heads down quickly and
busily.

The head of surveillance crossed the room, a
plump Choya'i of the House of Star, with more
gray than red-gold in her hair, and eyes of blue so
dark they were violet. "I was just about to send
for you." She drew Jorana toward the corner
where the monitors were busily tracking the foothills of Sethu. "Rufeen just called in."

Jorana sucked her breath in, suddenly appre-
hensive. She sat down at a bank of monitors. Rufeen was not on-screen, but her voices were
recognizable and confirmed as genuine by the
tracking computers.

". . . attack, right shield up and holding despite
damage. I seem to have driven them away for the
moment." A pungent swear word which *tezars*
seemed to favor flavored the transmission.

The Choya'i Melbar leaned over Jorana's shoulder to brief her. "Rufeen contacted us about eight
minutes ago, early for her status transmission. The
cruiser is under attack by forces from the temple."

"From the temple?" Shock underscored her
words. "Military?"

"Not that we've been able to identify."

She relaxed a tiny bit. The Houses had their own military, but had not used them in personal attacks for over three hundred years. She'd hate to be in office when precedents were being set. "What's going on, then?"

"As near as we can tell, and Rufeen speculates, the attackers are simply trying to drive her away."

"Isolating Palaton."

Melbar's indigo eyes considered her and then she nodded. "So it would seem."

Rufeen's burly and flushed countenance suddenly dominated the monitors. "Melbar—ah, Jorana. I see the reinforcements have been called in."

Jorana leaned forward slightly. "We may not have much time, Rufeen. Please give me status."

"Look for yourself." The pilot moved slightly out of frame. The camera had been set to look out of the cockpit, toward the temple and the purple mountains beyond. It was bright daylight, yet a stubborn haze appeared to be occluding the view of the temple.

"What is that?" muttered Jorana in irritation.

"That is the temple at Sethu on fire. Why the bastards came out here and attacked is beyond me, unless they want to commandeer the cruiser for evacuation." The camera view, apparently cued to verbal, refocused on Rufeen.

"Where are Palaton and Rand?"

The camera view shifted again. "In there somewhere."

Jorana sat, stunned, watching purple-black smoke begin to boil out of the ancient temple. "What in God's name happened?"

"I don't—uh, oh. Company." Rufeen disappeared abruptly.

"Take me with her," Jorana snapped to Melbar. Technicians around them began to transmit computer directions to the monitoring equipment aboard the shuttle. She could see a priest, dirty and disheveled, and unarmed, talking to Rufeen at the edge of the ramp. "Get me audio."

"Trying," a technician intoned even as he played his machinery for fine-tuning. "Coming up."

Fuzzy, but audible. "Blast each and every one of you bastards into desert lint—"

"*Tezar* Rufeen. My temple is burning, my High Priest is dead. My House is split against itself—I beg your forgiveness—I came to tell you that Heir Palaton is missing and presumed dead also. There were assassins. . . ." The Choya's voices thinned off and died away.

"Did you see the body?"

"Of Tela? Regrettably, yes . . ." The Choya swayed, as thin as a reed, and the high mountain wind seemed about to snap him in two. "Of *tezar* Palaton and his companion, no."

"Then they're not dead," Rufeen snapped, "until I see their bodies piled across my boot toes."

The priest bowed. "*Tezar* Rufeen, I cannot tell you where they might be within the mountain . . . but the assassins are many."

"Bring me a body. I won't be leaving until then. I don't know if you're one of the bastards or not, so I suggest you go work on putting that fire out. I find out you're one of them and you can join the High Priest."

The emaciated Choya bowed and scurried off before Rufeen could change her mind. She came back up the landing ramp in two jumps and secured the ramp. She seemed to be aware that the monitor had followed her.

"Missing," she repeated, "presumed dead." Rufeen stared into the lens. "I'll believe Palaton is dead if and when I see it. They wouldn't be hammering away at me if they knew ... they don't want transport available for a rescue if they flush him out. Got that, Melbar?"

Melbar intoned, "I've got that, Rufeen."

Jorana sat back in her chair, wetting lips gone sand-dry. "She's probably right." She stood up. "Gathon has to be notified. Rindalan, too. I'll take care of that."

The graying Choya'i inquired softly, "What will you tell them?"

"The only thing I know for sure. Sethu is in flames and Palaton is missing. You keep me up on surveillance. I'm sending troops out to assist."

Melbar nodded and bowed out of Jorana's way.

She stopped at the doorway face-to-face with Gathon. The Minister of Resource looked drawn and gaunt. It was apparent she would have no need to tell him of the events.

He put a hand on her forearm. "I must notify Panshinea."

She hesitated. Then she agreed. "If you must."

"Seal off surveillance. Let no one in or out of the palace."

Jorana had not thought of that. She nodded. "Rumor control."

"Essential now. Jorana, the commons on the streets will turn if they find out Palaton is missing."

"All right." She pivoted. "Melbar, seal your area. We'll release everyone as soon as the situation is settled."

A wisp of gray mane came loose and trailed across the Choya'i's forehead as she nodded in response.

Gathon's thin lips tightened. "Now I must do my duty to my emperor." He left the room ahead of Jorana.

Gathon hurried to his quarters. Anxiety tightened his chest. His undersecretary looked up curiously as he locked the door behind him, sealing the rooms for all effects and purposes. The Choya who served him was a good worker, for all that he'd come from the God-blind himself, and he sat now, impassively watching Gathon.

"Set up a subspace transmit to Sorrow. I need the emperor as soon as you can get him."

Chirek frowned. "What is it?" the undersecretary asked.

"Palaton has disappeared. There has been an assassins' attack upon Sethu. The ancient site is in flames, I'm told. We can fear the worst."

"But you have no confirmation?"

"No."

The undersecretary rolled his chair to the transmission console. "Then," he said soothingly, "there's always hope, isn't there?"

Gathon let himself slump down into a second chair. "So I've always told myself. But second chances come in precious small amounts." He rubbed his forehead wearily as his aide worked on spanning space and Chaos with the news.

*   *   *

Rindy visibly paled and rocked as though slapped. Jorana caught him by the fore-elbow. "Your eminence!"

"I'll . . . I'll be all right." Rindalan's hand shook as he pulled a pill vial from his pocket and fished out a caplet to put under his tongue. "Nothing is certain. Faith will play a great role in this."

He began to collapse slowly. Jorana got her shoulder under his arm and guided his spindly, yet solid-weighing form down on his chaise. Papers and books scattered as she dropped him down. He gasped once or twice and then settled. She pulled a pillow behind his shoulders. The color had begun to return to his cheeks by the time she stood.

He grasped her wrist. "They do not have him, or they would have brought the body out to Rufeen, either to display it or to transport it back here. Do you understand?"

She nodded.

"They do not have him yet!" Rindy lay back on the pillow and his eyelids fluttered.

She wanted to find comfort in the elder Prelate's words, but there was none for her. She pulled his robes about him, found him cold to the touch, and adjusted the thermostat slightly before leaving his rooms. The Earthans might not have him, but who knew about the fire?

Qativar came quietly into the rooms from the veranda, where his presence had been forgotten by Rindalan and unknown by Jorana. He stood at the head of the old Choya's divan and listened as Rindy dropped into fitful sleep. Then, chewing thoughtfully on his lip, he made his way out of the apartments. There were advantages to be

gained from this situation. Rindy's collapse was
only one of them.

Chirek waited until Gathon was immersed with
Panshinea, discussing possibilities and weighing
inevitabilities. He left the Ministry with very little
notice, a commons among Housed, unimportant.
His heart weighed heavily within him. Palaton
had, perhaps, been the very Being of Change he
had hoped to bring to his people. He had to think
out his course very carefully now.

Head down, he clattered down the imperial
steps and did not notice the wall of security going
up behind him, Jorana directing guards and having sonic barriers raised. He had to talk with Malahki—and it seemed likely he'd find him at the
hiring halls. Yes. That seemed a good place to
start.

Chirek put his head up and hurried into the hot
summer air, his heart beating quickly with his
urgency.

*   *   *

Nedar stared at Vihtirne and Asten, who stood
smugly at her heels. "Your source is reliable?"

Asten answered tightly, as if resenting being
questioned, "My source is impeccable." The two
glared at one another.

Vihtirne lifted a hand. "If the heir is gone, we
must move quickly, Nedar. Cho cannot be without
an heir. There will be havoc trying to fill the
throne, and havoc will draw attention we don't
want. Our time is near."

The pilot threw his head back, ebony hair cascading from the movement. "Don't count Palaton out. Never."

"Then what do you suggest?"

"We have our own satellites viewing Sethu, do we not?"

"The general regions only," answered Asten sulkily.

"Can we pick up the cruiser?"

Asten's eyes narrowed, and then he nodded. "I think so."

"Then do it. And let me know if it makes any movement at all." Nedar watched Asten stalk off, reluctantly leaving Vihtirne alone with him.

The beautiful Sky tilted her head to look at Nedar. "What is it you have in mind, my love?"

"The cruiser won't leave without a body or proof. We'll know nothing until it moves."

"And if Palaton is alive?"

"Then he'll board the cruiser to return to Charolon as quickly as possible to put an end to . . ." Nedar's lips curved, "speculation."

"So, if and when the cruiser takes off, we still know nothing."

"Ah. No, Vih, when the cruiser takes off, we know everything. Palaton is found, dead or alive. Until then, anything is possible."

"And if he's dead or alive . . ."

Nedar put an arm out and drew the Choya'i to him. He put his slight smile to the curve of her throat. "And then I take a fighter, and I make sure the cruiser never reaches Charolon."

Vihtirne leaned slightly out of his embrace, her eyes wide. "And the Earthans at Sethu take the blame for whatever happens."

"Does it matter as long as I give you the surety

to move on the throne?" His words buzzed pleasantly against her neck as he drew her close again.

"No," said Vihtirne with a great deal of satisfaction. "No, it won't matter at all." She gave herself to the pleasure he was offering her.

Chapter 22

Alexa stared at the small, silvered hand mirror she had hammered out for herself from scrap metal she'd smuggled from the docks. The Abdreliks disliked mirrors. They saw what they wanted of themselves in water. She did not know if they thought themselves ugly. In her dark times, she might know. She might think it was because mirrors could reflect and reveal the presence of a stalker, scaring off the prey. She had originally intended on making a dagger, but lacked the ability to make it strong enough to pierce Abdrelik hide and small enough to keep it hidden, so she had finally made the hand mirror.

She pinched a curl into place and lay back on her cot. The cabin walls gave her scarcely more room than she would find in a mausoleum. The bay station thrummed with power. GNask was back. He would be here for a short time and leave again, going back and forth between here and Sorrow. They were in a high, outer orbit above Sorrow. If she turned on the monitor permitted her, its narrow range of channels would show her the planet. She might even be able to catch a glimpse of debate being televised from the main floor on a second channel, but debates did not interest her.

They were waiting, both she and GNask, only the
Abdrelik had some inkling of why they waited and
she did not.

She suspected he was about to strike, something
he could not do from Sorrow's surface, where all
pretended neutrality. The bay station stayed in the
sector for easy access, yet out of range of Sorrow's
enforcement. But strike who and where and why,
she did not know.

Unless it were Cho. That was a target she knew
to be firmly ingrained in GNask's mind. Sooner or
later it would be Cho.

She let her mirror drop gently to the carpeted
floor. It landed with a dull thud.

These times were worse than the dark times.
This was when she knew how truly alone she was,
how abandoned by her race as well as by the Abdreliks, and how she had abandoned herself. These
times, thank God, had gotten fewer and fewer as
she descended into a dark well of hunger and
predatory desire. But they did happen, though less
frequently, and when they did, she despaired.

Where was Bevan, who'd loved her despite her
darkness, and where was Rand, beacon to them
both? Did heaven exist for any of them? Would
they remember to pave a way for her ... could
she ever hope to reach them?

A tear started at the corner of her eye and ran
down her warm cheek. It felt hot, and then cooled
as it terminated. A second followed, and then a
third, and then nothing. She had no more water
to shed for herself or her friends.

She lay quietly for a moment, then looked up
and saw a signal light blinking on her console.
Alexa hurriedly sat up and scrubbed her face dry.

She straightened her suit and stood up to leave as her cabin door received a signal to set her free.

She recognized fleet commander rrRusk and gave him a slight smile, nothing more, knowing it disconcerted the Abdrelik, for Droolers had little understanding of human body language. She went to GNask's side and stood quietly, waiting. His *tursh* sat on his bare shoulder. It gave a slug-like stir as she approached and two stalk eyes looked down at her. Did it recognize her, she wondered, as something it had penetrated once? Awakened, the *tursh* began to feed, slurping tiny, imperceptible fungus and bacteria off the Abdrelik's hide.

The two Abdreliks had been speaking in their own guttural language of hoots and humphs. When finished, GNask looked down at her.

"You will be pleased, I think."

As always, she wondered why he wished to please her. Was a happy spy a better spy? And if he kept her with hopes of returning her to infiltration again, why didn't he just get on with it?

Alexa masked her face to hide her thoughts and murmured, "What is it?"

"Our allies the Ronin have just presented us with some valuable cargo. It's in decon now. I'll have it ready for you in a moment. But that is only one piece of excellent news. The other is . . . we have intercepted a rather hasty, uncoded transmission. Eavesdropping, as it were."

She waited patiently.

GNask mopped the corner of his upper lip with the back of a purplish paw. "Panshinea's heir to the throne is missing."

"Which means?"

"The implications are boundless. Civil disorder, at the minimum. Chaos, perhaps." GNask looked at rrRusk and rumbled with pleasure. "What do you think?"

"I think we can be ready and then wait."

"Good."

"Ready for what?"

GNask put his beslimed paw on her wrist. "We are part of the Sorrow security council. It's our job to help when situations appear out of control. We will be ready to go to Cho on a moment's notice."

She saw only a slight flaw in that. "And where will you get your pilots?"

GNask grinned more broadly, revealing more of his tusks. "I only need one to lead the way . . . and I think I might have just what I need in decon."

rrRusk moved in response to the ambassador's gesture, pelting into a run with an odd grace for such a huge-framed being.

Alexa stood still. In her dark times, she would know and understand—perhaps even be light-years ahead of GNask in his plans. Now she felt slightly befuddled.

The bulkhead opened across the bay. She heard a high, singsong giggle amid the squeak of wheels as rrRusk grabbed a cart and pulled it their way. Whatever lay on the cartbed seemed to be in perpetual motion, kicking, rolling, and singing.

Alexa's bewilderment increased as rrRusk hauled the cart to them. GNask had been hunkered down. Now he brought his bulk upward and leaned over the cart. He looked to rrRusk. "Have you confirmed what the Ronin told us?"

"Yes, your honor. There's no doubt of it. We have tracking records on the life pod."

GNask made a smacking sound. "Good. Very good. Come here, Alexa. I think you might know our pilot. He's crossed Chaos all the way from Arizar. The *tezarian* drive in the raft shows it has been activated. I do not think the journey was accidental. Come see for yourself."

Half-cast in the Abdrelik's shadow, she felt a sudden, cold reluctance to approach the cart as whatever occupied it kept up a litany of giggles and singsong. She did not move. GNask reached out and flung her against the cart's side.

"Look!"

Her heart jumped. Had she died and not known it? Had the Abdrelik dealt her a lethal blow? She took a deep breath and felt mortality coursing through her as she recognized the occupant. Alexa looked down and saw Bevan, dirty, stinking, his dark hair in strings, and his face sunken as though he had died but his breath had not yet left his body. The man rolled onto his side and looked up at her.

He let out a high, pealing laugh. His eyes went up in their sockets and he collapsed.

Her legs folded under her and she, too, collapsed, but her mind stayed clear and her eyes open. Bevan, alive.

Insane, but alive.

And how in God's name could he have navigated Chaos to get here?

*   *   *

"Palaton!" Rand's panicky voice echoed around him, and the vibrations of it raised dust motes which crashed into the clouds ahead of him.

"A little quiet would be prudent," the Choya admonished, unseeable, yet only a stride or two away by the sound of it.

Rand forced himself to relax. He edged forward in search of his companion, saying, "You disappeared."

"Not for long." The immense horned crown emerged, capping Palaton's oval face which followed. Oddly, the rest of his body stayed curtained. The effect was eerie and ghostly. A hand strayed forward. "Come on."

Rand passed into the cloud, feeling the mix of fresh air hitting air that had grown close and stale. He felt like he was being pelted, the hairs on his arms standing on end from a kind of buzz.

"A light and sonic field," Palaton explained. "Mild enough. I don't know how old it is. Perhaps it's lost some of its lethal intent." He let go of Rand's hand. "If they did not want us dead before, they will now. We're in trespass here, of what I don't know, but it was meant to be kept hidden."

The natural tunnel and rock formation gave way to a vast gallery, carved and polished, with solar reflective panels that brought light down from some chimney stories above, passing it back and forth until it bloomed here. This was the grandfather of the lighting system for his own room. Rand blinked a little, his enhanced vision whiting out, overlit. He could not, however, miss the vast banks of tables and shelves and equipment sitting silent, arranged by some system he could not fathom. Palaton strode forward.

"There's a natural dryness in here. Most mountains don't have that. Moisture seeps in. There may be a salt deposit from the foothills tunneling

in here. This is a repository . . . and from the size
and depth of it, I'd say this encompasses most of
the records of the House of Earth from its very
origins. We Stars have one, too, but I have no idea
of its location." He pivoted. "We came in the back
way, I'd say."

"Then there must be a front." Rand caught up
with Palaton.

"Yes. And if they've figured out which way we
went, they'll know this is where we have to end
up. We can't stay, however profitable it would
seem to be in the short term."

"Profitable?"

"Yes." Palaton touched a table with his fingertips, brushing it so lightly that all he did was stir
the dust. "Too bad. I would never have thought of
anything so audacious. All I need is here."

"All you need for what?"

Palaton gave him a measuring look. "The House
of Earth," he said, "is famous for its balancing
act. It's taken on the role of buffer between the
Skies and Stars as far back as recorded history.
That neutrality was sometimes forced on it, and
sometimes assumed, and sometimes the Earthans
were able to force their neutrality on us. There is
information here, had I the time to ferret it out,
which could break that neutrality. I could impel
the Earthans to join with the throne, forming a
power bloc it would be damn near impossible to
break, two Houses against one."

"Then let's do it."

Palaton shook his head. "If we do, they'll be certain to be waiting for us at the end of the other
passage. We'll never live to use the advantage
gained."

"We can come back."

"The library will have been moved. The Earthans can't take a chance that I've found it." He lifted his chin. His nostrils flared slightly. "The fresh air comes from this direction. We should have light from here on out. Let me stay in front. You may need a shield."

He trotted down the wide aisle, reading off signs graven in the rock, detailing some of the histories stored in the vast gallery. One slowed him, in surprise, Rand thought.

"What is it?"

·"Look here." Palaton opened a book with covers of bronze. The paper inside had been protected with some kind of coating, shiny yet tough. He could not read the Choyan language, but the manuscript was peppered with pictographs, some modern and some akin to cave drawings. Rand moved his hand over the protective covering. "How old?"

"A million years, perhaps. Or more. Not the book, but the reproduced drawings."

"I understand." Rand watched as Palaton turned pages. "Look. It's a cleansing."

He could not mistake the tremor in the *tezar*'s fingers as he brought the huge book closer. Palaton became silent, turning to the next page.

"What is it?"

Palaton looked up, stark emotion in his eyes. "It seems," he said quietly, "that the cleansing is more than a ritual. Once, it was meant to work. It was devised because it *did* work. What have we become, that we no longer know what we are, or how to help ourselves?"

"Then it can work again. Read it."

Palaton gave a quick shake of denial, of frustration. "I don't understand," he said. "Not the words, but the intent."

"It has to be there!"

"It's not!" Palaton slammed the book shut and let it fall to the floor. Dust exploded upward, a huge cloud that made Rand's eyes water and tickled his nose. He rubbed his face vigorously.

"It's not there," Palaton repeated. "Lies, old lies, myths."

"Maybe not. Maybe not if the House of Earth thought it important enough to keep in here."

The Choya looked at him, his eyes hard. "You don't know," he said, "what it means to lose *bahdur*, never to fly again, to face the prospect of dying painfully bit by bit."

"And you don't know what it means never to have been offered any of that. Ever." Rand stood his ground.

His words were met with silence, and then Palaton retreated fractionally. "You're correct," he said. "I have no idea." He stared across the wide cavern. "Although there is knowledge enough here to teach us both. And if there is knowledge here, my own House may have something it can share with me. Come on. We need to make haste."

And Palaton began to move again, swiftly, sorting through the corridors and aisles of the warehouse as if he knew a way instinctively, letting nothing else stop him. Rand hurried to keep up. His leg began to ache, reminding him that it was not prepared for a stint like this. He rubbed his thigh as he jogged after Palaton, not daring to stop.

But it was a near-hidden alcove, in the shadows

even of the lighting system, that stopped Palaton in his tracks.

"What is it?" asked Rand.

"Flames etched in the rock, in the stylized manner of a house sigil. The Fourth House."

"I thought there were only three."

Palaton advanced to the alcove, drawn there despite the urgency of their flight. "There are. Not many know there might have been a fourth House, destroyed in the dawn of our technological civilization. I was told, but I didn't know whether to believe ... now the Earthans offer me proof. Is this the moment they hoped to erase from their future by killing me? Did they foresee this discovery?" Within the alcove now, surrounded by bookcases and cabinets, Palaton stretched over and above, to trace the sigil. "Flames out of ashes ... my mother knew. There is a tapestry and embroidery hanging in the palace gallery ... I'll show you one day, if I can. She was an artist. She reproduced this sigil without ever having seen it." Palaton slapped a palm down on a cabinet. He opened it and fanned through files, scanning at a speed which Rand's odd vision could not follow and there were no illustrations to interrupt the script.

Palaton slammed the cabinet shut. He swung to his left and pulled open a wooden cabinet, simple yet elegant in its lines. Inside the cabinet, drawers swung out. Palaton again began to thumb through the contents. "Listen here," he says. "A diary so old it would crumble if I touched it directly. It's been protected like the other manuscripts: 'The root which branched us all has grown dark and diseased and we must excise it, lest the branches too grow twisted and evil.'"

Rand could see a sheen overlying each page. "The House was corrupt?"

"So they thought." Palaton put the diary back. "It appears the three remaining Houses operated in concert to destroy the fourth. But what could have challenged them so?" He fumbled through other files, found another protected one and slid it out. Muttering as he read, he suddenly grew silent.

"What is it?"

Palaton looked up. "Nothing," he said, "that I can tell you." With pain etched on his face, he closed the folder. He relented, saying, "Some of the answers, though not most, and from them will spring the most agonizing questions. The Earthans are not innocent in this. There were hunts for decades, searching out and destroying whatever Flame stock could be found. The Earthans pretended to participate, but in secret they took in those they could find and interbred them in their own lines. The purest Choyan they could find they used for genetic experimentation." Palaton pushed the folder back into the drawer in disgust. "I thought we had grown beyond that."

"Maybe," offered Rand, "this is what did it."

"Perhaps." The Choya straightened. "All of this is priceless. I could not pick a single scrap of information to carry out with me." He paused. A tiny, white triangle of paper edged out from a cabinet near the side of the alcove. He went to it and opened that storage unit. A dossier had been examined, and recently.

Rand caught a stirring up his spine, a chill of fear and apprehension. He twisted abruptly. His ears thrummed. "Palaton. . . ."

"I hear them." He paused. "This is about me."
"What?"

He looked up, with a wide grin. "This is my
death warrant." He ripped it cleanly out of the
folder and slipped it inside his shirt. "Sometimes
paper trails are eminently useful." He closed the
folder briskly and slammed it back inside. "Like
any good philosophy, it creates more questions
than it answers. I have a name, if not a reason."
His neck stretched as he looked up and his eyes
gained a sharp purpose in their depths. "Can you
run, do you think?"

His bones ached. His lungs burned from the
faint drifting of salt in the air, but he denied himself. "I've got a second wind. Which way?"

Palaton pointed. Rand broke into a sprint and
he could hear the other at his heels. The gallery
drummed with their speed. They sounded, he
thought, like a herd of wild horses racing across
the frontier. He did not begin to gasp until they
reached the sudden maw of the cavern, jettisoning
them into the sunlight and the yelps of their pur-
suers as they were sighted. Palaton turned his
head a bit without breaking stride, pointed, and
altered his course. They must circle the mountain
if they wanted freedom. He could not do it if he
thought about it. Rand lowered his head and gal-
loped at his heels.

Rufeen met them at the loading ramp, the
cruiser ready to go. The vehicle vibrated with
power beneath their feet. Rand staggered, with Palaton propelling him forward. Purple shadows fell
across the landing strip.

"It's a good thing a *tezar* never leaves his ship,"

she said. "I've fought off two groups of unwelcome visitors. I wasn't much impressed by the reception committee, but they're throwing you one hell of a farewell."

Palaton fought for breath. "Just get us out of here . . . before they decide . . . to shoot us down."

"Strap yourselves in," she answered briskly, as she closed the portal and strode to the front.

Palaton made for a chair. He looked back to see Rand crawling determinedly across the liner floor. The boy's face was gray and pale. He helped him up.

The vehicle shot forward into taxiing motion with little preliminary. Rand collapsed into the chair and let Palaton fasten him in.

"Will you be all right?"

Rand wearily nodded, too spent to talk.

"I don't think this is a normal color for humankind."

Rand's lips worked and he got out, "Only the dead ones." He coughed.

Palaton found a cold drink and passed it to him. "If it counts for anything, your stamina impressed me."

Rand drained the container with one gulp. He paused long enough to say, "It counts," before melting into the chair.

Palaton looked out the window. "I should imagine we impressed the Earthans, too. We circled that mountain on foot, at a run, in less time than it took them to try to cut through it and cut us off." He put a hand to his chest. Paper made a crinkling sound. "I don't plan to do much more running."

"Good." Rand put the cold container to his forehead, chest still heaving.

The aircraft accelerated rapidly, making the thrust off ground and into the air. Rufeen let out a call of raw triumph.

Palaton said mildly, "I think we finally outdistanced them." He leaned back into his own chair.

Chapter 23

Dusk was nearing Charolon's skies, though it was still a few hours away, but this was summer's eve, hanging low over the city. Chirek wove his way between drunken commons staggering along the glidewalks. The walks had been shut down for the day because the solars of the city had already been drained to meet the demand of the cooling systems and none of these Choyan had the ability to psionically power the walks.

A beggar staggered into Chirek, and steadied himself by grabbing his sleeve. Chirek straightened. He leaned a little so the stinking Choya would hear him well, and pitched his voices although he had no *bahdur* to give them command.

"Find your home and go there. Palaton has no further use for you."

The beggar struck the palm of his hand upon his crown base as surprise pierced the veil of his stupor. Chirek added. "Our God watches and weighs you. Go home before He finds you lacking for the Change."

The beggar wiped his lips hastily on the back of his hand and bowed away. "I'm sorry, sir. I . . . I'm going." He backed into the flow of the crowd, was jumbled aside, and disappeared.

Chirek looked after, wondering if what he'd said would do any good. If it did not, then the ministry of his life had been wasted. He brushed the filth and grime, but not the stench of the other, away, found his bearings, and continued on.

The hiring hall was silent. A few Choyan read the monitor displays, their gazes furrowed in concentration. He made his way through the lobby and spotted Malahki at a far table, a bottle of fine wine in front of him as if the hiring hall were a sidewalk café, and he enjoying a view. Chirek cleared a path to him.

Malahki's eyes widened. He kicked his chair down as Chirek sat down next to him. "This must be important."

"This is disaster."

Malahki poured a glass of the sparkling yellow wine which matched the highlights of his eyes. His knuckles were scarred over, Chirek noticed for the first time, as if Malahki had hammered out a life for himself bare-handedly. "Were you followed?"

"I came on foot. The walks are still full enough that it would have been difficult to follow me. Also, other things occupy the imperial staff."

Malahki sipped at his drink. "What is it?"

"Palaton has disappeared at Sethu."

"What?"

"His pilot reports an attack on the imperial cruiser, in an apparent attempt to drive her away. Assassins hit the temple in force. Sethu is burning. Palaton is missing, presumed dead."

"Earthans," said Malahki as if he swore, and he slumped back in his chair, stunned.

"I think they mean to take the throne. It nears

their turn in the Wheel ... they will have the right, eventually."

"Shit. Earthans couldn't cope with the Compact. Who is their heir apparent? Ariat, no doubt. A young buckling, a nothing, and he's the best they can put forward. Where's their sense?"

"That matters little. What matters is, what are we going to do?" Chirek thought he saw a tiny veil cross Malahki's eyes, as if the other prepared to hide something from him. He blinked, disbelieving what he'd seen.

Malahki answered carefully, "What can we do? The House of Earth operates without our input, just as the others do."

"Malahki, our people still fill Charolon. If they think Palaton was killed, their fury will fill the skies. He spoke for them. He gave them hope that they might at last have a voice within their own government, *bahdur* or not. By the Wheel," Chirek said and pushed back in his own chair. "Sethu won't be the only site in flames. We could have riots all over the counties."

Malahki pushed his wine glass with a blunt finger. "We can't give the Houses an excuse to bring us down in the streets. All right. I'll spread the word the strike is over. I'll begin to pull them out."

"And I'll go to the priesthood. We'll do what we can, although we can only move one or two at a time." Chirek finished his wine. He put a hand out and caught Malahki by the wrist. "You're more than a commons, luminary. You see more import in this than I do. We each have secrets from the other—you do not know my life any more than I know yours—but don't seek to profit now. The streets will run with blood if you do."

Malahki smiled slowly. "Do all priests see so deeply?"

"I can only answer for myself."

"Then I will answer for myself. The Fourth House is trying to rise from its ashes. The Earthans hid survivors after the great scourging. What we may see happening now is the splintering, the sundering of the House of Earth, and the House of Flame being lit anew. If that is happening," and Malahki put his face closer to Chirek. "There isn't a damn thing either one of us will be able to do." He pushed to his feet. "Time is running out."

They had crossed the hiring hall when a scream rang out, its piercing wail cutting across the meager sounds of the street and the hall where they mingled. Malahki put a hand to a bulge in his vest which harbored an illegal enforcer. Chirek stepped back to give him room.

The hiring hall doors burst open. The scent and smell of smoke curled in and shouts and screams followed. A young Choya flung himself into Malahki. Malahki's fist swung and the other went down. His companions stumbled over him, still shouting, and ran off. Chirek could see Choyan running, the streets full. Store view screens exploded as they were smashed in across the street. No one stopped or paused as looters tore down the outer security wall, cracking open the warehouse behind the storefront like breaking open a melon.

"What's happening?" Chirek got out.

"We're too late," said Malahki. "It's begun."

*   *   *

Qativar watched the streets from his windows. The raw energy and frenzy of the rioters filled him. It carried a rush with it that only *bahdur* could approximate. The excitement and anger of the mob sounded and he could hear it all the way up to his veranda, as well as from the communicators covering the events on his monitors. He had their commentary turned low. Below him was the real thing. Like a tiny spark, he had torched the fires which raged below.

Qativar dropped a screen into place. There was a certain satisfaction to it, even if he could not personally enjoy running amok in the streets. And, in the aftermath, his men would pick up stragglers, new subjects for experimentation. He would profit on many levels if this riot continued unabated. Troops had been swallowed by the floods, inundated by sheer numbers, when their first appearances had been passive, as if hoping the sight of them alone would make the rioters desist. Violence meeting violence only begets more, or so the theory went.

But the commons saw no reason to respect or obey the troops, sweeping them up and carrying them along, disposing of the bodies downstream on another street or in an alleyway. They looted the stores in a feeding frenzy of longing to have what the Housed had, and could afford, and they could not. Greed added fuel to their anger.

Qativar might be a priest, but his Householding specialized in reconstruction and, from what he could see of Charolon tonight, there would be a great need for their services in the near future. As a consequence of their actions, he might even get government approval to test a drugging program among the commons. Yes, there were a great many possibilities.

*   *   *

"I can have a fighter ready," said Hat, "but I want to know why. You're asking a great deal of me."

Nedar knew that he did. To have a fighter taken from Blue Ridge, fueled, armed, and ready, without proper flight permits might cost Hat everything that he had earned in his service to the flight school. "It's necessary."

Hat's stolid presence did not flinch in the transmission. "That's not good enough. Charolon is in turmoil."

"My need has nothing to do with that."

Hat's deep brown eyes flickered. "Then what?"

"There is a traitor, Hat, whom I cannot let get away with trying to destroy Cho. That's as much as I can tell you."

"The Houses are calling for calm and a put down of the Godless."

Nedar could feel Vihtirne and Asten shift impatiently behind him. She had summoned one of her staff to assist him, and he also stood waiting, out of line of sight of the monitor. "There is a loyalty between us, old friend, which runs far deeper than the blood of the Houses. We are *tezars*! Without us, Cho has no destiny in the stars. Let the Houses destroy themselves with their foolishness. We only need each other."

"And the traitor?"

"A fellow *tezar*."

Hat flinched then. "Palaton—"

"You do not know," Nedar repeated firmly. "Can I have the fighter?"

Hat's square form appeared to compress with indecision, and then he put his shoulders back. "All right. I can have it ready in fifteen minutes."

"I'll be there," Nedar said.

"How—"

"Vihtirne has a teleporter standing by." It underscored the power backing which Nedar now had. Teleporters were extremely rare among Choyan . . . but Nedar had one as a resource. The pilot pressed. "Hat, nothing which has happened since Palaton was named heir has been accidental. *He* filled the streets with the Godless. *He* engineered this riot to prove his power. You and I both know he cannot be dead. This is a ploy to bring down Congress and strengthen him. I cannot stop him at Sethu if I cannot get to him."

"All right." Hat stepped back from the screen. "It'll be waiting for you."

"Good." Nedar ended the transmission. He turned to Vihtirne.

An odd smile played on the lips of his patroness. Asten had left, on some mission of hers, he supposed.

"And do you believe that, Nedar?"

"Believe what?"

"That the *tezars* have a greater loyalty to themselves than to their Houses?"

"If I believed that," he said, putting an arm about her waist and thrilling in the bend of her figure as he drew her close, "I would not be in your Householding now." He stilled her next question with his lips, but he could not help but wonder.

Could he build a House of *tezars*? And if such a thing could be done, how could the other Houses hope to stand against it?

Why had he never seen such a possibility before?

But Palaton's disposal remained foremost before any other plans could be made. If the Earthans had killed him first, so much the better. This time Nedar was not willing to trust to chance. "We must hurry," he whispered urgently to her. "Now is the time to strike."

*   *   *

Qativar entered the High Prelate's quarters gingerly. He had not been summoned, but the alarm did not stop him, for he still wore a security badge encoded to these rooms. As the badge gave him safe passage through the barrier, he did not feel the pressure. Perhaps old Rindy did not even have his security system on. Foolish, if trusting, of him.

It was not that he had no right to be here. It was that he hoped to come without foreknowledge, to surprise the old Choya, to perhaps strain the old heart even further. A subtle assassination, if necessary. Things would be a lot easier if the wily old priest were gone, his meddling nature stilled by the finality of death.

But Qativar had legitimate business to relate, news to bring, even if startlement did not do the work he hoped it would. He stepped quietly upon the wooden floor. Squares gleamed beneath his feet, polished to a high gloss by centuries of servants hand-rubbing the wood. One of the boards gave out a fine tone, a noise barely perceptible. If

Rindalan were asleep, it would not wake him. If he were drowsy, it would not alarm him. If he were awake, he would now be listening for another tone, another board to speak and tell him of intruders despite the alarm system.

Qativar kept his steps firm. He did not have Rindy suspicious of him, as far as he knew, and it behooved him to keep it that way.

Another board groaned gently, almost the sound of a Choya'i responding to lovemaking. The noise brought a prickling to the nape of his neck. He shivered in spite of himself. The room opened into a hallway, which curved seductively into a sitting room. He could see the glow of a dim light awaiting him.

Rindy had been awake then, sitting up, though perhaps he drowsed now. Qativar slowed, assembling his words within his mind.

"Palaton?" Soft, thin, yet still a strong inquiry from the parlor.

The young Choya stepped into its dim light with a bow. "Your eminence. Talking to ghosts?"

"Qativar! What are you doing here at this hour?" Rindy had been seated, his feet bare and crossed upon an ottoman, loose dressing gown about his spindly figure, and he closed a book upon one finger. "Do me the kindness of hoping for Palaton's return, as I hope."

Perhaps the news itself would be sufficient to do the damage. Qativar composed his face. "I have some news, your honor, which I thought best to give you in person."

Rindy did not stir within his upholstered chair, though his face grew wary. He had heard, Qativar supposed, a lot of news within his lifetime. "What is it?"

"The commons have heard. They are rioting. The streets of Charolon are being torn apart. No one seems able to call them to heel." This last was said with satisfaction which Qativar did little to disguise. He looked toward the small, decorative stained glass of the singular window of Rindy's parlor. "If you look, you can see the flames on the horizon."

Rindy swore then, a single, despairing oath. He sat back in his chair, leaning his horn crown upon its rest, and closed his eyes wearily. "Jorana left me to rest. She must have thought it best I not know." Then he looked a second time at Qativar, and this time his eyes seemed to bore deeply. "Why do you bring me this pain?"

"It's our duty," Qativar replied evenly, but his mind raced ahead of his words. If not this shock, then perhaps another. "If they won't listen to anyone else, perhaps they'll listen to the Voice of God. I came to ask if you'll go out there with me, to help."

Rindy took his finger out of his book, dropping the object upon the floor heedlessly. He stood and gathered his evening clothing about him. "If you'll give me a moment, Qativar, I'll get ready."

Qativar bowed, the better to conceal the flash of triumph across his lips. The mob would batter them. He would be safe, but he could not guarantee Rindy's life. It didn't matter to Qativar if Rindy's death produced a martyr. Eventually the events being shaped would make martyrdom useless and forgotten, of no consequence.

It was the immediate death which mattered, the

removal of a stumbling block to Qativar's plans. He kept his face averted as there came a din of noise from the other room, of Rindy dressing in haste. He did not straighten until he could wipe the look of triumph from his features and contain himself.

Chapter 24

"Nothing else explains the Choyan interest in humankind on Arizar. Nothing else would be worth breaching Class Zed restrictions on racial contact. Somehow, humankind are able to navigate Chaos as well as Choyan. They have been able to divine the *tezarian* drive." rrRusk straightened proudly at the end of his conclusion.

Bevan had crawled out of his cart and lay on the filthy dock floor, his head in Alexa's lap. She patted her fingertips gently on his face from time to time, loathe to touch the tangled dark hair which had once been so enticing. He twitched and sang to himself, unaware of her touch though he had crawled to her for comfort.

"We have nothing which indicates that. Alexa's own experience leads us to believe the Choyan seek a spiritual encounter." GNask lifted his lip in a sneer and sucked on a tusk, loosening a bit of his last meal. He spat it out across the bay. "Ghosts do not navigate FTL space."

rrRusk's beady eyes flicked a quick glance at Alexa before he countered, "We have had Choyan at our disposal from time to time. Even intense anatomical study of both the body and the drive has not given us the information we seek."

Alexa fought to contain a shudder at the implications of the commander's words. Torture, vivisection.

"I scarcely see where this *thing*," and GNask shoved a massive foot into Bevan's side, "will help."

"He doesn't need to help if he can pilot. If he leads the way, your honor, I can follow."

Alexa looked up in sudden shock. "Cho," she said. "You won't go in to protect them. You'll be attacking." And met GNask's gloating face.

"Exactly, little hunter," he said. "Now you understand."

She could feel her skin grow hot. He had been playing with rrRusk, waiting for her to draw the conclusion he and his commander had come to. She looked back down. "He is not capable," she said finally, unwillingly.

"Perhaps not by himself. But with you at his side, I have no doubt he will succeed."

Alexa shuddered. This gross thing which groveled at her feet had once shared the most intimate acts with her. How could she touch him intimately again, body or soul? Now he repulsed her. In her dark times, he would represent a miserable, craven prey . . . darting furtively, uselessly, from her hunger.

She did not let GNask see the repulsion in her eyes. "How much time do we have?"

"Now," said rrRusk. "We must prepare to strike now. It will take us some time to attain FTL and then cross Chaos."

Bevan jerked. His head snapped back and their eyes met, hers and the young man's. He had once had beautiful, dark, soulful eyes. Now they were like sunken cesspools.

"How do you expect him to get us there," Alexa said bitterly.

Bevan's face glowed as if her voice had awakened him. A death-grin split his filthy face. "Alphabet soup," he said. "It's like stirring alphabet soup. And we go from A to Z!" He cackled, lost his breath, and doubled over, wheezing.

Alexa leaned over suddenly, hugging him to calm him down as he fought to catch his breath. She looked back over her shoulder at GNask, defiance in every word. "I can't help him like this."

"What do you need?"

If he would do this to her, then she would punish him back. "Your bath," she said. "I need to clean and comfort him."

GNask's face grew stiff. The *tursh* which now rode the crown of his brow in lopsided fashion shrank in fear. Alexa watched him decide. He would not touch the bath again until he'd had the waters drained and cleaned, a difficult proposition in deep space, she knew that. She would be depriving the Abdrelik of one of his essential pleasures.

GNask turned his back on her, growling something at rrRusk as he passed. He slammed through the bulkhead leading to the living quarters of the bay station.

rrRusk cleared his throat. "Make it so," he said, but Alexa already knew she'd gotten what she wanted.

She pushed Bevan gently out of her lap and stood. "Carry him along," she ordered the war commander and brushed past him as well.

The Abdrelik let out a snort and then did as he'd been told.

*   *   *

Palaton looked over Rufeen's shoulder. "I thought you said you repelled the attackers."

"That I did, but I didn't say we didn't take any damage." Rufeen glared over the panel. Scorch marks scarred its normally pristine cover, and there were both dented and melted holes. Wires and fibers hung out in confusion. "I can't send and I can't receive."

"Neither can the panel," Palaton said wryly. He kept smiling at Rufeen. "Well, there's nothing that can be done. Try whatever repair you can. The security net will catch us coming in. You'll have no trouble landing, *tezar*, and we'll be home. In the meantime, they'll just have to worry about us."

"In the meantime," Rufeen said frostily, "no one knows the whereabouts of the heir and his charge and I can't get the scores of the five-team kick-down game."

"You play?" said Palaton, momentarily distracted. He showed his teeth and tapped one of the incisors with his nail. "Had to get it capped after a game, but I made the winning goal."

Her face twisted. "I played defense," she said. She sighed. "Cho may be collapsing, but they still play kick-down."

"Naturally." He put a hand out and clasped her shoulder. "I'll be resting in the back. Let me know if you need me up front."

The pilot nodded, dropped the com panel with a *tsk* of disgust, and swiveled about in her chair.

Rand was draped limply across the passenger lounge. Palaton sat down quietly, thinking the other slept, but Rand said, "What's wrong?"

"Nothing. The ship took a little damage in the siege. We can't communicate right now."

Rand swung his feet to the floor and sat up. "Anything to eat?"

"Still hungry?"

"Yeah. I'll take anything that's wrapped in that purple paper. Forget the gray stuff."

"Carbohydrates and sugar, huh, forget the vegetable matter?"

"Is that what it's supposed to be?" Rand wrinkled his face as Palaton opened the fuselage galley and rummaged about for short rations. "You couldn't prove it by me."

Palaton found several carbo bars and tossed them over. "This should hold you for a while. We'll be home soon enough."

"If we're not, you'll hear from my stomach." Rand unwrapped a bar and devoured it. He licked sticky crumbs from his fingers.

Palaton found a seat and settled down, and watched the humankind enjoy his food. There was a joy of life to these beings that transcended age and maturity. He sensed that if a humankind ever lost that joy, he would be a sorry creature indeed. Like water that ran deep and sure, it might go underground from time to time, but it needed to bubble up to the surface, ensuring life. He allowed himself to enjoy it now, that which welled unconsciously from Rand.

He had dozed off without knowing it. He awoke with a start to Rufeen's hand on his shoulder, thinking of dusty crypts and fountains which ran from broken pitchers, asking "Do You Remember Me?" That last he had just recognized as his mother's memorial when Rufeen shook him awake.

"What is it?"

"I'm getting a partial transmission on the backup. It's very weak and fuzzy, and we can't respond." Rufeen's face was carved in solemn planes. "I think you better come up front and hear this." She looked at Rand, who had also come alert. "You, too, perhaps."

They crowded the cockpit. Rufeen amplified the transmission as much as was possible on equipment meant only for stopgap emergencies. The pilot translated into Trade and Rand heard the news as it echoed after.

". . . barricaded the new Congressional Halls. Curfew has been set, but there are not enough troops to effectively maintain it. All citizens are requested to stay inside. . . . Firestorm has cut off efforts to save the eastern quarter. . . . Uncontrolled looting in the merchant's quarter. . . ." Static broke up the broadcast. Palaton looked sharply at Rufeen. "What is this?"

"Riots," she answered. "Over your assassination at Sethu."

"What?"

"It's been reported. The commons erupted."

"This has to be stopped. Is this all over Charolon?"

"From what I heard," Rufeen said grimly, "It's all over Cho."

"No. I can't allow this—"

"What can you do?" asked Rand evenly. "You can't get the truth through to them."

"I'll do whatever I have to."

Rand put his shoulders back. "Then come with me." He extended his hand, palm upward, to Palaton.

Rufeen said only, "I'll keep trying. We'll make the airstrip in three hours."

                    *   *   *

Hair wet from the damp, and wiry body, which had gone scrawny in its deprivation, squeezed into one of Alexa's old suits, Bevan sat hugging himself as she tried to feed him. The smell of the cooked food made her ill and she fought off the desire to hunt, to bring down her own meat, sweet and red with juices, body temperature, fresh.

Bevan put out a hand suddenly to clutch hers. The spoon in their entwined grasp quivered.

"I know their secrets," he said. "They poisoned me for it."

"What secrets?"

Bevan looked deeply into her eyes. "I can cross Chaos," he said. "I know how they've mastered it."

"Teach me."

He shook his head and dropped his hand away from hers. "You couldn't do it. Neither could the Droolers, if I told them."

"But you could."

Bevan gave a jerky nod. He took the spoon from her fingers and began feeding himself vigorously.

Alexa sat back on her heels and watched. "What about Rand?" she asked suddenly.

Bevan paused. A bit of applesauce ran from his

mouth. He wiped it up with a fingertip, then sucked the finger clean. "I don't know. Maybe."

"The Choyan have him. He's being held on Cho."

"Vampires," said Bevan vehemently. "They'll strip his soul away."

"GNask has a grievance before the Compact. It's about all of us . . . all of us who were taken and poisoned . . . but we need Rand, too. We need to save Rand if we can."

Bevan's gaze shifted back and forth. "You weren't poisoned."

"Remember Arizar? Remember the upper campus, with its dead and its crazies? They don't care what happens to us. We need to get Rand out of there."

Bevan dropped his spoon into his food tray. "You loved Rand more, didn't you?" he asked with sudden lucid insight.

Alexa winced. "I loved you both. I couldn't help it. But Rand never understood what you did. . . . He never understood what it was to give up all of yourself—"

"Even the dark side," Bevan finished.

Their eyes met.

"Yes. Even that," Alexa admitted.

"If we save him, will you let the Abdreliks have him?"

A sudden fierceness gripped her. She leaned close and vowed, "No. Never."

"Promise me?"

She put a kiss on his brow, saying, "I promise." And sat back. "And what about you? Do you promise?"

Tiny golden lights seemed to illuminate his

sunken eyes. "No promises. I can get you there," he said. "But it will be the death of me." He let out a trilling laugh and began to dig his fingers into his food and eat, slop running down his hands.

Alexa stood up. She faced the bulkhead viewer and signaled to be let out. The door blossomed open. rrRusk waited for her in the outer corridor.

"He's ready," she said.

"We'll be transferring to the launching cradles as soon as GNask is notified."

Alexa nodded. "Who goes with Bevan?"

"You do. You'll have a minimum crew. I have a wing of the fleet ready to follow."

The Abdreliks weren't risking anything if they could help it. But she and Bevan would be alone. There were possibilities in the situation, she thought, as she went to prepare.

*   *   *

Rindy clutched at Qativar's arm. The buildings rang with noise. Trash, torn from shops and streets, skirled around them. The face of Charolon had turned dirty and begrimed and morning would no doubt show an even bleaker aspect. Running Choyan swept past them, oblivious, intent upon other missions, looting, destruction, their arms full of goods and weapons and their faces etched with . . . what? Greed, joy, excitement? One of them hit Rindy hard, and spun away, scarcely turned in his frenzy. The elder Prelate clutched even harder at Qativar.

*   *   *

"How to catch them," Rindy said, his reedy voices hard to hear above the crowd. "How to catch them to hear us."

Qativar had begun to doubt his own safety. "They won't listen. I was wrong to bring you here."

Soot and smoke enveloped them as the shop they passed began to catch, its inside already gutted by looters, its doors hanging upon bare hinges. Qativar coughed and hurried Rindy past it. They had barely made it beyond the gaping maw when the catching fire roared and exploded outward, orange flame spewing at their backs. Rindy let out a gasp but hurried onward. Qativar looked back once, wondering what it was which fueled the fire in an empty building. Hatred, perhaps?

He found a satisfaction in the wonderment. For his works to be fulfilled, he needed that sort of fuel. He stored the memory for the future.

Rindy pulled away from him at the corner. The street swept into a circular drive. There was a greenbelt at the core of the boulevards, a strip of green which had stayed pristine, despite the destruction along the street itself. Rindy put his head down, thin hair drifting in a frizz about his crown, and loped to the park.

Qativar stepped off to follow him. He dodged a conveyance careening about the street, full of commons whooping and screaming obscenities at him. His eyes narrowed at the insults. They grinned back at him as if they might consider stopping to argue the matter. He shrugged deeper into his priestly garb and raced to catch up with Rindalan.

The old Choya had mounted a pedestal within

the greenbelt. The statue which had occupied it, one of Panshinea, lay crumpled on the ground, smashed to blocks of ungainly ruin. Rindalan flashed him a determined look. "I'll draw them," he said. "And then we'll do what we can. They may be God-blind, but they aren't God-*deaf.*" He spread his arms, sleeves falling back upon his knobby elbows, and began to sing.

It was then Qativar realized what he dealt with, what powers, what charisma, what belief. It staggered him to hear the chanting voices of the elder Choya. It stirred his own heart, despite the machinations Qativar dreamed of, and he knew he had an enemy he must defeat if he would go farther toward fulfilling his ambitions. But all he could do now was stare upward at the Choya on the pedestal and marvel. Above the sirens and screams, the crackle of flame and the shriek of alarms, Rindalan could be heard for blocks around—more than heard—his demand was one which *must* be answered, and the Choyan clawing at shielded storefronts began to turn in their tracks and listen.

The Choyan came, as Rindalan had said they would. Soot stained their faces. Anger and disappointment flashed in their eyes. Choya'i who wore rags held the hands of their riot-dressed children tightly, wariness on their faces. Youths bucked their heads on the fringe of the crowd, the noise like loud claps emphasizing Rindalan's chanting voices.

Suddenly, the old Choya stopped. He had been looking skyward, now his gaze blazed down to the immense crowd at his feet, crowding the green-belt, pressing upon the circular intersection.

Qativar felt his chest hurting from the inhalation of the smoke. Two burly commons leaned on him. He put an elbow back to remind them to give him a little room. One God-blind grunted as the elbow made contact, but his gaze stayed avidly turned toward Rindalan.

Power, thought Qativar. *He's using his* bahdur *upon them.* And what a kind of *bahdur* to have. A feeling of distaste rose in his throat. No one should have the power to sway anyone subconsciously. Not for good or evil.

Rindy held out one hand, palm down, his arm quivering from age or effort. He could not hold the hand steady, though his jaw tightened from the effort. "God hears you," he said. "God sees you, though you cannot see him. God weeps that you are suffering."

Someone shouted across the silence, "Does He tell you so?"

Rindy nodded. He dropped his trembling hand by his side. "He does. And why shouldn't He? He speaks to all of us. You can hear Him, too. Above the noise, the flames, the cries of riot, you can hear Him. Listen."

Qativar watched as Choyan looked skyward, their faces going innocent, in search of miracles, in search of awe and wonderment, their eyes aglow in the summer dusk. *How could the old Choya do this?*

Yet Qativar heard it, too. He told himself it was the summer wind, heated by the fires, choked by the flames, but there was another sound, a moaning, a keening, a gentle wailing which might almost be the voice of the city itself in despair. Whoever heard it could not doubt the agony.

A Choya'i threw herself to her knees, wrapping her arms about her two children. She sobbed into their manes. "Forgive me," she cried.

Rindy put his hand out again. "Go among your neighbors," he said. "Tell them what you have heard. Have them listen. Stop what you're doing. Go home and listen. We are all one people. Listen to the despair and answer in peace."

For a moment, Qativar thought he had done it, this spindly old Choya, his priestly robes flapping in the hot wind rushing through the greenwood park. Then someone threw a rock—a chunk of the broken statue—with a cry of anger. Rindy looked toward the cry. He did not duck. The missile struck him just below the crown. Crimson fountained and the priest swayed. He looked to Qativar who opened his arms just in time to catch Rindy as he toppled from the pedestal and the crowd erupted in hatred.

Chapter 25

Rand sat down in the fuselage. He put his hands on his knees. He could feel Palaton standing nearby, fighting to contain the anger and frustration and concern that he felt. Palaton's own *bahdur* told him that as he searched for it within him. He knew that if he searched deeper, he could find more answers to the things which had puzzled him, but he did not want to ask the questions.

"You can't take the blame for this," he said, looking up at Palaton.

The pilot bowed ever so slightly to listen. "And why is that?"

"You had no way of knowing what might happen at Sethu."

Palaton sat down wearily with a sigh. "Ah, but I did. The Earthans have tried to stop me before. I knew they were behind one of the attempts. Possibly the second, as well. So Jorana and I had discussed this possibility. It was more important to force the Congress to give me a vote of trust."

"More important than your own life?"

"Yes. And more important than yours. I'm sorry, Rand."

Rand shrugged. "I've been on borrowed time since Arizar." He turned his left hand over and traced the lines in his palm with the fingers of his right hand. The left hand showed possibilities, and the lines of the right hand revealed what he had done with them. The lifeline in both hands was admirably long. He wondered why. "Take it back," he said. "Take your power back. You can't hesitate any longer."

"I would if I could."

"You can." Rand watched Palaton's face steadily. Now the other's eyes turned from him slightly. "I saw it then, I see it now. You threw the book down, but it told you what you needed to know."

"You saw nothing!"

"Our *bahdur* tells me otherwise. I saw an answer, but you rejected it."

Palaton twisted in the chair. "I was right to do so."

"We're going back to a city in chaos. From what Rufeen said, everything you've been trying to prevent just exploded."

"Not quite." Palaton put a hand to his head and rubbed the base of his crown ever so lightly, and Rand wondered if its weight bothered him. Did Choyan have headaches? It seemed they must. "If the Houses join in open warfare, then what I fear most is happening. But not yet. The commons are warring against the counties, against what they perceive as injustice. We are a civilized people. We had come far and fallen far, but we're still here."

"You won't be if the scavengers come to pick at what's left of Cho after civil war."

"Don't you think I know that! Why do you think I came forward . . . just to save Panshinea's hide?" Palaton shut his mouth abruptly. He collected himself before adding, "You know more than you should. I won't endanger you further."

"It's too late for that," Rand said softly. "I know what you are. I couldn't understand the xenophobia . . . the fear of those who met me. What was I to be feared? I could understand the disgust, but not the fear. Then, at Sethu, I started to understand. You keep off-worlders away to hide your abilities. As a *tezar*, one to one, you can shield yourself. But you can't shield an entire race . . . nor can you fully explain a society in two distinct stratas. Those who have psionics and those who don't. This isn't just a religious difference for you."

Palaton said nothing, but watched Rand steadily.

Rand's mouth had gone dry. He swallowed, knowing that what he was saying would probably cost him his life. "And the level of your psionics ability is dwindling, generation after generation. You have appliances, machinery, whole cities that can't function the way they used to because no one has the ability to trigger them now. The *tezars* are probably the most talented . . . you used it to make the FTL drive function, which is why none of your enemies have been able to duplicate it. But at the same time, you're burning your talents out . . . out of yourselves, and out of your people."

"As for what I am . . . I guess I'm a human oil filter. I don't know. As a Brethren, I'm supposed to take this psionic power and filter it through me. Cleanse it. Refresh it and return it to you. Only I was never supposed to know just what it was I had."

"No," agreed Palaton. "None of you were."

"And because I do, I am now expendable. You can do what you have to."

"No."

"You have to, dammit! I won't be the only reason an entire planet goes down. Not for my world and not for yours!" Rand found his fists clenched and his heart pounding in his chest.

"That, too, we have in common."

"Then what are we going to do about it?"

Palaton looked at his own hands. "Whatever we can, I guess."

"Tell me what to do."

"Close your eyes and empty your mind."

Instead of emptiness, he found it filled with Chaos. He grasped for Palaton in fear like a drowning man and found nothing to catch.

*   *   *

Nedar heard the thunder of implosion as the teleporter sent him on his way. His head thickened and dulled with the rapid pressure change and although there was a hollow, terrifying moment when he was nothing, the next moment he could feel himself pushing out, being birthed into *someplace*. Nedar caught himself with a stagger as his boots made contact with solid ground.

He could not imagine a Cho where teleporting had been common. His stomach roiled at the abrupt method of travel and his head pounded. As his eyes cleared, he saw himself on the edge of the airstrip at Blue Ridge, the mountains sharp and clean behind the outline of a fighter plane.

Nedar smiled as Hat reacted to his sudden appearance. The other's eyes widened like a child's.

"Nedar! You're here. I . . . I've never seen that done." Hat looked him over as if fearful something might have fallen off on the way.

Nedar reached out and took his flight jacket from Hat's arm. "Another lost skill with some usefulness to it."

Hat shook all over in denial. "I could never travel like that." Still in motion, he pointed to the plane. "It's all ready for you."

"Good." Nedar mounted the wing ladder and settled himself inside. Hat watched with a mournful look. He gave a *tezar* salute. "Wish me luck," he called down.

Sadness etched Hat's broad face beyond his years. "If it were anybody but Palaton. . . ."

"A traitor, by any name, is still a traitor."

"I know." Hat dug his toe into the ground. "Fair winds, Nedar."

Nedar snapped the canopy shut and the plane roared into life.

* * *

Qativar absorbed the shock of Rindy's fall, going to his own knees as the Prelate toppled onto him. The elder's neck snapped back with a sound like a breaking stick, and the Choya advancing on them stopped abruptly.

Rindy wore the richly colored robes of the High Priest of a House, and though they were torn and dirtied from his efforts in the streets, they were unmistakable. The commons surrounding them now absorbed the fact that the Prelate might be dead, and they might be found at fault.

Their superstitions won and with shouts of de-

fiance and warning, they scattered. Qativar
abruptly found himself alone with the old Choya
in his arms.

He had gotten more than he bargained for. Why
hadn't he run off and left the old fool to the whims
of the crowd? He did not need to be found here
with Rindalan dying in his embrace. It would do
his cause absolutely no good at all if he died as
well.

But it had been the other's fervor which had
captured him, just as it had captured the other
listeners. Qativar's face burned in shame that
bahdur could be so perverted. He got to his feet
with a grunt and resettled his hold on the other's
spindly frame. He could not leave Rindy now. He
had been recognized as the old priest's companion. He would have to take him back to die.

Conveyances littered the streets, stripped and
burning. He began to walk back toward the palace, a whole city's quarter away, looking for a vehicle that had perhaps just been overturned and
left, abandoned, rather than destroyed.

Ashes and sparks drifted through the hot summer air. He could see, over building tops, where
the wind that came from fiercely hot and burning
buildings swirled into maelstroms of energy, but
here the air was relatively still. It settled in chok-
ing layers. Qativar found tears coursing down his
face.

He walked until his feet and knees and arms
went numb, then leaned against the nearest building, searching for a smooth panel to take his
weight among the jagged store and security fronts
torn open. The old priest stayed quiet in his arms,

but he could hear the noisy sound of Rindy's labored breathing.

Qativar squinted through the thickening dusk, now lit with an orange-red glow from within, like a glowing ember inside the gray drift of ashes. Moon or stars could not be seen ... black and white clouds funneled across the evening sky. Qativar coughed. It did no good. He spat out the taste of soot.

He turned his head. Above the dim cry of alarm and fire pumps, he could hear a drone. He turned and found himself in the service alley. The loading docks were in disarray, most of them stripped, but an idling ferry sat, its cargo long gone, its hovers still on.

It was better than walking the rest of the way. Qativar staggered toward it, arranged Rindy on the flat bed and sat next to him, punching out a new destination on the instrument panel. The ferry shuddered beneath them, then slowly rose higher and began to cruise down the alleyway.

Havoc met them in the streets before the palace. He could see that the commons had barricaded the new Congressional Halls. They were laying siege to the Congress. He rolled Rindy off the ferry and took the back glidewalk toward the palace, hoping that his movements would not gain their attention.

He stopped short of the sonic barriers surrounding the gray and black stone palace. Bizarrely, the atmosphere of the city surrounded it, camouflaging it, and the palace cum fortress could barely be seen at the edge of the summer night. Troops saw him as he sagged to the bottom steps,

unable to bear Rindalan any longer. They dropped
to their knees, enforcer muzzles targeting him.

Qativar found more than a sob in his chest as
he cried out, "Get Jorana. This is High Priest Rindalan, and he's dying."

*   *   *

Chaos swallowed him. He found his heart beating in time with a pulse of light which kept surging past him. He was not the center of this
universe. He hurtled through it, dropping. Rand
flailed, trying to halt his descent into—what? He
could not be in Chaos itself, could he?

And where was Palaton? Rand tumbled like a
parachutist in free-fall, spread his arms and legs
to slow the tumble. As he spun, he slowed, and he
could see a golden thread trailing out behind him,
a fine anchor line like that spun by a spider, and
he the four-legged arachnid.

The thought gave him a sudden jolt of fear . . .
but it wasn't him, it was that other who lived inside his skin, that thin skin which threatened to
rip now and then, spilling the other out. It would
be havoc to lose that other now, he knew, and he
held tight to the sense of him. The moment he
made the decision, he could feel Palaton's presence. He could not see the pilot as he could see
Chaos, but he could feel him, could hear the slow
steady beat of his heart, could smell the slightly
musky Choyan smell. The knowledge that the
other was near slowed his descent abruptly, and
he hung in the balance.

As he watched the random activity boiling
around him, he thought that what they measured

as random might not be random at all—but the pattern so vast that only across infinity might it be measured. Who was he to calibrate the infinite across the finite? The abrupt rise and fall of fractals might be nothing more than the peaks and valleys of a heartbeat, the span of space a pause between breaths.

He had attained calm abruptly. Yet, just as sharply, that other probed at him. *Danger.* Rand squirmed a little in the base of the tangled web his fall had woven. He was secure in Chaos until that time when Palaton had achieved what he desired, or let him fall to death. But he no longer felt alarm. A warm, drowsy peace enveloped him.

Danger.

He put a hand out. A shower of golden sparks trailed from it. He bridged dead space and touched another, briefly, so unexpectedly that he jerked with the thrill of it. *Someone not Palaton.*

"They're killing you, Rand. And they're killing me, too. But I know the poison."

The sudden recognition of the South American lilt brought a choke to his throat. It was Bevan who spoke . . . his voice trapped eerily here, as though this bit of Chaos was purgatory.

"Where are your senses? We're in this together. We're coming for you, Rand, me and Alexa. We're alive, and we're coming for you."

"Bevan? *Alexa?*"

The spiderweb holding him trembled with the sound of his voice.

"Coming for you . . . like alphabet soup. From A to Zee . . . the Choyan do it, too. Get this, my boy. We can do it better. Better and faster. We're coming in!"

Rand grabbed for the sense of something pushing past him, rushing past the web he'd strung, hurtling through Chaos as he had been only moments before, but whatever that something was, it slipped through his fingers. He had it for a shadow of an instant, long enough to know that it was Bevan and Alexa . . . and others, a dark hunger driving them. Abdreliks? He did not know what an Abdrelik felt like.

I do, said Palaton grimly in his mind.

Whatever it was rushing past him, it knifed the web strands cleanly. The anchor strings of golden light which held him safe ripped clear and he plunged downward.

Chapter 26

"We're losing him."

"No," said the physician. "He's stabilizing."

Jorana stepped away from the door of the Prelate's apartment. Rindy lay, his body shrunken and pale under the medical sheets, every fiber of the sheet which covered him monitoring a function, in a room of the apartment which Panshinea had years ago ordered made over for the aging Choya. It was a room she had hoped never to see in use. She could not imagine Rindy gone, his *bahdur* snuffed, his vigorous love of life and his people shut away.

The physician on duty, a narrow-faced, near hornless Sky, stepped away and eyed the monitors. "I like the looks of that," he said. "What we have to worry about now is blood clots in the lungs. He's taken quite a fall and a beating."

She could not stay, no matter how her heart directed her. Melbar's staff had spotted some air traffic disruption along the northern and easternmost edges of the county security net. She had to see if the traffic had been identified. And Congress was under siege, and she waited, with Gathon, to see if they asked for deadly force to be freed. Much as she thought Congress ought to be left to stew in its own juices, she would have to respond if the vote came through.

Qativar stayed just inside the doorway. He looked as if he'd been dragged through a pit of ash and smoke. "I'll stay," he said, "if I may."

Jorana hesitated. She was still uncertain of just why Rindy had left the palace, and how Qativar had found him. But Qativar was the Prelate's aide, his chosen protégé, his own heir to the throne, as it were. If Rindalan trusted him, who was she to question the point?

She was, by the very nature of her training and her position, suspicious. Still, with the medical monitors in place, Qativar could scarcely harm Rindy further. Either the elder made it—or he didn't. "All right," she said. "Let me know how he's doing."

Qativar nodded, and she left the apartments. Traskar joined her in the hall. She turned to face him and set her jaw. Traskar was one of the mistakes she had made which she had had to face every day for the last five days. He should have gone with Palaton and Rand to Sethu, and damn the protocol of a cleansing. If the High Priest had allowed an alien within the temple, she might also have allowed a guard.

"They're beginning to cordon off the imperial grounds."

The grounds were vast—so vast—and yet the numbers of the commons seemed to multiply by the hour. Done with burning and looting the other quarters of the city, they were now flocking to the palace and the new Congressional Halls. "I want lifters on the back grounds, fueled and ready to go. Make sure one of them is a med-evac. And I

PATH OF FIRE   315

want every Choya with the talent to throw illusions on a roster, in my hands, in fifteen minutes."

Traskar nodded. He broke into a run.

She did not want to think they had come to
burn the palace, but the reality of the situation
told her it could very well be otherwise. Would
Malahki sacrifice her for such a powerful
movement?

She thought he would.

She broke into a trot again, heading toward the
surveillance wing.

The medical techs left him alone with Rindy
after a quarter hour, convinced that the Prelate
finally had lapsed into a comfortable rest. The
head physician took a critical look at Qativar,
touched a bruise on his cheekbone which had not
hurt at all before and smarted sharply when
touched, and said, "Get yourself cleaned up so I
know what to treat on you."

"I'm all right." He did not take his eyes off
Rindy.

"Nonetheless, we've made him sterile." The Sky
looked Qativar up and down. "And you're not."

The young Prelate knew when to relent. "All
right," he said. "I'll use the refresher here in the
apartment."

"Good. You can sit with him, if you like, but I
doubt he'll wake till morning. The monitors will
let us know if there's a problem." The physician
brushed past him, joining his tech in the hall.
They shared a low laugh and moved on.

Qativar knew they did not laugh at him, yet
heat rushed to his face and he half-turned, think-

ing of a challenge. An unpriestly response, he told himself, and turned back to look at Rindy.

He could feel the *bahdur* from across the room. Not banked or shielded by dint of his personality, the power seemed to emanate from Rindy as it had while he had tried to reach the God-blind. Perhaps, in his coma, he still tried to reach them, to save them from themselves, those too blind to see what it was they destroyed. Qativar had served the elder these past seven years, hand and foot, as undersecretary and aide and even servant, as well as protégé, yet he had never felt the *bahdur* unleashed as it had been this night.

And the vigor of it threatened him even as it resolved him in his course. No Choya, by chance of birth, should be so gifted while millions were not. Nor should a Choya be allowed to reign by virtue of that power. Equality was the only answer and Qativar was more determined than ever to achieve it. But could he when Housed talents like Rindalan stood in his way? He, who had become a Prelate because his talents were so sparse that he'd been lucky to have even passed the tests for that, could not stand against them one by one. He patted his sleeve, testing for the tiny vial of *ruhl* he always kept with him. It was still the only hope he might have.

If Vihtirne of Sky won back her water recycling patent, the Water Resources of every county would be thrown into disarray and all the counties would become vulnerable to his schemes. He had only to keep testing his drug and wait patiently.

But what a boon it would be to his plans if Rindalan were to pass beyond now, leaving him the High Priest of the House of Star. He would have access to the House library and to the very network of power he hoped to bring down. He had only to stand and wait and let nature take its course. For it was obvious that, though Rindalan's spirit was strong, his flesh was weak. The vessel might prove too aged to contain the power within.

Rindy stirred. Despite the cradle holding his injured neck and head steady, he thrashed a bit, then subsided. Then, eyelids fluttering as if he attempted to wake, the elder whispered, "Water."

Without thinking, Qativar moved to the pitcher on the medical stand. He poured a glass and then it struck him. What chance for recovery did Rindalan have if his *bahdur* abandoned him?

Carefully, so that monitoring cameras could not catch his sleight of hand, he removed the vial from his sleeve and tipped its clear liquid into the glass. He did not carry a toxic dose—as a poison, it left residues in morbid flesh, though it passed so quickly through the system that if Rindy lived but an hour or two longer, its traces would be gone. He swirled the glass to mix its contents, then stepped to his Prelate's side.

Rindy, half-conscious, rallied enough to drain the glass. He lay back in the cradle, his horn crown immense and his thinning fringe of chestnut hair wild among its curves, the planes of his face sharp-cut. Qativar dropped the glass in the disposal and stepped back to watch the poison work.

The deep lines etched in the other's face began to smooth out as the *ruhl* intoxication soothed whatever half-conscious dreams he had. The fretfulness with which he had begun to stir left him. Satisfied, Qativar turned to go shower and change clothes, the smell of the fire still on him, smoky and pungent, when Rindy spoke.

They did not have an auditory monitor on him. What he said would be of little importance. The medical equipment surrounding him constantly evaluated his vital statistics and left his audible ramblings in privacy. Qativar paused, wondering what value a *ruhl*-induced dream might have, and he listened.

"Palaton?" Rindy moved a hand and his brows arched as if he tried to force himself to wake. His eyes fluttered open, unfocused. "Palaton, is that you?"

"Yes," answered Qativar. He stepped back toward the bed, offering a hand which Rindy gripped tightly.

"I did a foolish thing."

"Not to worry," Qativar said. "Get your rest."

Rindalan tried to move his head and failed. His unfocused eyes sought Qativar's. "I'm very tired."

"Then sleep."

"This is a sleep I fear I might not wake from. Palaton, I have something I must tell you."

Qativar debated, then squeezed the hand he held tighter. "What is it, Rindy?"

"I will not go as your mother did, without your knowing. You don't remember me . . . but I tested you when you were just a child. You were the youngest candidate I ever tested, but your grandfather insisted."

Qativar knew of Palaton's grandfather Volan, a domineering Star who had bankrupted his Householding, depending too heavily on the financial fortunes of the *tezars* his bloodline produced. Early testing would have been typical of the Choya.

Rindy paused, wet his lips, and then said, "I found out that you had no acknowledged father. Your mother refused to name your sire. Your grandfather feared the genetic lines had been soiled, but you tested well and truly. But what he did not know was that I and the Earthan priest who worked with me identified the out-cross. You come from the Fourth House, Palaton, the House destroyed. Your lineage from that House is true and clear. The Earthan priest confirmed it. We were sworn to secrecy, he and I. Your grandfather dared not touch me, but he had the Earthan priest killed later. Yet, from the attempts made on your life, the priest must have told what he knew. The lineage of a Flame is greatly feared, and with reason. You must know yourself, Palaton, and protect yourself. They will not cease until you are dead." Rindy halted, breathless.

Qativar eyed the heart monitor. It showed the beginning of an erratic beat. "I'll remember, Rindy."

"Take care, Palaton. Forgive me for keeping a secret." Rindy's eyes fluttered shut. Slowly, he released the grip he had on Qativar's hand.

Qativar stood a moment longer, but the old Choya had merely lapsed into sleep. He watched the heart monitor. It stayed erratic.

He smiled. By the time he'd showered and changed, the deed should be done.

Pondering what rewards he might reap from the unexpected confession, Qativar left the room.

*   *   *

"Palaton, don't leave me!" Rand screamed as he plummeted, heart drumming, breath tearing his lungs as it seared outward. He would never stop falling, not even after death, he knew and he clawed in desperation.

He could feel that other leaving him, pulled out by the pressure of the fall. It was as if his insides were being ripped out, through his screaming mouth, the pores of his skin, his eyes, golden sparks pouring outward, the very substance that kept him alive.

He had to let it go, he knew that. But he could not help himself. He shoveled his hands through it, trying to hold on, trying to stop the inevitable. His heart beat faster and faster, deafening him, swelling in his chest, causing incredible pain.

He clutched his chest. He could feel his heart bursting, the pulse in his eardrums booming. He was dying, and he knew it.

And then the golden fire leaving him arched through space, bridging from him to another, and he saw the other, a proudly horned figure, and they were connected, intimately, through the umbilical of power. What flowed from him, flowed into the other. Palaton looked at him and fear carved his face.

"No," he said and pushed back.

Rand lost consciousness of even Chaos.

Palaton went to his knees. A bitter sob tore through him. He choked a second one back and took the boy in his arms, the boy who had been barely breathing, and he held him tightly. He could not do it—he knew he could not do it—and now he held the other tightly and felt the racing heartbeat that had been pulsing wildly begin to steady.

The *bahdur* had been streaming back into him. For a wild, unfettered moment, he had its full strength, pure and renewed, coursing inside him. But it had not come without a price, and with it had come another soul, as tied to its power as he was.

But he could live without it, while, losing it, Rand had plunged rapidly toward death, and so he had let it go.

There was a small hope to be gained from this failure. His *bahdur* prospered. It had been cleansed and refined beyond all his dreams. It waited for him still. One day, he might be able to regain all that he had lost and more.

Until then, there was Rand to be considered.

Stranger from another world, in his arms, rocked back to life.

Palaton.

His soul blossomed at the voice within, joy beyond any he had ever known at the Congress, and then startlement, as the two touched minds.

He answered tentatively. *I have you.* With mental irony, adding, *And it appears you have me.*

The *bahdur* had tied them together in a knot of souls, bridging the distance between flesh with that rarest of psionic abilities, pure telepathy. Only death would part them now.

Palaton was wondering what the future could hold, when the cruiser rocked under a violent assault.

*   *   *

"Sequencing the net matrix," the tech told Jorana. "Two inbound, one a cruiser and the other a fighter. Both unID'd at this point."

"Give me a point of origin for the cruiser." She bit her lower lip, not daring to hope.

"They're in an evasive pattern. I can't pinpoint the vector of origination."

"Could it be Sethu?" Her voices raised, vibrating with impatience and frustration.

The tech looked coldly at his screens. "It could be, choya'i, from anywhere. The fighter, however, appears to have come from the area of Blue Ridge."

Why Blue Ridge? And, if the cruiser was Palaton's, why wasn't it broadcasting its ID?

"Uh-oh," the tech said. He narrowed his eyes. "The fighter is engaging the cruiser."

"What?" Jorana felt her throat constrict. "Scramble a flight. Get them up and see what's happening."

The tech's stony gaze wavered. "I can't, Minister. The commons have the airfield. We can't get anyone up locally. Only the deep space berths and cradles are free."

A deep space cruiser would do her no good. Jorana swore and slammed her palm down on the tech's desk. The furniture shuddered under the blow.

"Find out what the hell's going on and let me know as soon as possible." Jorana left, and broke into a run, covering the marble corridors of the palace.

It had to be Palaton, or Rufeen bringing the bodies back. The Houses were keeping their troops back now, waiting for the morning and the confusion to clear. There were no other cruisers out. It *had* to be Palaton, dead or alive.

And if he were alive, then someone from Blue Ridge was doing his best to bring him down.

But *why?*

She came to a halt at the front doors. A troop of guard in full riot gear stood just within the doorway. A similar troop was just outside, and a full line had been stationed at the sonics barriers.

She chose a Choya with approximately her build. "Soldier, hand me your gear."

The Choya blinked, then impassively began to shed his body armor and shield and vest battery pack. Jorana suited up quickly, taking every piece of gear almost before the guard could surrender it.

"Soldier, I want you to find Minister Gathon. Inform him that a ship I have reason to believe is the imperial cruiser is attempting to come in. It's under attack. I am going to the airstrip to see what I can do. I'm going alone because I think I'll have better success making my objective. Is that understood?"

The Choya nodded. "Repeat it back to me."

He did so, haltingly, with care.

"All right. Hold your station," she told the others, and stepped outside.

She was not prepared for the sight. The skies in all directions flamed and smoked. It hurt to breathe. The skyscape crumbled in blackened, falling ruins wherever she looked. The Godless had all but destroyed Charolon.

And the commons stood ringed about the palace, just as they held the Congressional Halls, determined to wreak even more destruction. They raised their voices in taunts as they saw her.

She paced to the line holding the sonics barrier.

"This is Security Minister Jorana. Let me through." She put up her visor to confirm her identity.

The guard saluted, but said, "Choya'i, they'll pull you down."

"I don't think so. You have your orders. Let me through, then get that barrier back up—and take it from stun to stop."

He fumbled at the control post. The laser lines delineating the sound waves blinked and then faded. She stepped through. The barrier went back on with a sizzle behind her.

Jorana sat down cross-legged on the steps before the commons could move. She kept her visor up and said calmly, with all the *bahdur* reinforcement she could muster, "Bring me Malahki. It's time to talk."

Rand's pulse fluttered weakly in his throat as the ship veered. Palaton loosed him and fastened the safety webbing close. He gained the cockpit, almost pitching in headfirst.

"What is it?"

Rufeen said grimly, "We're under attack."

"What?" Palaton grabbed for the threshold to steady himself as she took the cruiser evasively about again. "By Charolon?"

"No . . . I don't think so. He intersected us just outside the security net. The net is down . . . we can come in, although the visual on the airstrip looks to me like the rioters have it."

"We can't land and someone is busy trying to blast us out of the sky."

"You got it." Rufeen swore as the plane rocked,

catching the outer burst of another attack. "Who-ever is flying is good."

Palaton thrust himself inside and sat down. He drew a harness across his chest and lap hurriedly. "What's the ID on the plane?"

"It's out of Blue Ridge."

Palaton felt as though his throat had been cut. Words left him. He reached for the controls in front of him and brought up an ID. It was a training fighter from Blue Ridge. The cruiser had no hope of continuing to elude the needle sharp form on its heels, no matter how good a pilot Rufeen was.

He thought fleetingly of Nedar. Then, as the fighter closed, he was too busy to think.

* * *

Malahki came in on a jet sled, his thick dark mane tangling with the night, the crowd parting before him. He stepped down and gave a hand to Jorana, helping her to her feet. He had answered, as she'd hoped, so quickly he must have been quartered nearby, waiting and watching.

He drew her aside. "You asked for me, to talk. Are we talking of surrendering the palace?"

"No."

Anger crossed his face. Gold glinted deep in his eyes. "Then what?"

"I want safe passage to the airstrip."

"The strip? Why? We've embargoed the city. I don't want *bahdur*-blazing Houses to come riding to your rescue. At least, not until we're ready for them."

"Palaton's trying to land."

"Palaton? Are you sure?"

She could not meet his eyes. "No. We've had no contact. But it's a cruiser, and it's the only one due back."

"And if he's dead?"

"I'll come back and talk to Gathon about surrendering the palace before anyone else gets hurt. Rindy is upstairs . . . in critical condition. I want permission to med-evac him."

"We have no quarrel with the Prelate. And if Palaton is alive?"

She looked at him then. "He'll have more control over them than you, and you know it. He'll send them back."

"Then why should I let him land?"

"Because this is not the time for revolution."

Malahki's mouth curved in a one-sided smile. "You are so sure of yourself, Jorana." He considered a moment. "I will give you passage . . . on one condition."

"What?"

He pressed a vial into her hand without words. She looked at it.

"Use it on Palaton. Give me a child of your lineages."

She swallowed tightly. Then Jorana closed her fingers about the vial. It would not matter if Palaton were dead. And if he were alive . . . she would face the future later. Malahki knew he had his answer as soon as she closed her fist about the drug. He strode back to the jet sled and kicked it into high.

"Time is short," he said.

She mounted the sled behind him.

*   *   *

"Bring it about!" Palaton's voices rose above the whine of instruments.

"What?" Rufeen spared a split second to glare at him. "Are you crazy?"

"Attack back. He won't expect it. Be aggressive."

The Choya'i shook her head in despair and then said, "Oh, what the hell." She kicked the throttle loose and brought it to manual, taking it off the autopilot evasive pattern. The cruiser answered smartly to her demands on it.

Palaton's gut protested the loop of movement, but he kept his eyes on his monitors. They were just outside Charolon, within range of the strip, and its broadcast was filling his screens with electronic demands he could not answer. He could also see that most of the air lanes were blocked, filled with infrared heat that could only come from living bodies.

The commons were literally lying down on the airfield to control it.

A cruiser could not land on a thumbnail like a lifter. Nor could it continue to outmaneuver a fighter. Rufeen would have to bring it down soon. Palaton brought up his map, scanning the area, and located a maintenance field which appeared to be empty. The lanes were short. Rufeen would have to brake sharply and finesse a taxi.

Getting there in one piece would be as much of a challenge as landing in one piece.

The cruiser shuddered. Rufeen said, "He's dodging me."

"But at least you're on the offensive." Palaton brought up his coordinates. "Can you bring it down there?"

"Unless we're scrap metal by the time I need to make the approach, yeah."

"Let me take the guns."

"I thought you'd never ask." Rufeen let go of the gunfire control abruptly and applied all of her attention to maneuvering.

Palaton laced his fingers into the gunnery panel. Without *bahdur* to guide him, he felt odd, no warming tingle to let him know instinctively when to fire. The grid tracked over his left eye. He normally wore it over his right, but he normally piloted instead of copiloted. Before he could get accustomed to it, the fighter in front of him looped off suddenly and disappeared from sight.

But he knew where the fighter was going before instruments could pick it up. "Yaw," he yelped at Rufeen and set his sights for the fighter he knew would appear there.

She did not answer. The cruiser swooped in answer to the helm. And the Blue Ridge fighter came up in his sights as he had known it would.

They fired at one another simultaneously.

Chapter 27

Smoke and flaming metal filled the sky. Palaton felt the cruiser give a shudder like a death rattle and begin to plunge downward. Shearing off the target grid, he saw the fighter tumble downward, somersaulting like a fallen comet.

Rufeen laid in the coordinates of the abandoned strip and then slumped over the panel. Palaton put a hand back to rouse her without success. The cruiser went nose-down, vainly trying to answer the autopilot. He braced himself as the cracked windshield gave way and the earth and the night tore in at him.

The impact as they hit blacked out every thought he might have had.

* * *

Malahki skewed the sled about on the road as explosions rocked the sky. "There!"

Jorana threw her helmet off to see. The two planes nearly collided with one another and shrapnel filled the air. It rained down about them as the scream of diving planes tore at her ears. Malahki did not wait for her response. He gunned the sled toward the cruiser as it hit the ground,

skidding, and split in half. She had never heard
anything so awful in her life. Yet as she sent her
bahdur spiraling out, there was still life inside the
wreckage. Flames died down and then flared up
again.

She did not know she could move so quickly in
riot gear. She reached the cockpit, which had
spilled open like a cracked egg, white smoke billowing out of it and found a *tezar*. She was pale,
but breathing shallowly. Jorana recognized Rufeen under the blood.

She pulled her from the wreckage, muttering,
"Oh, God, oh, God," for the other Choya slumped
over the controls had to be Palaton. She spread
Rufeen out on her back, wondering where Malahki
was, and went back for Palaton.

A wave of commons rushed toward the wreckage. Malahki secured the jet sled and saw them
coming. He'd sent Chirek out to handle the airstrip and, looking for him now, was relieved to see
Chirek carried among their numbers. He flicked
a glance toward the downed cruiser. Jorana had
brought out one body and was diving in for another. He could barely see the outline of the
crowned head through the shattered canopy of the
foresection, but he recognized Palaton in silhouette as flames in the fuselage section lit up the
night.

She would have her Palaton, alive, if battered,
he thought. And what would he have?

Chirek gained his side. Malahki waved the
crowd off, shouting for calm and quiet. "Your *tezar*
has come back. The Housed at Sethu did not bring
him down!"

To Chirek, he said, "Damn the luck. Put them

on fire control. We don't need this spreading out of hand. We need the airstrip open for emergency supplies."

Jorana stood up, Palaton across her shoulder. Dazed, he looked about and then called, in voices of sheer terror, "Rand!"

Malahki grabbed Chirek by the shoulder. "The humankind must be in the fuselage. Get him out. Get him secured. Take him to my quarters."

"Malahki—"

"Don't question me! Do it!"

Chirek gave a nod, grabbed the arm of the Choya closest to him and plunged toward the fuse-lage which lay shuddering and flaming yards away from the foresection of the cruiser.

Jorana put her hand to Palaton's face. "We'll get him. Now come on." She smelled leaking fuel. "We're in danger, too."

"Rufeen . . ." Palaton turned confused eyes on her.

"Already out. *Palaton*, please. Help me. I can't carry you out of here alone." Her *bahdur*-augmented strength threatened to leave her.

He leaned on her heavily, limping and breathing raggedly. He winced as they jumped clear of the foresection, going to his knees and nearly taking her down as well. She pulled him up, struggling.

The smell of raw fuel filled her nostrils. It set her head reeling. "Come on!"

At her urging, he broke into a shambling run across the rutted air lane, putting open, torn land between them and the foresection.

The cockpit of the plane went up with a roar as

they reached the sagging tree under whose branches she had lain Rufeen.

The fuselage was crawling with Choyan. Palaton leaned back against the tree, taking his weight off Jorana. He watched avidly, blinking, blood-swelling threatening to close his left eye.

"What about the other pilot?"

"I don't know. I don't see it. It went down."

"I saw the pod go. He jettisoned." He looked about, saw a dim fire. "There."

"Maybe. All Charolon is in flames tonight. The Godless have the palace and the Congressional Halls surrounded. We are all hostage."

Palaton blinked. He felt his brow, still dazed. "I need to know who it was."

"It's over."

"No. No. But it will be tonight." He patted his chest, then winced. "I think I've broken a couple of ribs," he added and felt again gingerly. Then he froze, minutely, as if distracted. His face relaxed. "Rand's alive," he said.

Jorana wondered how he knew. She watched the frantic activity of fire crew and commons working on the fuselage. "They're bringing a litter out."

"Good." Palaton lurched upright, stumbling across the wreckage-strewn airway.

Commons saw him. They shouted his name and, like a tide rushing to fill an empty shore, swelled up, blocking him from the litter.

"Palaton," Jorana took his arm. "He's out."

The fuselage gave a belch of smoke and fire and the Choyan scattered. They came back with determination, using their hands and makeshift shovels to pile dirt on the flames. The litter passed from hand to hand, and Rand disappeared from sight.

Palaton tightened his grip on Jorana's shoulder. "Who has him?"

Malahki appeared out of the furor. "I have," he answered calmly. He handed Palaton a clean square of cloth. "Have her wrap your brow. You're bleeding, hero."

Jorana took the cloth and bound Palaton's head gently. Palaton stood impassively, as if bearing her touch. He did not take his eyes from Malahki.

"Your ward is safe enough with me," Malahki said.

"Neither he nor I are the pawns you hope we are," Palaton remarked. "I'm taking the jet sled."

"Are you?"

"I have business with Congress. I understand your people have kept it in session for me."

The two looked at one another. Jorana held her breath until Malahki dipped his chin slightly and stood aside. "I advise you to hurry," he said. "The people are in dire need of the news of your arrival."

Palaton claimed the jet sled. He paused as Jorana swung up behind him saying, "I'm going with you."

Rand felt the fanning of fresh air almost before he knew that he was being carried free of the cruiser. His limbs would not obey him. His mind called out in fear and Palaton answered, reassuring him, he was alive, safe, being carried free. He lifted his head and realized he was being borne on a sea of Choyan. Not one of them shrank from touching him in his blanket sling.

They laid him on the floor of a conveyance. A Choya smiled down at him as the vehicle jolted into motion. "I'm Chirek," he said. "And you're safe."

Rand took the hand he offered and pulled himself onto a seat. His bones ached and his mind spun. For a moment, he could hear nothing but Bevan's mocking voice, "we're coming to rescue you."

He opened his eyes wide, trying to clear his mind of past and present. He saw the wreckage of the cruiser as they passed it. "Rufeen?"

"It is my understanding all lived through the crash. Emergency vehicles are being brought in." The Choya had quiet, mannered voices, yet Rand sensed something more. The conveyance was taking them from the crash site as quickly as possible.

"Where's Palaton?"

"All in good time." Chirek looked out the window. "Everything in its own time."

Rand sat back on the seat, too weak to protest, wondering if he had been rescued or imprisoned. He put his head back on the cool, slick fabric of the vehicle's seat. Images rushed at him: of Chaos, of Palaton, of Alexa and Bevan. Of Bevan piloting. Of starfighters coming screaming in. Of fire. Of Bevan.

Rand closed his eyes and tried to still his mind. When things were quiet, when he felt better, he knew he could reach Palaton. Time to wait now, until he understood what was happening and what they might be up against.

*   *   *

Nedar lay in crippling pain for long moments. Then he forced himself to his feet. He kicked open

PATH OF FIRE 335

what remained of the shell of the jettison pod. He'd
lost part of his horn crown, its jagged edge lying
before him. Nedar looked at it. It could be grafted
back if he found a physician soon enough. He put a
shoulder to the wreckage of the pod, letting it bolster him. He knew who had fought him in the skies,
knew those maneuvers and strategy as well as he
knew the palm of his hand. Palaton lived! And Palaton was destroying him piece by piece. Nedar left
the bone fragment where it lay and staggered out
into the night, ignoring the warm sticky stream of
fluid down his face and along his neck.

A Choya came out of the night. "Sir, are you
hurt? Let me help you."

A commons, but a commons with a blurring of
talent. Nedar reached for him, his grasp like steel.
The Choya let out a yelp and went to his knees,
quivering with fear. He begged for his life but it
did him no good.

When Nedar had drained him of the meager
bahdur he carried, he let the empty body slump
over and fall to the ground.

He straightened and took a deep breath. He
would need shelter until he could find Palaton
again. But there was havoc in the streets, and as
long as confusion reigned, there would be a chance
to strike again. He had not lost Palaton. Not yet.
The Choya had left an idling ferry in the bushes.
He took it and struck out in the direction of burning Charolon.

*   *   *

Bevan's skin burned as though a fever raged
below its surface, threatening to crackle the deli-

cate translucency into char. Alexa tore off the hem
of her sleeve, wet it and put it across his forehead.
The open shield showed her Chaos; she could not
watch it, despite the drugs given her. Yet Bevan's
dark eyes sank into it avidly, he would not look
away, and his fingers played on the keypad of the
black box which had been attached to the control
panel. He muttered as he piloted, things she could
make no sense or inkling of, other than, "We're
coming, Rand."

The tiny instrument in her ear spoke. She listened and then said to Bevan, "Commander
rrRusk wants to know how much longer."

"We're nearly there."

"So soon?" It had only been a matter of hours
since they had reached FTL. She had not crossed
Chaos that often, but even she knew it was a matter of days, at least. "Bevan, that can't be."

He looked at her, eyes smoldering in a death's
head, and she shrank back. "I'm better at this
than they are," he said. "They didn't know!"
And he laughed, that high, crescendo laugh
which she could not bear to hear. Abruptly, the
sound truncated and Bevan looked back to
Chaos. She did not cool his forehead again,
afraid to touch him.

She relayed his message to rrRusk. The commander grunted in disbelief and said, "We'll be
ready." She hugged her knees to her chest, feeling
her dark side rising, aware of a hunt about to
begin, unable to control that part of her which
had become Abdrelik. Tears began to flood from
her eyes, but her face stayed frozen, unaware of
what it was which struck it.

*   *   *

Rand opened his eyes as the conveyance hit something with a jolt, and then the platform bed of the vehicle began to sink rapidly. Chirek put a steadying hand on his shoulder.

"It's all right," the Choya said.

Rand eyed him. The Choya looked common to him, without the distinct characteristics of the Housed he was beginning to learn to pick out. The horn crown was coarser, the hair and eyes light and nondescript. It was a pleasant enough face for a Choya. He looked for, but did not think he found, any ill intent in it.

"Just who are you?"

"I," answered Chirek, "am a Godless. A hard-working, God-fearing commons. And you?"

"A battered and bruised Terran. And I think I have about as much cause to fear God as anybody."

"Do you?" Chirek smiled warmly. "We shall have to talk religious philosophy sometime, you and I." He crossed his legs and looked out the window of the conveyance. Rand abruptly realized they were in a shaft and dropping. "But not tonight."

"And what do you have planned for tonight?"

The conveyance came to another halt, and this time sat, shuddering. Chirek leaned over and opened the door on Rand's side. "Tonight, all plans are confounded. All hopes and all fears realized. Tonight, we wait for the end."

That did not sound as promising as Rand could wish. He stepped out of the conveyance and stood up . . . and saw himself facing the Emperor's Walk, in the ruins of what had once been Congress. A great pit from an Abdrelik bomb yawned near him. Rand looked into it, and a sudden, dizzying rush claimed him.

Abdreliks. Bombs. Again. Bevan. He began to sway and sweat broke out on his forehead, plastering his hair to his skull.

Chirek came quickly to his side. "What is it?"

He didn't know. "I—" Rand could not tell him. His voice froze in his throat. "I—I—Bombs."

"These are old craters. Come inside with me. I'll make you as comfortable as possible. You've been through a lot."

Rand swung a hand at him, to grasp him, and fell through the other's handhold. As he went to his knees, he found himself on the rim of the crater. He wrapped his arms about the bronze railing encircling it.

"Bombs again," he got out. He knelt panting, about to vomit into the crater, his throat raw with rising gorge. "Again!"

Chirek knelt beside him, confused, dabbing a sleeve at his sweat-soaked forehead. "What is it? Are you hurt?"

Rand clutched at him. *Bahdur* ached in him. Like a volcano, it rose, lava-hot, ready to spill out. He held the other's cool hand desperately as if it could absorb the overload. *"See,"* he begged, and put forth the visions which came swimming past his eyes. Chaos opening, spilling forth Abdreliks, new bombs, new horrors.

Chirek screamed. He put his head back and howled, like a wolf of old Terra, in chilling notes and Rand in cold fear let go of him. The Choya crawled, staggered away, and let out another cry, of sheer, gut-wrenching pain.

Rand held to the bronze railing for his life, watching the Choya, unknowing of what had happened, would happen, to the two of them. He turned his head and spewed, head pulsing with the fervor, and when his stomach had emptied and he looked back to Chirek, the Choya had crawled as far as the dormant fountain sculpture by the Emperor's Walk.

"Chirek!"

The Choya looked at him. He reached to the sculpture to pull himself to his feet, saying, "We must warn them. We must tell them. . . ."

As he climbed, the fountain lit. Branch by curving branch, fiber by graceful fiber. A silver trail of fire marked the path of his hands. That which had not been activated for generations came alive with a brilliance which made Rand blink. Chirek pulled his hands away and the fountain abruptly went out.

They looked at one another. The Choya shuddered, saying, "I do not understand."

Rand said only, "Hurry. There isn't much time."

Palaton kicked the doors of Congress down, the interior guards taking the barricade away too slowly for his taste. His ribs protested and he took a sharp breath in reward for his pains. Jorana, at his elbows, said, "Careful."

The vast lobby was empty of Congressmen. It contained only personal guards and secretaries, armed, wary, bewildered. He threw up his hands, saying, "I have no weapons."

"Heir Palaton." They recognized him with relief.

He strode through and they fell back. He entered the Halls and a sudden hush fell on the din of conversation. His gaze swept the rows and aisles, looking for a shock of distinctive, snow-white hair, and the Choya which carried his Earthan heritage as he carried his horn crown. He saw him.

"Devon of Householding Kilgalya. Come forward."

The air inside the Halls was hot, stifling, stinking of nervous sweat. These gentle Choyan had crouched here for hours, Palaton thought, while their capital burned down around them. All because they would not admit that the Godless had a voice as well as they did, and deserved a hearing as well.

All because they were craven, hovering cowardly in the shadow of their powers. They had tried to deny him Cho, they had tried to deny him his birthright. No more!

There was a flurry and then Devon of Kilgalya stepped into an aisle. His uniform was stained with sweat and wrinkled from sitting too long, but his eyes were still dangerous.

"Heir Palaton. It pleases me you were not lost at Sethu."

Palaton slipped a hand inside his jacket. Torn, soiled, bloodied, it yet carried the paper he had secured inside its pocket, and he pulled it out. He looked at it for a moment. It seemed a lifetime ago he had pulled his death warrant out of the House library. "Are you sure, Devon, that it pleases you?"

"Bring this mob to heel and it will please all of us."

The square jaw set. The white mane of hair stubbornly defied gravity, straight and spiking.

"Before all of Congress, before this *night* session," and Palaton imbued his words with irony, "I accuse you of attempting my murder. Not once, but three times. Within the sacred walls of Sethu, within the neutral grounds of Sorrow, and a third time outside the city, by the hand of the imperial guard. I accuse you, and I ask you why."

No answer could have been heard over the din which followed his accusation, but from Devon's set jaw, it was clear the Earthan would not answer.

The tiny Choya'i at Palaton's elbow yanked at his jacket sleeve impatiently saying, "On what grounds?"

Palaton let the warrant drop into her lap. She promptly put the document up on her monitor, transmitting it to all monitors on-line, across the hall and across Cho.

The document was unmistakably genuine. Devon staggered back a step, but the written proof of his deed was reflected a thousand times over at him. Nowhere could he turn and not see the warrant.

His thick, square hand slipped inside his own jacket and pulled out an enforcer.

The elderly Choya'i screamed and ducked in her seat. All about, Choyan hit the floor. In the sudden silence, Devon smiled without humor.

"I do not choose," he said, "to answer your accusation."

He put the enforcer in his mouth and triggered it.

* * *

Palaton left the Halls, censureship lifted, Jorana at his side. He paused on the steps. The commons waited, gathering, so huge a crowd they could not all have possibly heard him. They filled the square from the new Congressional Halls all the way back to the palace, as far as his eye could see.

A movement caught the corner of his eye. He saw a communicator moving furtively. Palaton closed ground between them before the Choya could escape, and pulled the broadcaster from him.

He put it to his throat. "Censureship has been lifted. Tonight, you gain both an heir, and a voice in Congress. You can speak, and you will be listened to."

His crown rang with the answering vibration of their voices. He dropped the broadcaster to the steps. He saw Malahki at the fore of the crowd, listening.

They met one another on the stairs.

"Now give me Rand," Palaton said.

Malahki nodded. Shoulder to shoulder, they descended the bottom steps of the complex. The Choya led him to the Emperor's Walk, to the tunnel mouth, and they stepped on the glidewalk.

Jorana stayed silent, but she remained in her riot gear, and her palm rested on the butt of the enforcer on her hip. Malahki noticed it with humor in his eyes, yet did not remark on it.

As the Walkway opened up into the ruins, Palaton could see Rand and another Choya, walking, holding each other up, making painstaking progress toward his end of the tunnel. He broke into a run to meet them.

Palaton caught Rand up. "It's over," he said.

Rand's turquoise eyes reflected pain and fear. "God, no," he said. "Not yet. You have to let me pilot. I'm the only one who can get to the Abdreliks."

*   *   *

Nedar huddled at the edge of the spaceport. A launching cradle dwarfed him. The obsidian sands were slick and hard below him. The port was nearly empty, staff driven out by mobs of commons, only a few staying to protect the mechanical bays where chemicals, as well as valuable parts, were stored in abundance. He debated stealing a craft and fleeing Cho. Common sense told him it was best. Vengeance would not let him go.

He could feel his stolen *bahdur* trickling away. If he wanted to pilot, he would have to feed again, and soon. He hugged the shadows, moving cautiously, seeking out warmth in the darkness.

Berthing alarms came on. Nedar crouched, frozen, listening as bootsteps pelted past him.

"Incoming. It's a scramble." Breathless voices.

Nedar's senses knotted inside him. As much as he hated Palaton, he loved Cho. The cradle began to rock as the mechanics lowered it into launching position.

"The heir himself. . . ."

"I don't see anything on the screens," a mechanic interrupted his fellow abruptly.

"Out of Chaos—"

"Not in centuries. . . ."

"God be damned Abdreliks!"

The metal groan and clank obscured whatever else Nedar might learn. He put his back to the framework. He could not stay where he hid—this vessel would be launched within minutes. Already he could smell the beginning burn of fuel.

Out of Chaos.

Nedar broke into a shambling run. He made the lowered ramp of another starfighter, this one quiet, acquiescent, and gained the cockpit. From inside, he began the cradling sequencing to position it for launch. It rocked into motion.

Palaton was not going to do this without him. Nedar would not be left out of the acclaim and the heroics this time. He fastened his harness and brought the instrument panel up.

* * *

Palaton sat down in the pilot's chair. He frowned as the cockpit shield gave him an overview of the launching field. Another ship appeared to be warming up. Rand sat down, distracting him. Palaton opened up the instrument console for him, and activated the black box. Rand looked at it. "Can I do this?"

"I'm here. The launch will be rough—we're not going out of a bay station. You'll have to take the G's and stay alert."

"What if I'm wrong?"

"Then we've wasted a few tons of fuel. But if you're right, GNask's finest are about to make an approach out of Chaos, and Cho has never been more vulnerable."

The starship shuddered as the final stage kicked in. The berth turned the ship into position and he lay on his back. Dully, Rand heard the call for lift-off and the cradle rocked away, freeing the ship.

For a moment, there was a sensation, not of flight, but of something stomping on him, pushing him deeper and deeper into his seat until he could not breathe. He heard Palaton's hissed intake of breath and felt, through their *bahdur*, the pain of broken ribs shifting and piercing. Long moments passed, Palaton's agony stabbing through his own fear and discomfort and then, suddenly, he could feel the flight and knew they had reached escape velocity.

The ship curved and they came slowly upright in their seats. Palaton's hands went out immediately to the screens.

"There's been another launch behind us," he said, and frowned in puzzlement.

"Who?"

"I don't know. Another *tezar*, perhaps, answering the alarm. None of us would stay aground unless we had to."

Rand turned his sight forward, through the velvet of deep space. Palaton said to him, "Reach for Bevan. A pilot can always taste the *bahdur* of another pilot."

Rand looked to him. "I'll draw him to us."

"If he's coming through anyway, an enemy we can see is better than an enemy we cannot."

Rand closed his mind. He thought of Arizar, mountainous, piney Arizar, with skies of blue and white-wisped cloud, and of the campus and Alexa and he and Bevan, like puppies, curled together after lovemaking, and at the back of his mind he realized he and Palaton were still linked, but the time for embarrassment was long past.

Bevan and Alexa, sharing and then shutting him out. Alexa and Bevan, trust and then deceit.

How had Alexa survived Arizar? How had Bevan? And why did the Abdreliks now have them both?

With a jolt, Bevan entered his mind.

Alexa felt Bevan stiffen suddenly. He dragged his hands off the instrument pads and thrust them to his temple, grabbing fistfuls of hair and yanking them out. He let out an ululating moan.

"Bevan!" She threw an arm about his shoulders.

He stared starkly into her face. "Get into the pod," he said.

"What?"

"Get into the pod! Now! Or you'll die with me!" He shook off her embrace.

Hands shaking, afraid not to obey him, she got out of her webbing. "Bevan . . ."

"*Now*, Alexa. They've poisoned me and they've poisoned him. The only way through is death." He put his pale, trembling hands back on the controls. He brought the ship into abrupt deceleration.

Alexa said, "Commander rrRusk, we're leaving Chaos." She yanked off her wiring and walked into the life pod. She sealed the door behind her, and sat, waiting, listening to dead silence, wondering if the pod would survive whatever Bevan had planned.

Rand's eyes flew open. Chaos ripped in front of him. Palaton let out a startled curse as the edge of it yawned, and they had not reached FTL to gain it. "What has he done?"

The Abdrelik vessel, built by Choyan, twinned the starship they rode. Behind it, he could see a wing of five more, but Chaos lipped at them, and they disappeared from view momentarily.

Palaton said, "Now, Rand. Together."

He *saw* and fed it to Palaton. Palaton worked the control panel. The starship gained on the first, as it erratically flew the tsunami-edge of Chaos.

"He's leading us *in*," said Rand.

"I've got us."

Bahdur cut a path across space, across black velvet and Chaos, bridging the two ships. It was a fiery path of destruction and when Rand saw it, he knew what Bevan was attempting to do.

"He's opening up a hole," he said. "A hole big enough to swallow Cho."

Five wingships appeared again. Palaton hesitated. Rand said urgently, "Palaton, we've got to get *him*. Or Cho is gone."

The starship behind them veered off suddenly, armament blazing. Whoever the second pilot was, the unknown *tezar* who had launched with them, he was not afraid to take on the five wingships. Palaton saluted him mentally.

Rand leaned forward in his straps. He gathered his *bahdur* even as the other spent his, following the path of fire searing across Chaos, cooling it, mending it, bringing it back. He wove light and dark and sent random segments spinning back into random sectors. He felt the heartstrings of the universe tugging through his fingers. He looked and he saw the patterns of Chaos through which he might someday pilot, the signposts of reality which impacted Chaos despite its unreality.

And they drew nearer the ship of destruction.

Palaton said, "I have a target."

For a moment, his heart failed. "Bevan," he

said, and all his friendship and betrayal rode that word.

Rand.

The heavens exploded. A single white dot cascaded away, before Rand's eyes burned and he could no longer see. Blindly, he rewove the last edge of Chaos shut.

Epilogue

GNask looked at rrRusk. "It is well, commander, that out of every failure, a grain of success may be obtained."

rrRusk stood sweating. He had lost three of his finest wingships, and if he had been to the fore of the attack as he'd wished, this ship would have been lost also.

GNask sat in a vat of mud and water. "We came very close to ending the stranglehold of Cho upon us. And perhaps, with this tiny grain, we might yet do it." He smiled benevolently at the captive trussed and sitting in front of him. "It pleases me, dear Alexa, that Bevan did not take you to the abyss with him. As for you, Nedar, I have something very useful planned for you. My intelligence reports tell me you disappeared some time ago. You are already lost to Cho. Therefore, your Brethren won't be searching for you. You are mine. All mine."

And the Abdrelik stroked his *tursh*, drool cascading from his tusks.

DAW

Charles Ingrid

PATTERNS OF CHAOS

Only the Choyan could pilot faster-than-light starships—and the other Compact races would do anything to learn their secret!

☐ **RADIUS OF DOUBT: Book 1**   UE2491—$4.99

☐ **PATH OF FIRE: Book 2**   UE2522—$4.99

THE MARKED MAN SERIES

In a devastated America, can the Lord Protector of a mutating human race find a way to preserve the future of the species?

☐ **THE MARKED MAN: Book 1**   UE2396—$3.95

☐ **THE LAST RECALL: Book 2**   UE2460—$3.95

THE SAND WARS

He was the last Dominion Knight and he would challenge a star empire to defeat the ancient enemies of man.

☐ **SOLAR KILL: Book 1**   UE2391—$3.95

☐ **LASERTOWN BLUES: Book 2**   UE2393—$3.95

☐ **CELESTIAL HIT LIST: Book 3**   UE2394—$3.95

☐ **ALIEN SALUTE: Book 4**   UE2329—$3.95

☐ **RETURN FIRE: Book 5**   UE2363—$3.95

☐ **CHALLENGE MET: Book 6**   UE2436—$3.95
